RESCUED BY THE FAE

SIREN'S BLOOD CHRONICLES

BOOK ONE

JESSICA WAYNE

Rescued By The Fae
Siren's Blood Chronicles, book 1
Vampire Huntress Chronicles, world book 10
By Jessica Wayne

Edited by Dawn Y
Proofread by Rachel Cass
Cover Design by Bewitching Covers by Rebecca Frank

To the scarred.

The broken.

May you find the one whose pieces fit your own.

PROLOGUE

I can't breathe.

Every intake of oxygen, even as shallow as it is, might as well be sandpaper against the inside of my throat. The very air around me weighs down on my naked, broken body, hundreds of pounds of pressure pinning me to the cold stone beneath me.

Stone that rises up on all sides, keeping me trapped in this tiny, personal hell where they can fetch me when they need my body. My magic.

A sob rips from my chest, though I barely recognize the sound. It's so much hoarser than my voice, so much dryer. I've grown numb to the cold by now, but when they pull me out then plunge me into the warmth again—only to violate my body and lower me back in—I'll face the uncontrollable shivering that accompanies the climate change.

If only they'd just let me die, already. Except, as twisted as it is, I'd rather be the one plunged into hell than an innocent. After all, I was the one who walked into the monsters' den.

I'd been a fool. And this is my penance for that mistake.

Sure, they'd spun stories, but I'd devoured them; excited to move into the next phase of my life after being forced to hide what I was for my entire life. I'd been raised on stories of horrific things that had happened to sirens throughout the ages.

Being kidnapped from their cavernous homes and raped by the crews of ships, only to be blamed for the sailors' untimely destructions. Being harpooned and laid out for the world to gasp and point in horror.

I'd ignored all the warnings. All the stories.

The darkness above me is comforting, at least. See, my nightmares don't dwell in the night; they walk freely in the day. Loved and adored by all who look to them for guidance.

Something scrapes overhead, and light floods my cell. Curling in on myself, I aim to remain as still as possible because any movement will let them know I'm still breathing. My hope is that maybe if they think I'm dead—if they believe they've finally killed me—they'll just fucking leave me be.

"Hello?"

A masculine voice calls down, but I do not recognize it. That should bring me hope. Maybe someone is here to save me? But I immediately shove that thought away.

My captors, they love to play with me.

So I don't move.

Don't breathe.

"Are you alive?" he calls down, accent thick. "I'm not here to hurt you, lass." The wheel above squeaks as he turns it, raising the platform I'm lying on. My stomach lurches, forcing bile to rise, though there is nothing for it to void.

The clicking as iron chains raise me higher is torturous, but still, I remain perfectly still.

As I always do, I attempt to process what's to come so I can find a way to fight back. Once among the most powerful supernaturals in existence, the bastards holding me have found a way to render my power useless. They keep me sealed in this room with barely enough oxygen to survive. There is no moisture in the air, nothing that could bring me even a spark of power.

And even if there were nearby weapons, I have no strength to fight back. They'll simply flip me over and drive into my body, breaking it more and more each time.

Until they've had their fill.

One, two, three more seconds pass until, finally, the platform stops, and I'm level with the floor of the dry chamber.

"Oh, lass," the man whispers, voice full of emotion.

I almost believe it.

"I'm going to tear them apart," he growls. His hand touches my side, and the broken nerves near the area send pain burning through my body. I use all the energy I can to roll over, to move away from him, but that only brings me new pain.

At least, now I can see him though.

He doesn't look like the others. He's handsome, his crystal blue eyes illuminated with power. They tell me he's a supernatural, though what kind I'm not sure. His hair is long, to his shoulders, and a wavy brown. His clothes are what really set him apart, though; he's not dressed in robes like the council members. Instead, he's wearing trousers and a white linen shirt covered with a brown jacket.

"Easy," he finally says, holding up both hands. "I'm not here to hurt you."

I can't talk because my mouth is dry, but I glare back at him from where I lie on my side, not trusting a single damned word he says.

They'd made me promises, too.

Promises they'd broken within moments of luring me here.

The stranger reaches into his pocket and withdraws a glass bottle filled with a clear liquid. For the first time in who knows how long, hope warms my chest. After all, giving water to a siren you plan to harm is foolish, at best.

At worst, it's suicide.

"What they did to you—it's monstrous," he says. "I will get vengeance for you, but first, we need to ensure your safety. I don't know how much longer you'll last, and I cannot imagine this is nearly enough."

My gaze darts from the water bottle, back to this face, then to the bottle again. It's been so long since I tasted anything more than a tiny drop of water fed to me from a syringe after each 'session'.

What he's offering will heal me. Give me the strength to murder those who will haunt my nightmares forever.

He opens the water bottle and presses it to my lips.

The moment the moisture hits my tongue, my body flares to life. My strength returns quickly, and I grip the bottle and turn it up, sucking it completely dry. When I finish, he offers me another. I finish it, too, and sit upward, feeling the aching already subsiding as my body absorbs his offering.

"That's all I have, but there is more outside in the carriage." He glances back at the door. "Shite, you must be cold. Here." After shrugging out of his brown jacket, he offers it to me. I stare at it. This act of kindness is the first I've experienced since I was taken from my home in Ireland—the same place this stranger is from, based on his accent.

Do we know each other? Is it possible I've simply forgotten everyone I once knew?

"Who are you?" I manage, the throaty sound unrecognizable to me. It burns to speak, but breathing is becoming easier with each passing moment.

"Elijah."

My nostrils flare as my magic returns, allowing me to sense his nature. *Blood.* "Vampire."

"Yes. But doona' hold it against me, yeah?"

I want to throw my arms around him, cry into his shoulder, and thank him for rescuing me—but doing either would show weakness to a man I'm still not sure I can trust. So instead, I pull his jacket on. My arms are so much shorter than his, so it dwarfs me... but it's warm, and thanks to the water, the fabric scraping against my skin is not painful.

"Thank you," I tell him.

His eyes shimmer with power that does not belong to a pure-blooded vampire. "Doona' thank me for this. I did what any decent person would do." He reaches for me, but I pull away, because the very idea of having hands on me makes my stomach churn. "I'm just going to help you down. We need to make sure you can stand."

His eyes are kind, but I still hesitate.

What if this is a trick?

But the water, I remind myself. There's no way any intelligent creature would give water to a siren. And I don't get the impression this man is anything less.

So, even though it makes my skin crawl, I reach out with a shaking hand and grab the one he's offering me. The contact churns my stomach, but I hold firm as Elijah pulls me to my feet. My legs are heavy, but for the first time in recent history, I can stand. Tears spring to my eyes as my chest aches with the heaviness of hope, so unfamiliar to me now.

At least until my gaze lands on bloodied chains across the room. My chest seizes, lungs forgetting to fill with air, and I stumble forward. Black spots invade my vision, and it's all I can do to not pass out. The heart beneath my breast hammers so heavily I'm sure it will break free.

"Easy, easy, Siren, you're safe," his thick brogue is soothing, and I focus on it as I try to recall a moment in time when I wasn't terrified.

And then it hits me. Soft green eyes, a handsome smile, a dance. Bringing the man I've not allowed myself to think of once since I was captured into view soothes the ache enough for me to gain control.

"Eira," I choke out, as I turn my face up to him. "My name is Eira."

"Eira," he repeats, softly.

It's been so long since someone called me by my

name, I'd nearly forgotten it myself. So, to hear it now, on the lips of my rescuer, it's a gift.

"Let's get you into some fresh air, shall we?" he asks, holding out a hand. I take it, the contact becoming a bit easier to stomach this time. Keeping my gaze on the floor in front of me, I avoid looking at all the places I've been tormented.

It's damn near impossible.

"I'm going to cloak us," he tells me.

"Cloak? That's not vampire magic."

"You are right about that, lass. It is a gift from my witch of a mother." He winks. Trusting him could be a mistake, but what more do I have to lose?

"Okay."

"They won't be able to see us, but don't get too far from me, or it won't work."

I nod so he knows I understand. Then, I let him guide me through the door.

Together, we make our way out of my prison cell and into a long white hallway. My body aches with every movement—not a single part of me left unscathed by my tormenters—but with the water in my system, in the air around me, I'm beginning to feel more and more like myself with every step.

Alarms pierce the silence around us, and I throw both hands up over my ears. The sound is deafening when I've been stuck in the quiet for so long.

"Seems they got my message."

Before I can ask what message, dozens of supernaturals race toward us. Elijah pulls me out of the way, and my back hits the wall. He releases me quickly, but even still, I can feel the panic inching forward, the fear.

He won't hurt me, I repeat those four words, hoping with everything I am that I am not putting my trust in another monster.

As soon as they pass, he moves away from the wall. "We need to go. They can't see us, but if they run into us—it's going to get a lot more complicated." He looks down at me. "Can I lift you?"

My vision swims. Images of being lifted from my platform assault me.

"I promise I won't hurt you, Eira, but if we don't get out of here, they're going to get you again."

I know he's right, so even though it makes my mouth fill with saliva as my stomach lurches, I whisper meekly, "All right."

Elijah wastes no time. He lifts me into his arms, and before I know it, the air is whipping around us as he blurs toward the exit. I'm expecting him to step outside into the fresh air, but instead, he comes to a stop in what looks to be a large room boasting a massive fire.

The warmth reaches me, even here, and it's so much more welcoming than I remember. But then *his* voice fills my ears, and every bit of hope I had is crushed.

The one who captured me, who tricked me into believing I would be helping others as a member of the Council.

My main tormenter.

The warlock who would visit me every single morning. Every single evening. Sometimes he'd bring others with him, but when he wanted to rape my magic as he did my body, he came alone.

He stole my dignity.

My soul.

And my power.

For that, he will pay.

"Find the bastard, now," he orders. *Get on your knees, siren whore. Open your mouth.* "Hawthorne is not going to get his hands on anything that belongs to me."

Hawthorne. I've heard them mention that name a time or two; they've been hunting him, too, looking for a way to lock him up like they did me. Or maybe not quite like they did me.

"We can't leave until they do," Elijah whispers. "The place is warded, so it's going to take everything in me to get past them without alerting them."

"Put me down."

He does as I ask, keeping a hand on my shoulder. My gaze lands on the bastard who spent years breaking my body. My soul.

I can't leave here until I know he and the others will never, ever hurt another.

Elijah knows it, too. Because he leans down and whispers, "I am behind you, Eira. Whatever you wish to do."

With a deep, steadying breath, I roll my shoulders, allowing my magic to pull moisture from the air around us. This close to the front door, the area is saturated, and I allow myself to draw all of it toward me. I absorb it through my skin, and within seconds—I feel the power surging through me.

"That is magnificent," Elijah whispers in awe, as he stares up at the droplets surrounding me.

"What the—" My captor turns in my direction.

"Release the cloak over me," I order Elijah.

He does. My captor's eyes widen, and he gasps. "You."

"Hello, whore," I tell him.

He opens his mouth to say something, but I'm tired of hearing him talk. With little more than the force of my will, I call forth the saliva in his disgusting mouth. Angry tears sear my eyes as I choke on my rage. "How does it feel to not have any liquid in your body?" I ask, my voice so steady it's a shock to me.

His eyes turn red as he sputters.

"Here, let me help you with that." I change the course of my magic, and instead of pulling it out of him, I send liquid slamming into his system. From the outside, you'd never see it, but as his body fills with liquid, he coughs and chokes.

"The very blood in your veins is beginning to pool in your lungs," I tell him as I take a step closer. His body convulses. I move even closer, noting the blur of movement to my right as the door ahead opens.

The body of an unknown man slams into the ground moments before Elijah comes to a stop beside me. His speed gives him an edge over any warlock in this room.

Even still, my captor's gaze never leaves mine.

"You will never hurt another," I tell him. "I only wish I could make this more painful than it will be. That I could torture you the way you tortured me. You evil, vile man. Burn in HELL!" I scream. Somewhere, glass shatters, but all I can see is the liquid pulsating through his body.

The sound of his lungs filling with water is music to my ears.

The sound of his heart slowing is the melody to my vengeance.

And too soon, he falls slack.

I drop the body and turn to him, power snapping through my veins like a downed electricity line in a thunderstorm. This thirst for blood—for vengeance—is entirely new to me.

And more than welcome.

Leveling my gaze on Elijah, I urge him to sense the

sincerity of my words because, if he doesn't, if he tries to stop me, I don't know what I'll do to him. "I want the others."

There is no hesitation, no attempt to keep me from getting the revenge I desperately crave. He simply nods and says, "Then let's go get them."

I spent a lifetime in hell as these monsters tortured me.

Now, it's my turn to make them burn.

CHAPTER ONE
EIRA

PRESENT DAY

The chill of the mid-January air surrounds me, but I feel very little of it from beneath the heavy weight of the coat I have wrapped around my shoulders. I *despise* the cold. Which likely makes no sense since I live in one of the coldest places in the United States.

With careful precision, I make my way up the icy steps of the shelter, carrying a tray of coffees in one hand, bagels in the other. Before I can even reach it, the door swings open, and I'm greeted by the wide smile of the woman who manages it. A smile that quickly morphs into exasperation.

"Eira! You're going to crack your head open trying

to balance like that," she scolds as she reaches out and relieves me of the tray of coffee.

"Nah, I'd likely just get a bruise. I'm fairy thick-skulled." The warmth of the shelter closes around me, thawing my frozen nose the moment we're inside.

"That you are," she says, with a laugh. "I, for one, am looking forward to the warmth of summer. This year was particularly brutal."

"That it was," I agree. And for reasons I can't even begin to explain to the older woman. Her silver hair is pulled up in a tight bun like always, and the lines beside her mouth are evidence of a woman who laughs a lot—which she does.

Despite the ugliness she's seen, Maribel is one of the happiest women I've ever met—and I've been around a long-damned time.

"How are things today?" I ask as we move down the hall toward her office.

"Not bad. The children are still having some nightmares about monsters and other creatures that go bump in the night, but we're managing."

"Poor things." My heart aches for them. Living your entire life, and then learning that the monsters you read about in spooky stories—the ones you fear live under your bed—are actually very, very real—it's life-altering to be sure.

And that's exactly what happened at the end of the last supernatural war last October. The fight was caught by humans and streamed via live video to everyone in the nation. Since then, traffic to Billings, Montana has increased ten-fold, though it did die down a bit with the colder weather.

I guess that's one thing to be grateful for.

She opens the door to her office and sets the tray of coffees down. I do the same with the bag of bagels and then begin shrugging out of my jacket. "Maybe you could talk to them?" she asks. "Let them know there's nothing to be afraid of?"

I know what she's getting at, but letting everyone in on my secret is not something I'm prepared to do. Not now, not ever. "Maribel, they think I'm human. Talking to them will be about the same as you doing it."

"You know you don't have to hide anymore," she says, sadly. "And within the next ten years, I could be gone, too."

I turn toward her and offer a slight smile. She's been with my shelter since she showed up here at twenty-three with a young daughter and nowhere else to go. As far as humans go, she's my oldest friend, and the one person I trust with nearly every one of my secrets.

Still, some things really are better left buried.

"I do still need to keep my identity under wraps. Otherwise, this place would be crawling with press and people who have no business being here. We need to keep it a sanctuary," I remind her. "And if I let anyone else in on the truth, it will become anything but."

She sighs heavily. "I know you're right. I just wish the supernatural worms had been left inside the can."

I bark out a laugh. "You and me both, Maribel. You and me both." As soon as I've hung my jacket up on the coat rack, I retrieve the coffees, hand her one, then grab the bagels and head out through the doorway.

"Everything else going okay?" I ask as we make our way down the long hall toward the dining area.

"Residency is up ten percent, but with the new addition finalized last month, we have plenty of space."

"Good, good. Are we going to need more space?"

"Possibly?" she says. "But, to be honest, we may need to simply move to a larger location if we keep growing the way we do. I know you don't want to put a stay limit on them, but—"

"No. These women are here for help. They can stay as long as they need. I'll get with my realtor this afternoon and start looking for some property. Then, we can keep expanding as much as we need. Maybe even put in a pool for the summer months. A garden. Things like that." The idea begins to take shape in my head, and my excitement grows.

All the people I can help, the children who get to go to sleep at night, feeling safe...it's what gives my life purpose. What makes suffering through the nightmares worth it.

Otherwise, I likely would have ended things more times than I can count.

"Look out! Monster alert!" a little girl screeches as she comes racing around the corner. On sock-covered feet, she slides around and raises a banana at us. "State your business."

We both hold up our hands in mock surrender.

"Olive, what are you up to today?" Maribel asks with a smile.

"I'm going to be a monster-hunting detective! Like the one on TV!"

Unable to help myself, I drop my hands and kneel. "Just like Detective Astor, huh?"

The little girl's grin spreads. "Yes. I bet no one ever messes with her. Ever." She sniffles, and I note the fading bruises on her cheekbones.

My heart aches for little Olive. So much pain in such a small body. It's heartbreaking. "Well... What if I told you I could introduce you to her?"

She gasps, drops her banana, and rushes forward. I barely have time to set the coffees down before she's slamming into me and wrapping both tiny arms around my body. The contact jolts me, and my stomach drops.

I hate being touched.

Even when it's a completely innocent little girl

giving a hug. Still, I manage to remain calm enough to not completely lose myself here in this hall.

Finally, she lets me go. "You really can?"

"I really can." Forcing a smile, I retrieve the coffees and stand again. "I'll try to get her to stop by sometime over the next couple of days. Does that work?"

Olive's eyes light up the hall. "Yes, yes, yes! That would be so awesome! Oh my gosh, I have so many questions! I need to go write them down!" She turns and bolts down the hall.

Maribel chuckles and lifts the forgotten banana. "She's a sweet girl."

"Rainey is going to love her."

"You really think you can get her here?"

"As long as she can fit it into her schedule, it won't be a problem. I can give her a call." Continuing down the hall, I can feel my heart rate begin to decline back to normal. I hate that I still feel the way I do—hate that the contact still makes me physically ill.

Honestly, I doubt that will ever change.

"Hey, Eira," Mel, my head of security, sticks her head out of her office. "Can I have a minute?"

"Sure, be right there."

"I'm going to go check in on the group therapy," Maribel says with a smile.

"See you later." I carry the coffee and bagels toward Mel's office, slip inside, and inhale deeply. The aroma of lemon and pine fills my nose, bringing a smile to my face. Somehow, the woman always manages to make her space smell like whatever season is currently outside.

It's a magic of its own, really.

After setting the coffees and food onto her desk, I offer her a cup. "For you."

"Thanks." Mel doesn't waste any time before she turns it up and drinks. The only supernatural on my staff, she is who I trust to keep all of my tenants safe. Born a human and murdered by her new husband on their wedding night, Mel now walks the earth as a Revenant. She's essentially a spirit, though she can choose to be corporeal.

"How are things going?" I ask, taking a seat in the leather chair across from her.

"Overall, not bad. We've had some troublesome phone calls recently, though." Never one to beat around the bush, she opens a manila folder on her desk and pulls out two white sheets with dates, times, and numbers listed.

I take the paper and study the numbers. "These are all nearly the same."

"Except the last number," she says. "And, that's what is really bothering me. I hacked into the police system and ran it through their database, and *none* of them actually belongs to anyone."

"That's not possible." There are only so many

number combinations; somewhere, someday they had to belong to someone.

"That's what I thought, too. But I triple-checked them. It's the area code. It's not an actual area code."

"Did you extend the search to outside of the US?"

"I did. There is no area code like that anywhere in the entire world."

My stomach drops. "Has the caller said anything?"

She shakes her head before reaching over to the phone on her desk and pressing the messages button. The room fills with a crackling sound, something akin to a fan being on in the background when you're on the phone. And then, after a few seconds, someone begins to breathe into the line.

A few moments of that, and everything falls silent.

I shift my attention back to Mel. "Weird, right?"

"Just some asshole being a creep," I tell her. "Can you block those variations from calling?"

She nods. "I blocked them all from calling, but if they change numbers—"

"Then we'll know we have a much bigger problem on our hands," I tell her with a smile. "Just keep me in the loop if anyone else calls."

"Will do."

"See you later."

Mel waves at me as she shoves a bagel into her mouth. I'm just stepping out into the hall when my phone dings. I pull it out of my pocket and awareness washes over me before I even have the chance to look at the name on my screen.

Fearghas. A smile spreads over my face as I tap on the text message and pull up the image of a villain as he stares up from a dark hole. The words *'When I go out and there are people everywhere'* are typed across the top with the thought bubble below reading, *"This is a nightmare."* I snort and send him an eye-roll emoji back.

The fae is the most social person I've ever met. It's ridiculously charming, really, and ever since he stopped being able to dematerialize everywhere and simply began using his phone for text messages, I get at least one meme a day.

One to make me smile, and the goodnight message I get every single night makes my frozen heart thaw, just a little.

After shoving my phone back into my pocket, I head back out into the hall and back toward Maribel's empty office to retrieve my jacket and hat. Then, giddy with excitement for the fae I know I'll be seeing later, I step out into the cold.

Somehow, this time, it doesn't bother me nearly as much.

CHAPTER TWO
FEARGHAS

"Seriously, Fearghas? Do you not know how to blow up a balloon?" Rainey snatches the green latex from me and goes about it herself.

Grinning, I set my phone aside and watch as she exhales, her cheeks turning pink as the balloon gets larger.

I *could* tell her that all it would take is a snap of my fingers and I could inflate them all, seeing as how we fae have minor control over the elements. Note—minor. I can't bring a thunderstorm crashing down, but I can sure as hell mess up someone's hair or fill up a balloon.

But where's the fun in that? "What can I say? Your human ways are lost on me."

She glares at me, dark eyes narrowing on my face.

"Listen, first of all, *not* human. I could kill you in the next five seconds. And secondly, I *will* kill you in the next five seconds if you don't start helping."

Chuckling, I lift a balloon and pretend to blow into the hole. Rainey rolls her eyes and snatches it away from me.

"She's going to kill you, brother." Elijah's warning does nothing but further amuse me.

"Probably one day. Thousands of bounty hunters, fae, and supernatural, alike, have failed, but Rainey Astor will be the death of me."

"Keep joking, fairy boy," she snaps as she blows up yet another green balloon.

"Okay, how many of these things are you going to put on the ground? At this rate, Delaney won't even be able to walk in. She's already at a disadvantage given that she can no longer see her feet."

"We needed some kind of decoration for the floor." She ties off the end and tosses it to the ground.

"This is looking like a scene from a horror movie. Except, instead of fog, it's an attack of green latex."

"I think I saw a porno like that once," Brad, the head of Tarnley's cleaners, calls out from the corner where he and the pub owner are trying to hang streamers.

"Only you," Tarnley chuckles as he applies tape to the corner.

"Listen, there is no telling if there will be any other babies born into my family. You guys are going to help me give this little nugget a welcome party fit for a king."

"You don't want any kids?" I question as I let go of the balloon I just inhaled. It squeaks and flies toward Rainey as it rapidly deflates. She simply watches me, little sister annoyance etched in every line of her face.

I love it. There may not be much joy in my life, but being around the Astor sisters has given my life new meaning.

"I don't know. But, to be fair, I also have no idea what I want to have for dinner tonight."

"Lasagna," Elijah calls out.

She snaps. "Sounds perfect."

I grin, looking between the two with nothing but admiration and jealousy for what they have. That connection? Love? It's what I want more than any damn thing right now. My thoughts shift to Eira—to the secret I know she's keeping from me.

"What's up your asshole?" Rainey questions.

"Girl trouble." I wink and she rolls her eyes.

"You two really just need to get after it already. It would put you both in better moods."

I'm getting ready to retort, but the door opens, and a young hunter strolls in with a petite witch at his side.

"Sorry we're late," she says as she rushes forward and hands Rainey a bag that's practically bursting at the seams with green and yellow decorations. "Drex just *had* to stop and take out a vamp on the way here."

The hunter shrugs. "Listen, it's my job."

Rainey narrows her eyes on him. "You're on probation, Drexel. Or need I remind you of the shifters who almost ripped your face off last week?"

He grimaces, his cheeks flushing crimson. "They got the drop on me. Won't happen again."

"You're not supposed to be out hunting solo," Rainey reminds him. "Do it again, and I'll lock your ass up for a few days."

Drex groans. "Someone put me back up on the auction block," he retorts.

"Don't tempt me," Rainey replies.

"Streamers are done." Tarnley claps his hands. "What else?"

"Bar is stocked?"

"It is."

"Food?"

"Ready to be fried."

Rainey takes a deep breath. "I think we're good, then." She turns to me. "Eira is coming?"

"As far as I know. I'm not exactly her keeper."

"No, but you are her stalker."

The word leaves a dry taste in my mouth, but I don't show it. Smiling instead, I shrug. "I'm trying to change my ways."

She snorts. "Yeah, okay." With a deep breath, she steps back and studies the space. "What do you think?"

"She's going to love it." Elijah wraps an arm around his wife's shoulders and leans in to press a kiss to her temple. "You did good, Rainey."

"Thanks." She beams up at him before leaning into his embrace.

I turn away, suddenly needing more fresh air than is currently available. "Okay. If that's all, I have some things to look into."

The huntress I've adopted as my little sister arches an eyebrow. "A siren to stalk?"

"Believe it or not, I do have other things in my life."

"I don't believe it," she retorts. "But thanks for your help. What little you did do, anyway."

I flash a smile before heading toward the door and calling out, "Anytime!" Noticing some empty balloons sitting on the table beside the door, I lift one, turn toward Rainey, and snap my fingers. The balloon steadily inflates at roughly the same rate her cheeks flush with red.

"You bastard!"

"See you all tonight." I let it go and rush out into the sunlight where she wouldn't dare kick my ass. Probably. Who knows, she might actually follow me out and do it on the street. I slip dark sunglasses onto my face and step onto the sidewalk.

While I do miss possessing the ability to dematerialize and appear somewhere within the beat of a heart, human travel certainly does have its perks. For one, it gives me time to process thoughts that would otherwise plague me once I lay my head down at night.

Not that I'm getting much sleep these days, but that's a problem for another walk. After hitting the unlock button on my key-fob, I slip behind the wheel of my car, then fire up the ignition. The classic muscle car roars to life, the loud sound echoing off the exteriors of the buildings around me.

As I pull out into the flow of traffic, I let my mind drift to Eira. To the sight of her sitting across from me in the booth I will be occupying in only a few minutes. Rainey calls me her stalker—they all do—and while I know it's meant lightheartedly, there is a grain of truth to it.

When we're not together, I'm thinking about her, dreaming about her. It's ridiculous, this heart-stopping affection I have for a woman who may never want me, and whom I definitely do not deserve.

As I pull into the parking lot, the current between us intensifies. I can sense her just inside the warded walls, feel her humor, her joy, and it makes me so damned happy, I'm all but running toward the doors.

Lovesick puppy? Apt description. But this puppy knows all too well what happens to the things he cares for most.

And Eira will never again be broken. Especially not by me.

CHAPTER THREE
EIRA

Even with it barely being nine in the morning, my club is already packed. Since I stay open all the time, most of my clientele cannot venture out without bursting into flames. Plus, there's the added benefit that it keeps them off the streets so hunters like Rainey Astor don't have to put them down.

I move through the crowd, enjoying the looks of joy on the faces of some of those who are simply enjoying themselves. Of course, there are those who lack any conscience. My only rule: No violence. If that gets broken, I have plenty of guards who ensure the offender doesn't get a second chance to step out of line.

After waving at the bartender, I step into the back hall leading toward the dining hall. I'm only half-way there when I feel him—his power reaching out and caressing mine. It soothes my anxious heart and sets my blood pounding.

My reaction to him—the power he holds over me—it's terrifying.

I step through the threshold and spot him in his usual booth, wearing a dark suit. Hair styled perfectly atop his head, he looks more like an elegant businessman than the deadly fae I know him to be. Moss green eyes find mine, and my stomach warms, leaving heat pooling low in my belly.

He's the only man who has ever made me feel this way; the only one who manages to keep the want inside of me from shriveling up and dying. And even though I know acting on it is out of the question, the feeling is enough to help me feel alive.

So I stalk toward him as he watches me, strong jaw set, hand on his steaming mug of coffee. "Fearghas, how nice to see you."

"Eira," he replies with a lopsided grin. "You're looking warm."

"Had to venture out."

"Everything okay?"

"It is," I reply.

"Can I get you anything, boss?" Jackie, my morning waitress comes to a stop beside the table.

"Coffee, please, thanks."

She rushes off with a nod as I continue stripping

out of my coat, hat, and gloves. Tossing them to the booth seat beside me, I slide in across from Fearghas. "How are things this morning?"

"Good. I find I have a lot more time on my hands these days."

Chuckling, I nod in agreement. "So many ways to spend time when we're not fighting for our lives."

He grins, though it doesn't reach his eyes. The last year has been incredibly stressful for all supernaturals, given the rise—and fall—of the original witch, Heather, and then the toppling of our structure by her daughter, Lucy, that followed.

Those I lovingly referred to as the *Scooby Gang* fought hard to ensure neither witch was able to come in and take over. But the cost of their success—it was higher than anyone really cares to revisit.

And now that the final battle was caught on camera and supernaturals have been outed to the humans? Well, things have gotten a lot more complicated for the hunter, and now police captain, Rainey Astor.

"How's Delaney doing?" I ask, referring to Rainey's sister, who is pregnant with her shifter mate's son.

"Ready to pop," he replies. "But happy. She looks good."

His expression shifts to pure, blinding joy, and it nearly melts me. After taking on the Astor sisters as a surrogate brother, of sorts, his pride is apparent every time he speaks about them. And for a man like Fearghas, who has avoided attachment for over a millennia, that's a big shift.

"Here you go, hot and fresh." Jackie sets the coffee down in front of me, then disappears before I can even thank her.

"I'm so excited for her." Lifting my mug, I take a sip of the hazelnut flavored caffeine then set the mug back down in front of me.

"Same. She and Cole are more than ready. Bronywwyn just finished warding their house. Which reminds me, she asked if you could come by soon. They want to add you to the magical guest list so you can get inside without setting off the wards."

I cannot hide my appreciation for being included. Just like Fearghas, I've fought to keep everyone—he and my oldest friend, excluded—at arm's length. When you have few people in your circle, fewer people can break you.

A rule I live by. Or...lived by. "How are you doing?" I ask as I take another drink. Fearghas's expression darkens for a moment, but it's so swift to pass over his handsome features that I wonder if I'm not imagining it.

"I'm dandy," he replies. "Ridley and Rachel haven't returned from Faerie yet, but as soon as they do, I'll know a bit more."

The only other two light fae in Billings, Ridley and

Rachel went to Faerie, looking for Fearghas's sister, who was mortally wounded by him in a fight just before we were outed. She'd been prepared to kill Bronywyn, and he'd chosen good over familial ties.

While he won't admit it, I know that not knowing whether she survived or not is killing him. I long to reach over and touch his hand—to offer him any sort of comfort—but doing so would open a can of worms I desperately need to remain closed.

"I'm sorry, Fearghas."

He shrugs. "They'll find her. One way or another."

My answering smile is half-assed, at best, but I offer it anyway then take another drink of my coffee. "Meme was funny, especially for a guy who hates being alone."

Fearghas's grin is real this time, and it momentarily steals my breath. "That was one hundred percent accurate for you."

I chuckle. "I'm constantly surrounded by people."

"Sitting up in your tower doesn't count." He winks.

"Fair point." Truth is we both know he's not wrong. While I hate being alone, I also desperately crave separation from those who are around me. Yet another instance where having fewer people around means less of a chance of me getting hurt.

I've learned far too many times that betrayal rarely comes from those you expect.

Fearghas leans further in and drops his voice

despite the warding I have around his table. No one can hear anything we say—even with supernatural hearing—from inside the warded lines. "Rainey said things are starting to heat up between humans and our kind. Please be careful when you go out."

"No one knows what I am," I tell him.

"Anyone who looks at you can tell you're not human," he replies.

As it so often does, his deep voice sends my heart pounding. "While I appreciate that compliment, I can take care of myself."

He leans back, expression faltering just a bit. I hate that I do that to him. This constant push and pull between us, exhausting as it is, is the closest we can get to an actual relationship. My scars are far too deep, too jagged, to have anything more.

"Just keep an eye out. They're apparently hunting us these days."

My brows draw together in irritation. "Hunting us?"

He nods. "They've put together task forces to patrol at night. Anyone who doesn't pass a heartrate test is as good as dead. And those who have fought back? Rainey said they're putting out wanted images in chatrooms so everyone can hunt them."

An ache spreads through my chest. There are bad supernaturals out there, plenty of them, but there are also good ones. People who are just trying to live their lives—family, friends. I've seen hatred come from humans before; they're always quick to condemn what they don't understand.

But technology has made them far more dangerous than ever.

"I'll be careful."

"Thank you."

"You need to promise the same," I tell him. "You're still out hunting at night, aren't you?"

"They need the help. As much as she wants to be in the fight, Delaney has to stay out of it. Cole helps where he can, but he's afraid to leave her alone."

"Bronywyn?"

He sighs. "She's back working full time in her clinic. We need it more than ever now with the increase in injuries."

"This is so insane."

"It is."

"Rainey's doing okay with all of it?"

"She's managing. Frankly, I'm surprised she hasn't gone postal and just started offing humans."

"Are they hunting her, too? Since she's a supernatural?"

"They've left her alone—for now. Though I think that has more to do with her being such a high-profile person. The government is supposedly sending a liaison in next week to work alongside her."

The mental image of Rainey being forced to work

alongside a paper-pushing diplomat is hilarious, though I try to hide my amusement because I can all but taste Fearghas's unease. "She'll be okay."

He nods. "Just be on the lookout. They're getting bloody ballsy. Just last night, we ended up at a vampire den right after they'd cleared it out. There's no telling how many of them there are now. And we found silver blades."

"Silver."

"Someone is feeding them information on how to kill supernaturals."

"You really think so?"

He nods. "Rainey said she's recovered silver shackles, blades—all kinds of stuff on the bodies of the humans who don't make it."

"Who would do that?" I ask, disgusted. "Who would feed information on how to kill their own kind?"

He shrugs. "Possibly someone who wants to bargain for their own life? There's no telling at this point." Fearghas runs both hands over his face, and I track the movement, wishing like hell I could stand his hands on me.

How might that feel? To not panic every time someone gives me a hug or wants to shake my hand?

"You okay?"

My gaze meets his, and I swallow hard. "Yes. Sorry, I'm fairly tired."

"Is something bothering you?"

"Nothing in particular," I reply. "Just have a lot on my mind."

"Eira—"

"I promise I'm fine," I assure him with a forced smile. "You'd be the first one I'd tell if something was wrong."

He opens his mouth to respond, but his phone goes off, the song *Eye of the Tiger* filling our small warded booth. "Rainey," he replies with a grin.

"Of course." I laugh as his cheeks flush with color, and he presses the cell to his ear.

"Fearghas here." His gaze meets mine and darkens. "Be there in a few." After ending the call, he turns up his mug and downs the still-steaming liquid. "I have to go."

"Everything all right?"

"There's a mob forming outside Tarnley's pub."

"I'll come, too."

"No." He shakes his head as I start to stand. "Please. I need you to stay out of this, Eira."

"Haven't you learned? I don't stay out of things when I can help."

"Please. They don't know about you yet. Let's keep it that way as long as possible. They get your face, and every supernatural in here is going to be at risk."

Truthfully, I hadn't considered that. And that's a problem. Outing myself to the humans would mean they could try to track me, not just here—but at the shelter, as well. The latter has me nodding in agreement. "I promise."

His shoulders relax and shrug into his jacket. "Thank you." He starts to turn away, and fear for his safety has me pushing to my feet.

"Fearghas?"

He turns, his body so close to mine I can smell the fresh pine of his aftershave. I suck in a breath, and his nostrils flare. "Yes?"

I meet his mossy gaze and swallow hard. "Please be careful."

The corner of his mouth lifts in a grin, and he reaches forward, lifting a strand of my hair and dropping it behind my shoulder. There is no direct contact with my body, but need pools in my belly in response. "I promise I'll see you later for a drink."

Then he turns away and leaves me standing, staring after him and wishing like hell I was someone else entirely.

Someone who could be what we both need.

CHAPTER FOUR

FEARGHAS

"Supernaturals do not belong! Supernaturals do not belong!" The chanting crowd fills the street outside of Tarnley's pub. On the steps, I see Rainey between Elijah and Tarnley with her ex-partner, Walker Allan, just in front of Bronywyn.

"You all need to leave!" Rainey announces through a megaphone. "This is private property."

"We're on the public street!" a man yells, loudly.

I push through the crowd, making my way toward Rainey and the others. As soon as I do, a uniformed officer I hadn't been able to see before raises the yellow caution tape so I can duck down below and head up the steps toward Rainey.

"Thank you for coming."

"No problem. What do you need me to do?"

She leans in. “Think you can work your magic on this crowd?”

I look out over the two dozen or so humans. “I can try. Though erasing their knowledge of us would be foolish given they just have to turn on the news.”

“Just make them forget about this place,” she tells me.

My gaze drifts past her to the shattered window. Then, I turn my attention to Tarnley’s dark expression. “Was anyone inside?”

Jaw set, she nods. “Two vampires died, including his bartender, Mollie.”

Anger motivates me now, so I turn toward the crowd. Calling my power forward, I allow it to saturate the air around us. Then, I turn toward Rainey and the others. “You’re going to want to go inside,” I tell them.

They nod and turn toward the door.

“We know you’re in there!” a man yells.

“Come out, or we’ll come in!” a woman hollers right afterward.

“Human rights are not supernatural!” Another man yells. He raises his hand, holding a red brick in his grasp.

“Drop it,” I tell him.

His brown eyes fall on mine now, his pupils dilating so far they obliterate all color. The brick clatters to the ground.

“There are no supernaturals inside,” I tell them.

"You've made a mistake that cost a human her life. If you want to avoid any charges, you will never come back to this place."

They stare at me then mutter my words back to me.

"Oh no."

"I'm sorry."

"This was a mistake."

"That poor woman."

Slowly the crowd dissipates, turning and dropping their signs and bricks on the sidewalk right in front of the pub. As soon as they're down the street, Rainey steps out beside me. "Thank you."

"Yeah." The power to coerce others disgusts me, and I rarely use it. Even on my enemies, it feels wrong to rob someone of their right to choose. "If any of them have known about this place longer than twelve hours, they'll be back. I need herbs to enhance magic larger than that."

"Let's hope that's not the case." She takes a deep breath. "This is getting out of hand."

"We have to hope your liaison friend will be able to do something."

"Doubtful. She'll be here this afternoon. I do not have high hopes."

"Things have to work out," I say as I watch the humans continue retreating down the road. "You figure out who's leaking info yet?"

"Not a damned clue. I even tried asking them. One man let it slip the information is coming from an email address, though he wouldn't divulge how he got it or how the addresses are being exchanged. My tech team is on it, though."

"I'm sorry you're having to deal with all of this."

She shrugs, but I see the defeat in her shoulders. When supernaturals were outed on camera in a fight less than a year ago, none of us could have seen the repercussions coming. Sure, we'd known there would be fall out. And since I've been around longer than damn near any living creature, I've seen the torches and pitchforks turned against supernaturals before—but this level of engagement, it came as a surprise. Though, I suppose it shouldn't have given people will believe damn near anything on the internet these days.

"I just want normalcy again. Or something like it."

Elijah steps out and slings an arm around her shoulders.

"Thanks for helping out."

"No problem." I look down at her, our height difference putting the top of her head at my shoulder. "I wish I could have done it on a much larger scale."

"You and me both."

"We've got another issue," Walker announces as he steps out beside him. The flaxen-haired detective holds up his cell, his mouth in a tight line. "Family of shifters found dead in their home."

The drive across town to a suburban neighborhood takes less than twenty minutes, but each set of sixty seconds might as well have been an hour. Rainey's white-knuckled grip on the steering wheel shows her rage as she moves in and out of traffic, siren blazing.

Elijah sits rigidly in the passenger seat, while Walker and I take up residence in the back. Already, the place is crawling with press; newscasters with cameras shoved in the faces of the uniformed officers who've blocked off the place.

Outside, a woman stands in a man's embrace, her eyes red and swollen as he tries to comfort her. We climb out and follow Rainey to the other side of the caution tape.

"What do you know?"

"Who's inside?"

"Was it supernaturals?"

The press fire questions at Rainey, and she whirls on them. "Since I am just arriving at the scene, I have absolutely no comment for you."

"But can you just tell us if it was monsters?" one of the reporters calls out.

Rainey takes a deep breath and turns. "I can tell

you that humans are just as capable of monstrous and horrific acts." She turns away and ignores the onslaught of questions. The moment we step inside the house, my anger boils to a full-on rage.

"Oh my—" Rainey chokes and covers her nose as we move into the house. Seated at the table, cold, rotten dinner in front of them, a man, woman, and teenage girl all have their faces down on their plates. Dried blood crusts their noses and pools at their feet, giving away that they've been dead for at least a day—possibly more.

Scrawled in crimson on the rose wallpaper behind them is a message telling us exactly who committed this horrific act.

The word *Cleansed* is drawn above a trident.

"This is murder," Elijah snarls.

"How did you know they were wolves?" Rainey asks Walker.

"I got the call and had a Vision." Psychics are a dying breed—nearly extinct—thanks to the supernaturals who feared them.

The parallels between the genocide of his kind and what's happening to all supernaturals now are apparent and fucking disturbing.

I have no tolerance for those who hurt others. For bullies.

"They died painfully," he chokes out. "The father was the last." He walks behind the chair and gestures to something, so we follow, taking in the sight of the silver blade still embedded in the shifter's back. "They incapacitated him."

Rainey closes her eyes and clenches her fists. Her nostrils flare, and Elijah moves over to press a hand to her back. Last year, she likely would have blacked out and killed everyone outside, but with her Lunar side—the dark power—closed, she maintains control. "We need to meet their force with force," she says. "It's time to step up our patrols."

"Doing so will make them feel threatened," Elijah warns.

"I don't give a shit," she growls.

"Captain Astor?"

We all turn as a petite redhead moves into the room, wearing jeans and a black leather jacket. *Human.*

"Who the hell are you?" Rainey snarls.

"I'm Jillian Regner," she holds out a hand with black painted fingernails. "The liaison."

Rainey stares at her a moment—likely trying to get a read on the situation.

I may never have met a government liaison before, but this woman would certainly have been the last thing I expected. Rainey takes her hand. "Rainey Astor." She releases her and gestures to Elijah. "This is my husband, Elijah Hawthorne, my partner, Detective Walker Allen, and my consultant, Fearghas."

She turns her crystal blue gaze to me. “No last name?”

“Never needed one,” I tell her.

“Okay, so you’re a hunter, your husband is a hunter, partner is a psychic, and—” She turns to me. “What are you?”

“Powerful,” I tell her. No need to let them know fae exist anytime soon.

I’m expecting the woman to be annoyed. Instead, she grins. “That I can tell just by looking at you.” That smile vanishes as her gaze drifts over my shoulder to the deceased behind me. “Oh my, this is—”

“Horrific,” Rainey finishes.

“More than.” Jillian moves into the dining room, her eyes misting. “I’ve seen a lot of horrific shit, but this—killing because you don’t understand, that is another level of evil, altogether.” She turns to us. “I’m so sorry this is happening to you. My hope is that we can stop it by bridging our differences.”

“I don’t need a speech,” Rainey snaps. “I know why you’re here, and I’ll cooperate, but don’t expect us to be friends. Stay the hell out of my way, and we’ll get along just fine.” Rainey shoves out of the room, leaving me standing with Walker and Jillian.

“I said something wrong?”

“Rainey has been dealing with this for months,” Walker explains. “And so far, it’s only getting worse.”

Jillian glances behind her. “I see that. There’s

nothing that makes this okay. We'll fix it." She turns and heads outside, and I glance at Walker.

"That is not who I expected."

"Same here. Think she'll be helpful?"

He shrugs. "I think she'll try, but the damage has already been done. You and I know people don't change." With a sigh, he steps out into the sunshine, and I turn back toward the horrific scene behind me.

More times than I care to count, I've seen humanity at its worst. Destroying what it doesn't understand, running over those it deems too weak. It never seems to fail that the most horrible of all are the ones who step forward to lead the charge.

This time, the pitchforks came for an innocent family seated around their table, eating dinner. And I cannot help but wonder who they're going to come for next.

CHAPTER FIVE
EIRA

"We cannot be expected to sit idly by while they murder our kind!" A female vampire roars from the back of the council room.

I sit beside Walker—who looks like he'd rather be anywhere, but here—while Delaney sits front and center, Willa to her other side. Deissy, the only human on the council, is seated just to my right.

I have a sneaking suspicion Delaney put her here so I can help ensure she's not attacked.

"We're not asking you to do nothing. We're asking you to not go out on a hunt like they are."

"They killed my cousin and his family!" a female shifter in the back chokes out, as tears slip down her cheeks. "They'd never hurt anyone, not even an animal," she adds. "They didn't deserve to die." She collapses down to her chair, and a man wraps an arm around her shoulders.

"No one deserves to die," Delaney says sadly, her hand perched atop her swollen belly. "Rainey is handling it. The government just sent a liaison. She's going to—"

"Another *human* is not what we need," someone snaps.

"She'll just take their side."

"She's not here to help us."

The back door opens, and Fearghas steps in. My magic buzzes in response to his presence as warmth spreads through my body. He eases my nerves, his presence alone comforting to me even when he's clear across the room.

But then a woman steps in behind him, her eyes wide in response to the scene before her.

Chaos erupts. The supernaturals jump to their feet, and Fearghas steps in front of her, shielding her petite form with his muscled body.

It shouldn't make me jealous. Shouldn't make me want to rake my fingernails across the desk in front of me, but it does. A hundred percent.

"Everyone sit down!" Delaney roars.

Nothing happens.

Willa gets to her feet and whistles so loud the shrill sound hurts even my ears. All eyes turn to the alpha. "You were told to sit down. I'm sure there is an explanation for this."

Those in the audience begrudgingly take their seats, though their gazes never leave Fearghas, even as he and the mystery woman make their way up toward the front.

He doesn't look at me, and the strained expression on his face has my nerves flaring to life again. Something happened...something big.

Fearghas comes to a stop in front of Delaney's seat. "This is Jillian Regner. She's the liaison sent to us from the humans' government. Give her respect. She's here to help." He nods to her, and she smiles in response. Then he steps away, moving back until he's directly in front of my chair. From the height difference of the stage our table is seated on, the top of his head is right at table height.

Jillian clears her throat, and I force my attention to her. "I know tensions are high right now, and I can completely understand your unease when it comes to me, but I assure you that I am here to help."

Someone in the audience snorts. "We've heard that before."

"From a human?"

"From a witch who later tried to murder half our population," the man shoots back.

"Well, I am not a witch, so you already have the upper hand," she says as she clasps both hands in front of her. Confidence practically oozes out of every pore of this woman, which is surprising seeing as how she's a human standing in front of an entire room packed wall-to-wall with supernaturals. "I am here because I believe an understanding can be made between humans and supernaturals. I believe that we can learn to live together, without this fear."

"So, you believe in fairytales?" a woman calls out. "Because that's what you're suggesting."

"I do not," Jillian replies. "In fact, I pride myself on being fairly pessimistic." She begins to pace in front of the stage. "I saw what is happening to your kind first thing this morning." Her voice cracks, and she shuts her eyes tightly to compose herself. If it's an act, it's a damn good one. "That kind of horrific thing is exactly why I'm here, but in order for me to do my job, I need you to remain neutral. As badly as you want to go out and kill these assholes—and believe me, I get it—that is not the right answer. You have to be the better person in this case."

"Easy for you to say! They aren't murdering your kind!"

"Humans have murdered humans since the beginning of time," she reminds the room. "Serial killers exist in all realities, unfortunately. As we speak, new laws are being drafted that will cover supernaturals, as well as humans. I will be here to hand them over to your council when they're done and I'm ready to present them to the media." She clears her throat and comes to a stop in the center. "But, again, in order for that to happen, I need you to remain calm. Don't give in to the monster label they've created for you. You do not fit in that box." She pauses then smiles again. "Thank you for your time." As she leaves, she passes by Fearghas, and he falls in line behind her, the two of them moving into the corner.

Delaney clears her throat. "Thank you, Jillian. Does anyone have any other questions?"

The room is completely silent, so I stand, and gazes shift to me. "Be safe. If anyone needs shelter, if you're feeling scared, please head over to my club. It's open twenty-four hours, and as we speak, my team is setting up a family-friendly area. Your kids are welcome. Head around the back, and the guards will let you in so you don't have to move through the club."

"Thank you!" someone calls out.

"Meeting adjourned," Delaney announces. The room fills with murmurs and the sounds of chairs scraping against the floor. As it clears out, we all stand and head straight for the corner where Fearghas waits with the human.

"Fearghas," Delaney greets as she hugs him.

"You are very pregnant," Jillian announces.

Delaney chuckles. "I am. Delaney Astor-Miller," she introduces herself with the offer of a handshake.

"You're Rainey's sister." The human takes her hand and shakes gently before releasing her.

"That I am."

"Don't hold it against her, though. Del's the nice one." Fearghas winks at Delaney, but I see the humor doesn't fully resonate with him.

"What happened this morning?" I question. "Is Tarnley okay?"

Now, he finally meets my gaze. "He's okay."

"It was the family, then? The shifters who were killed?"

He nods at my question, and I long to be able to reach out and hug him without losing my mind. Just one quick embrace...but even that is not possible. Not with demons like mine clinging to every move I make.

"We are going to make sure it doesn't keep happening," Jillian promises. She reaches out a hand. "I didn't get your name?"

"I didn't give it to you," I reply, sweetly. "It's Eira," I add when Fearghas takes a deep breath.

"Nice to meet you. You're a—"

"Powerful," Fearghas replies, and Jillian grins.

It grates on my nerves.

"Got it."

"Willa Akacheta, shifter." Willa holds out her hand, and Jillian takes it.

"She's the alpha of a local pack," Delaney adds.

"Alpha, I bet that's an insane amount of responsibility."

"I manage."

Jillian turns to Deissy. "You are?"

"Deissy. Human."

This seems to genuinely surprise the human who is acting as though she already has all the answers. "Human? I didn't realize you already had a human on your council."

"We added her when we rebuilt," Delaney explains. "Figured it was important to have one."

"This is wonderful. We need to get you in front of a camera."

Deissy pales. "Excuse me?"

"They will be much more open to this merger of our kinds, knowing you thought to include a human from the get-go."

"We are not putting our faces on the news," I tell her. "That's asking for this gang to come after us."

Jillian turns to me. "We need to humanize all of you."

"I'm not going on camera," I tell her. "Period."

She glances back at Fearghas, who shakes his head. "It needs to be their choice."

Her red-painted lips press together before she faces me. "Okay, understood." Then, she shifts her attention to Deissy. "I really think it would help if you spoke to them," she says. "It might be the connection we need."

"They are slaughtering families in their homes," Willa replies. "I doubt Deissy giving them a pep talk on hand-holding is going to help."

Jillian nods in response to Willa's disagreement. "I'm not expecting it to be what fixes everything, but it could be a start. Will you do it?" she asks Deissy.

The young woman's cheeks flush.

"Don't feel pressured," I tell her. "You should take time to think about it. Talk to Felix about what it might mean."

At that, Deissy nods.

"Yes, definitely, take time," Jillian adds. "I don't want you to feel pressured." She flashes a smile. "I think it's amazing what you're doing, and I'd love to have a coffee with you so you can tell me how this happened."

Deissy relaxes slightly and returns the gesture. "That would be good."

"Great." Jillian turns to me. "I'd love to see your club."

"No."

Jillian is completely taken aback by my refusal, and if I'd been a pettier person, I might have smiled victoriously. I don't like her. There's something—

"Why not?" she interrupts my thoughts.

"Because you're a human. Humans are not allowed

in my establishment for good reason. Some of the supernaturals who hang out there are newly-turned, and the scent of your blood could put them into a frenzy."

Fearghas glares at me because he knows I'm lying, but thankfully, he doesn't say anything. Not yet, anyway.

"Well, if there's any way I can get inside and see, I would be grateful—even if it's just from afar." She turns to Fearghas. "Where to next?"

"Where to? Are you babysitting her?"

Fearghas's expression darkens, but Jillian is the one who answers. "Not babysitting—escorting and introducing. It was so nice to meet you all," she says. "I look forward to getting to know everyone." She heads down the aisle, and Fearghas hesitates just a moment before following, his gaze not leaving my face until he turns away.

"You don't like her," Willa says. It's not a question, and I don't bother lying.

"No. But I'm wary of everyone."

"She seems a little too confident, right? As if she's been around our kind before?"

"Certainly appears that way," Willa replies to Delaney.

"We just need to keep an eye on her. I'm glad Fearghas is the one Rainey assigned."

"Why?" I ask, turning to Delaney.

"Because he can handle himself."

I know she's right, but there's a part of me that churns with unease, a rock settling in my gut preparing me for what's coming.

It's a storm, that much is apparent, but the damage that will be left behind is still yet to be seen. And I'll be damned if Fearghas is part of it.

"Jillian?" I call out right before she steps through the door Fearghas has opened. He glances up at me with wariness etched in every line of his face.

She turns toward me, wearing a smile plastered on her face. "Yes?"

"Go ahead and come by the club later. Be sure you come around back, though."

That smile widens. "Great. See you later." She turns and heads out into the sun while Fearghas lingers a moment, his gaze on mine. The air between us is pregnant with tension, so I force myself to look away and gather my things.

"You okay?" Delaney asks, voice low. "You know Fearghas—"

"Fearghas is my friend," I tell her as I lift my purse. "He can do whatever he wants. My concern for him is platonic, I assure you."

"Uh-huh," she replies. "Well, if you need anyone to talk to, you know where to find me."

I swallow hard. "Thanks. Fearghas mentioned you needed me to come by the house?"

She lights up, completely and totally joyful. "Yes, I want to add you to the wards so you can enter whenever you need to."

"When works for you?"

"What are you doing right now?"

Worrying about Fearghas. The distraction would be nice, though, so I force myself to appear relaxed when I'm the exact opposite at all times. "Nothing."

CHAPTER SIX
FEARGHAS

"I know what you're thinking."

I spare Jillian a glance as we cross the street toward *The Bean*. "Oh? You a psychic, too?"

She smiles and steps onto the sidewalk. I follow suit and shove both hands into the pockets of my slacks. "You're thinking that I'm not worth the trouble. That I'm going to fail in my quest for diplomacy."

She pretty much hit the nail on the head, but for whatever reason, I choose to spare her feelings. Perhaps I'm feeling generous—or perhaps it's the simple fact that she stepped up when others chose not to. "Nope. Actually, I'm wondering what kind of coffee you like to drink."

An auburn eyebrow arches, and she tilts her head to the side. "Really?"

"Yeah. You can tell a lot about a person when you

take into consideration what type of coffee they drink." I grip the handle and pull the door open, stepping to the side so she can move into the aromatic shop.

"I drink mine black. What does that tell you?"

"That you mean business."

Her cheeks flush with color, and she nods as she takes her place in line. "I do. And I promise I will be successful."

"You're confident. For a human," I add low enough she's the only one who can hear.

She throws her head back and laughs, and the throaty sound lifts my spirits. When Rainey first asked me to escort the human liaison around, to keep her safe, I'd been pissed. Glorified babysitter? Find someone else.

But truth be told, Jillian is oddly refreshing.

"What can I get you two?" the woman behind the counter asks as we step up. Her eyes rake over me as most women's do—not arrogance, truth—so I flash a smile.

"Drip coffee for me, please."

"Cream? Sugar?"

"No, thanks."

"You got it." She taps something on the pad in front of her then looks to me. "What about you?"

"Same."

"No cream or sugar, either?"

"Don't need it." I throw her a wink, and her cheeks flush red. "That'll be four-seventy-five."

I hand her a twenty. "Keep the change."

Then, Jillian and I turn away and head for a small table in the corner. "So you can just afford to toss twenties out there, huh?"

"When you're as old as I am, money is no issue. I'd rather give it out as I can."

"What exactly do you do?"

"This and that. Real estate, I own a shit ton of stock in different companies—basically whatever strikes my fancy."

Chuckling, Jillian shakes her head. "Well, thank you for the coffee."

"Anytime."

"Here are your coffees." The barista who took our order approaches our table with a coffee in each hand. As she sets them down, I notice the phone number scrawled on the side of my cup.

"Thank you," Jillian tells her with a smile as she turns away, walking incredibly fast as two other baristas giggle and watch on.

They all turn and look at me when she reaches them, so I hold up the cup and smile.

"Quite the ladies' man, aren't you?"

I shrug. "Nothing ever goes past flirtation, but I have fun."

"Nothing? Does your kind not do—"

I throw up a hand. “First of all, my kind can do anything your humans can do, except better. Second, it has nothing to do with that and everything to do with the simple fact I don’t get involved.”

“With anyone but Eira?”

I swallow hard and turn toward her.

“I saw the way she watched you, the way you tried not to look at her.” Jillian takes a sip of coffee. “If my ex-husband had looked at me like that—well—let’s just say we would probably still be together.”

“Divorced, then?”

“Majorly divorced. Last year.”

“Sorry to hear that.”

She shrugs, but the way she runs the tip of her finger around the base of her coffee mug tells a very different story. “We got married way too young,” she says. “And had we not gotten divorced and I hadn’t gotten the chance to throw myself into work to cope, I wouldn’t be here.”

“I’m not—”

She laughs and throws up a hand. “I know what you’re going to say, but I am not hitting on you. I promise. I have sworn off relationships in any form.”

I lean back in my seat and take a drink of my coffee, grateful I read that situation wrong. Not that Jillian isn’t attractive. She certainly is, but there’s only one who catches my attention that way. “Well, then, here's to not hitting on me." I raise my travel cup in a mock salute, and she does the same.

"Now that we have that tension out of the way, what can you tell me about Rainey?"

My walls go right back up. "If you're looking for me to give you some kind of gossip on her, you're in the wrong place."

"No, of course not. I want to know how to get her to trust me, to talk to me. If I can't get a clear picture of what's going on, I don't know how I can help."

"Well, I can tell you she doesn't trust easy, but starting by pumping her friends for information is a poor way to go about it."

"She seems so sure of herself, but also overwhelmed."

"She's currently sitting at the epicenter of a massive upheaval. Overwhelmed doesn't even begin to cover it, but Rainey is damn good at navigating choppy waters."

"Look. I'm not here for any other reason than to help. Rainey's department is handling things the best way possible, given the circumstances. I just want to see where I can assist."

"By watching and staying out of her way." I don't mention the fact that Rainey might put a bullet in her if she steps out of line; figure that piece of information is probably better locked down.

"Noted. What can you tell me about the fight that led to your kind being plastered all over the news?"

Rainey gave me permission to answer any and all of Jillian's questions honestly if I felt like it. And if she truly is here to help, then having the knowledge she seeks can't hurt. Shit, even if she's a wolf in sheep's clothing, I don't see what it would hurt to tell her, so I lean in. "Not here."

"Shit. So the original witch created all supernaturals?" Jillian asks from my couch.

"Yes."

"Who created the original witch?"

"The fae."

"Fae? As in fairies?"

A muscle in my jaw ticks. "Not fairies."

She cocks her head to the side as her eyes narrow on me for a moment. Then, she jumps up and claps her hands. "Yes! You're one of them, aren't you?"

"One of what?"

"The fairy—I mean *fae*."

"Why do you say that?"

"Because I know you're not a shifter or a vampire, and you feel far too powerful to be a hunter."

"Feel?"

"It's this gift I have," she explains as she sits down.

"I didn't realize what it was until you guys were outed, but it's why I wanted to join the I.U.E."

"I.U.E.? Isn't that a pregnancy thing?"

She snorts. "Investigation of Unexplainable Events. The branch of the government I work for."

"There's an actual branch?"

"Oh, yeah. Mostly it's been investigating reports of aliens, but when you guys were outed, I *knew* I wasn't crazy."

"So you can feel power?" Intrigued, I lean in.

"Kind of? For example, when I'm near you..." she trails off as though she's searching for the right words. "I can feel a shift in the air, almost like static electricity."

"And when you're around Rainey?"

"It's the same, but different?" She covers her face with both hands and laughs. "I sound crazy."

"Hardly. I've just never actually met one of you before."

"One of me?"

"You're a *Faic*."

"Excuse me?"

"It means 'see' in Gaelic. You're a human who can sense supernaturals. Very rare."

Jillian leans back on the couch and crosses her arms. "You're not kidding."

"No. You're lucky we overthrew the previous council. They would hunt and kill your kind." I get to my feet and head into the kitchen for a drink of water.

"This is insane."

"Welcome to the club." I reach above the fridge and retrieve my whiskey, then pull out two glasses from the cupboard. "Want some?"

"Definitely." After pouring some into each glass, I hand one to her.

Jillian is silent a moment, brows drawn together as she stares into her mug. The freckles lining her nose and cheeks scrunch with each shift of her expression. "So the original witch was created by your kind, and she, in turn, created all supernaturals."

"Yes. Would you like to hear the story?"

Her eyes all but light up. "Hell yes."

I move around the counter and head back for my chair, and Jillian returns to her seat on the couch. "As I said, witches are the oldest supernaturals that exist in this world. The original witch sold her soul to a fae in exchange for immortality and power."

"Sold her soul? Like a dem—"

"No," I interrupt. "While fae have both light and dark courts, the dark fae typically cannot leave the Veil. Unless they manage to slip out."

"The Veil?"

"A place where supernaturals' immortal souls go as they travel between worlds."

"So, purgatory."

"Essentially, yes." I take a drink of whiskey. "The original witch had her heart broken, and she wanted to make the human man pay for what he'd done. But after vengeance had been had, the witch grew lonely. She sought companionship and discovered affection for a human. She longed to possess him so he couldn't break her heart the way her last lover did. In order to do that, she sought a magical way to bind him to her—to make him immortal.

"She used a blood exchange where he drank from a human while she carried out the spell. This brought about the first vampire."

"Woah. This is a twisted fucking fairy tale," she says. "No offense."

"None taken. This time." I take another drink, then continue, "Years passed, they loved each other, but her lover's bloodlust soon became insatiable. It was all he thought about, and the lives he stole brought the humans closer to discovering her nature. So, afraid, she found another human and bestowed a portion of her power onto him, creating the first hunter."

"Like Rainey."

"Her great, great, great—however many greats—grandfather."

"Holy shit."

"The hunter slaughtered the vampire as he'd promised, though not before the vampire discovered how to create more of his own kind. The witch didn't know this, though, and was so grateful she wanted to give her hunter a gift. A way to keep him tied to her. She knew a blood sacrifice wouldn't do it; that had backfired before, so she began to turn humans into animals for her hunter to track."

"Shifters," she whispered. "She created the shifters as trophy hunts for him?"

I nod.

"That's awful."

"It was. But it worked, for a time. Not too long into it, the shifters became aware of what was happening. They went into hiding and created their own packs."

"That sounds like an incredibly twisted *Grimm Fairytale*."

"Essentially, it is," I tell her. "Our past is not free of stain. The fae are what brought this blight upon the human world, and it's why I've remained here—well, one of the reasons."

"You stay here to protect?"

"I remained here in Billings to protect the most powerful ley line in this world."

"Ley line? Those are real?"

"Very real."

Eyes wide, she shakes her head in disbelief, even as I know she's absorbed everything I've told her. "This is insane. I can't tell you how happy I am to know it's all real."

"Really? You enjoy knowing monsters are real?"

Jillian snorts. "You're no more a monster than I am."

"I could be."

"What can your kind do?"

"More than I can say in this conversation."

She pales slightly.

"What is it?"

"Someone—"

The air shifts, and I feel it then, too. The change—the charge. I whirl and come face-to-face with someone I really hoped was dead.

"Hello, big brother."

CHAPTER SEVEN
FEARGHAS

"Sheelin," I growl, placing my body between her and Jillian.

"Brother?"

Sheelin leans around me and grins at Jillian. "Keeping a pet? Don't you know they make messes when they bleed?"

"What the fuck are you doing here?" I demand as I reach behind my back for the blade tucked safely in my belt.

"Figured I'd do a check; it's been a while. That and your dog keeps coming for me."

Ridley. "You should be dead."

"Because you tried to kill me?" She laughs. "I'm so much more difficult to get rid of." She disappears, and I turn to Jillian.

"Get over here, now."

She starts to run toward me when Sheelin appears in her path. "Boo!"

Jillian stumbles backward and withdraws her firearm.

I rush forward and slam my body into Sheelin's. We tumble forward, and my head slams into the corner of my coffee table. Pain explodes as warmth begins a steady trickle down the side of my face. "Get close to me," I tell Jillian.

She does, putting her back against mine.

"I don't suppose you have iron in those bullets, do you?"

"I don't think so."

Sheelin laughs, and we whirl, facing where she sits on the countertop. "So much fun. See you very, very soon, brother. Brother's pet." She waves and disappears. My vision wavers, and Jillian wraps an arm around my waist to guide me toward the chair.

"We need to call—"

A knock on my door sends my pulse pounding.

Jillian sets me down and heads for the door. "Hey—"

"What the fuck did you do?" Eira's roar fills my ears as Jillian stumbles backward into the room. She falls to the ground as my siren moves into the room, violet eyes blazing with power. She takes one look at me and turns her full attention to Jillian.

"It wasn't her!" I yell from the couch. I attempt to

stand, but my vision swims, and I fall back to the couch. Fuck what I'd give for hunter-speed healing.

"Who did it?"

"Sheelin."

At the mention of that one name, Eira's power dies down. She looks down at Jillian, who watches her warily. "My apologies."

"Don't mention it," the human replies as she gets to her feet.

On heels as tall as short stilts, Eira glides across the floor toward me. "You okay?"

"Sure. Dandy. Hit my bloody face on the edge of the coffee table."

"May I?" she asks as she reaches forward.

I would have said yes even if there'd been a blade in her hand and she'd been ready to cut out the heart that's belonged to her for over a millennia.

The cup of water I'd abandoned for whiskey sits on the end table, so Eira reaches toward it, and the liquid inside dances out to meet her fingertips.

"What the—" Jillian's amazement falls on deaf ears as I focus only on the feel of Eira's fingertips against my forehead. I breathe her in, the ocean breeze she carries with her filling my lungs.

The pain subsides as she uses the water's energy to knit my broken skin back together. Her fingers linger against my skin. I open my eyes and stare up at her as she looks straight at my forehead. I don't breathe—

don't move—and if it weren't for the third party, I might have tried to brush a strand of hair from Eira's shoulder.

Soon, though, she swallows hard and pulls away. "Better?"

"Yes. Thank you."

Eira nods and steps back so I can stand.

"Are you a fae, too?" Jillian questions, and Eira shakes her head.

"Siren."

"As in mermaid?"

"No." Eira doesn't bother to elaborate. "Sheelin's back, then?"

"Sheelin is your sister?"

"Yes." Sheelin's return is far more problematic than I care to mention in front of the newcomer, but based on Eira's tight expression, she understands the words left unsaid.

"Don't see a resemblance there," Jillian comments.

"You would have once upon a time," I say.

Eira and I stare at each other, the expression shared one full of unspoken words.

"I'm going to head to my hotel. Anything I need to be worried about?"

"I'll take you," I offer.

"Cool. Um. I'll meet you in the hall." Jillian retrieves her jacket and heads for the door. "See you tomorrow, Eira."

Eira doesn't respond, her lack of respect toward the human completely unlike her. "Are you okay?" she asks as soon as Jillian has shut the door behind her.

"Fine. Now we get to deal with my psychotic sister on top of the human gang attempting to carry out genocide against our kind. Why are you here?"

"I wanted to check in—"

"You were worried about me?" I ask, attempting to arch an eyebrow in flirtation. But it seems I don't even have the energy for that.

"I'm always worried about you." She takes a step closer, and I freeze in place. For Eira to move toward me—for her to touch me—it's rare. "I need you to survive," she says, softly. "Watch your back, Fearghas. I don't trust her."

"Sheelin? None of us do."

"Jillian."

"She's a *Faic*."

That gets her attention. "A *Faic*? As in—"

"A human who can sense the presence of supernaturals."

"That's rare."

"It puts her in danger."

"From who? The old council is either dead or on the run."

"She's a divining rod for supernaturals. If word gets out and the humans discover—"

Realization dawns on her, and she nods in understanding. "Who all knows?"

"Just us. I'll tell the others in our group when I see them, but we need to keep a close eye on her."

"Did you explain to her how important it is she keep it to herself?"

"I did. Going to cover it again on the way back to her hotel."

Eira's eyes flash violet. Is it really just concern? A part of me, the twisted part to be sure, senses a hint of jealousy. "I really wish you weren't tasked with being her guard dog."

"I'll be fine, Eira. I promise."

"Says the guy who was bleeding when I showed up."

The image of Sheelin slams into me. "She would have come here whether Jillian had been here or not."

"What's the plan?"

"I'm going to find and deal with her," I tell Eira. "Alone."

"You can't—"

"Sheelin is my responsibility. I'm the reason she is the way she is, and the reason why she's back in Billings. No one else needs to get involved."

"You're not to blame for her choices."

If only you knew, my love. "I'll bring Jillian by your club tomorrow. Personally, I've had enough excitement for an evening." Moving past Eira, I pull open the door. Jillian stands in front of Barr and Marx, the two gargoyle shifters who escort Eira damn near everywhere.

"So you're literally made of stone?"

Marx grins. "Hard everywhere."

Her cheeks flush, and I roll my eyes. "That one is quite sure of himself," I tell Jillian.

She turns to me, and the color of her cheeks deepens. "Gargoyles? There are living gargoyles?"

"Them and so much more." I gesture toward the elevator, and we climb on. The doors are shutting as Eira leaves my apartment. Through the sliver, we lock gazes, and for a brief moment, time stands still.

I reach up and press my fingertips to my now unmarred forehead as the doors shut completely. The feel of her fingertips will not be one I forget anytime soon. Even if Sheelin does manage to kill me, the sight of my siren, lips parted, fingers against my skin, will be the thought that sends me into the Veil.

CHAPTER EIGHT

EIRA

I have never actually been inside the Billings Police Department, but it's exactly the way I always imagined it. Officers move around the inside of the building, to and from their desks, some on phones and some not.

Meanwhile, humans and supernaturals alike sit in the waiting area, some of them looking a bit more down on their luck than others. As my gaze travels over them, it lands on one young woman in particular.

Her blonde hair is cut nearly to the scalp, and she's clutching a backpack to her chest like a lifeline. Bruises cover her cheekbones, and her eyes—a dark brown—are haunted in a way very few will ever understand.

My senses tell me she's a young witch, but before I can move toward her, I spot Rainey stepping out of her office with Walker beside her. With his height difference, she barely makes it to just below his shoulder blade. Her with dark hair, him with a delicate sandy blonde, they couldn't be more opposite. But together, they're a formidable team, and he's proven himself to be more loyal than most.

Deep in conversation, they don't see me right away, giving me a brief moment to study Rainey's expression. She's exhausted—that much is apparent—and when she shakes her head, it's anger I see. My study session ends there, though, because then she sees me and raises a hand in greeting.

Ever since Elijah brought her into my club last year, I've had a fondness for the hunter. She's strong, powerful, beautiful, smart—honestly, she's exactly what I'd always wanted to be, and what I've fought to become since my release from captivity.

Then there's the fact that being around her is always a unique experience. She doesn't bullshit, and therefore, you never know what's going to come out of her mouth.

"This is a surprise," she says with a smile, as she makes her way over to me.

"Eira," Walker greets.

"Detectives." I throw them a wink, hoping to let them both know this is not a serious call.

Walker's cheeks flush, and Rainey grins. "Come on back to the office, and we can chat."

"I'm headed out to check on that call downtown," Walker adds. "Let you know what I find. Bye, Eira."

"Bye."

The handsome detective waves and turns away, so I follow Rainey into her office where she shuts the door and takes a seat behind a mahogany desk that spans most of the room length. "Everything okay?"

I nod as I take my seat across from her. "I'm actually here for more of a personal favor."

"Okay." Her tone is slightly hesitant, though I know that's more to do with the fact that she is likely picking up on my excitement.

"Has Elijah told you of the establishment I run?"

"The shelter?"

"Yes. There's a little girl there who is absolutely enamored by you."

Her grin spreads as color rushes to her cheeks. It's the greatest thing I've seen recently—a complete transformation from the stressed-out homicide detective. "I have a fan club?"

Chuckling, I nod. "Essentially, yes."

"Go on."

"She would like to meet you, and I kind of already said I could make that happen."

"Absolutely." She pushes up from her desk. "Can we go now?"

"Now?"

"Yes. I need a break, and that sounds like a perfect

distraction from the craziness that has been my life since we were outed."

I can already picture little Olive's grin as she stares up at Rainey. "Now works."

Maribel is already waiting for us by the time we reach the door. "Morning, Eira." She turns her attention to Rainey. "You must be Detective Astor."

"Just Rainey." She offers her hand, and the two women shake right before Maribel steps out of the way so we can move inside.

"How are things running?" I ask, noting the brand-new Valentine's decorations lining the hall. Bright pink, red, and white tufts of paper hang from the ceiling while shiny hearts line the hall.

"Smoothly. Nothing to report on."

"Good." We move further into the hall and head around the corner toward the dining room. We've barely made it two steps, though, when a little girl with dark hair is bursting around the corner, banana in hand.

"State you—oh my gosh." She drops the banana, and I nearly laugh in complete delight at the shock all over her face. Mouth slack, she stares up at Rainey as though the woman is a complete celebrity. Though, I suppose to Olive, she is.

"You must be Olive." Rainey kneels, and Olive nods. "That was some great form you had right there, clearing the corner with your weapon level. I'm impressed."

Olive's little cheeks flush crimson, and I cover my mouth to keep from embarrassing her with my smile. One glance at Maribel shows me she's trying to avoid the same.

"Detective Astor, I have so many questions for you."

"You can call me Rainey."

"Rainey," she all but whispers.

Mel comes around the corner, wearing a grim smile on her face. "Eira, can I talk to you a sec?"

"Of course. You two have fun."

Olive takes Rainey's hand the moment she stands and starts pulling her down the hall. "You have to come meet my mom. She's awesome, too."

I fall into step beside Mel. "Another phone call?"

"Yes. Another voicemail. This time, a bit longer."

We step into her office, and the aroma of coffee fills my lungs. "Still just the breathing?"

She nods and sits down behind her desk. I move farther into the office but remain standing as Mel reaches forward and presses the button on her recorder.

The room fills with static—heavy, old-tv style static. Then, comes the breathing. It's ragged, forced, as if the caller is purposely breathing louder than normal. Then, the voice comes out of nowhere.

"Coming for you, my whore."

My entire body goes rigid; muscles freezing as the blood in my veins turns to ice. I can't breathe, my lungs seizing even as black spots invade my vision. The entire room falls away, and all I can see is *him*. My main tormenter glaring down at me.

"No. No." Scrambling back, I pay no attention to the potted palm tree as it spills, sending dirt and debris all over the floor. My power blazes to the surface, and I barely register Mel jumping up to slam the door shut.

A shimmering shield forms in front of me, a murky brown from the coffee that was once in her mug. It took no rational thought, and still takes none to keep it formed.

Because, rationally, I know he can't hurt me. He's dead. Gone. Hundreds of years in the past.

And still, hearing those two words strung together...I don't know that there is anything ever that would terrify me more.

"Easy, Eira." Mel is in front of me, on this side of my barrier. Her hair is still dry, which tells me she passed through it using her abilities to momentarily lose all substance. She holds up two hands, and I focus on them instead of my panic, trying to zero in on the ice-blue hue of her nail polish, the way her white hair is perfectly pinned atop her head.

Those things are reality.

She is reality.

He is not.

Not anymore.

The door flings open, and Rainey bursts in, gun drawn. The moment she sees me, though, she lowers it and moves in far enough to close the door. Having her here gives me another person to focus on—another *real* person.

So, with steadying breaths, I manage to bring my heart rate back down. The water shield dissipates, the liquid returning to the air around us and the cups I brought in with me.

"Easy," Mel repeats. She knows better than to touch me, even if she doesn't know exactly what it is I've gone through. So, she begins to lower her hands as my gaze levels on hers. "Better?"

Still not trusting myself to speak, I nod.

"What the fuck happened?" Rainey demands. "There was a surge of power. I thought—someone want to fill me in here?"

"We've been getting strange phone calls," Mel tells her.

"You are—"

"Mel. Head of security."

"Nice to meet you—"

"Rainey Astor. Homicide detective, hunter extraordinaire—I know." Mel grins and Rainey turns back to me.

"The phone call caught me off guard," I lie.

Mel shakes her head. "Nothing but the breathing. Same as before."

"Another unknown number?" Rainey asks, holstering her firearm.

Mel nods. "Different area code this time." She turns to me. "I'm so sorry. I didn't know you'd react that way."

"It's okay," I manage. "Not your fault." I move toward the phone and push the eject button to remove the tape. For once, I'm grateful for the old school system Mel insisted on when I brought her on. I study the tape then shove it into my pocket. "The caller sounded familiar."

Thankfully she doesn't point out that it was a robotic voice, not an actual person, and simply takes a seat back at her desk. Her brows draw together. "Caller?"

"The voice."

"Someone spoke this time?" Rainey crosses her arms.

Mel shakes her head then looks back to me. "I didn't hear any voice, just the heavy breathing." Her tone is cautious, her gaze watching me with concern and—if I'm not mistaken—a little pity.

My cheeks heat, embarrassment for my momentary show of weakness outweighing my fear—for now. I've no doubt when I take this tape home and listen again, that terror will return. But I *need* to hear it again. "I must have heard something in the static."

Neither woman presses, though Rainey and Mel do share a look. Rainey reaches into her back pocket, withdraws a leather case, and retrieves a card from it. She offers it to Mel. "Call me if it happens again. I'll get a trace team in here."

Mel glances my way, and I nod, letting her know it's okay to loop Rainey in. "You got it, Captain." She sets the card on her desk.

Together, Rainey and I move into the hall, neither of us speaking until we're outside, standing on the sidewalk.

"Are you okay?" she questions.

"I—I don't know."

"You heard something?"

"Maybe. I'll listen again when I get back to my office...see if I might have misheard it."

"Want me to take it? I can listen."

I shake my head. "I need to do this." Swallowing hard, I attempt to shift the subject. "You get a chance to talk to Olive?"

Rainey grins. "That is the coolest kid ever. I'm coming back for her birthday party next month."

"Thank you so much for doing that."

"Anytime. She's a great kid, and it was a fantastic break from my real life." She lifts her wrist and checks her watch, then groans. "Speaking of. Meeting with the mayor in ten minutes. I better get going."

"Thanks, again."

She waves to straddle her bike. Within minutes, she's pulling away from the curb, and I'm moving quickly toward my car, heart still hammering.

I *know* what I heard.

No matter how impossible it seems, he was there.

Layered beneath the recorded portions.

The heavy breathing.

I heard him.

CHAPTER NINE
EIRA

"*Coming for you, my whore.*"

I rewind and listen, again.

Then two more times, sure I must have heard it wrong. It's impossible. There is literally no way he is back. I watched him die.

Then again, Delaney came back from the dead.

Cole.

Rachel.

Delaney's situation aside, the others had a fae pull them out, and the only two fae in Billings would never do anything like that. Which means either another fae I've never met managed to track him down in the deepest, darkest parts of hell, or someone is screwing with me.

I'm really hoping it's the latter. And if it really is

him on that recording, how am I the only one who can hear him?

Pushing to my feet, I begin a mental list of my enemies. Thankfully, it's a rather short list since most of them are already dead. The soundproof walls give me the silence I need to continue my thoughts, even as the floor-to-ceiling windows separating me from my club make way for the strobe lights to cast constantly moving shadows over my floor.

While the voice is different, animated, the words are so familiar that it took me half a dozen times of listening to it over and over again to curb the panic—and even still, it was only enough to keep my magic at bay.

I can still feel my heart hammering within my chest, feel the chill of my blood as my anxious mind transports me back to a place where I'd been weak. Vulnerable.

And even though I know, without a doubt, I will never be back in that place, my mind is fucking with me. Even now, in the safety of my office, at the very top of the empire I've built, I can see him hovering above me, chains in hand— *Easy, Eira. You are safe.* I repeat those words over and over again, hoping that the next time I think them, I'll actually hear the truth.

The door opens, and I freeze, sensing my magic pooling to the surface. It washes over me, a cleansing rain that soothes my fraying nerves. Nerves that ease as soon as the handsome fae crosses into my office. My panic subsides, my anxiety retreating just as it does every time I'm near him.

Which, as selfish as it is, is why I keep him in my life even though I know I can never be anything more for him. Some broken things are simply impossible to put back together.

"What is it?" he asks as he tosses his suit jacket onto my tall white chair and closes the distance between us.

I take a deep breath and focus on his forest-colored gaze and the way he watches me with the intensity of someone taking in the sight of the most important treasure in their life. It's how he's always looked at me.

Ever since the moment we first met. Of course, back then, I'd been happy. Innocent. *Unbroken.* My rose-colored glasses had let me see the good in everyone...in the world. Those damn things have now been shattered a thousand times over.

"Nothing, why?" The lie is smooth, but I know he doesn't believe me. Somehow, he always knows when something is wrong. How? I've no clue, but he's always nearby whenever I need help, and still gives me the space he also knows I need.

I am not good enough for him, and a part of me hopes he never realizes that.

His gaze narrows on my face. "You're upset. Why?"

"Fearghas—"

"Don't lie to me, Eira."

I sigh. Lying to him will do no good. And while I'm unwilling to go into full details, I can at least be partially honest.

After turning back to the desk, I slide onto the cushioned chair behind it. Then, I grab the list of numbers and offer it to him. "This is bothering me."

Never letting his gaze stray from mine, he takes the folder and opens it. As he does, I take note of his sharp jaw, of the way his clothes give the appearance of someone completely and totally in control.

I really wish I was the same. I may look it on the outside, but inside, I'm a complete and total mess of anxious nerves and nightmarish memories.

"What are these?" His gaze scans the top sheet. Then he lifts the bottom and looks it over, too.

"They've been calling one of my establishments," I tell him.

His green eyes find mine again. "Did you have Rainey look into it?"

"No need. My head of security hacked into the police database. The numbers shouldn't exist; the area codes are not real. She is aware of it, though. Mel is going to call her if it happens again."

His brows draw together. "Not real?"

"No. Somehow, someone is using impossible numbers."

"Have they left any messages? Said anything?"

Swallowing hard, I weigh the options of playing the message. Either he's going to hear the voice or not, but this could be a good test. I pull out my tape recorder and press the button on the top.

The crackling is what I hear first, it fills my office moments before the heavy breathing starts. *"Coming for you, my whore."* Swallowing my fear, I close my eyes against the sound of it, and soon, the message stops.

When I open my eyes again, Fearghas is staring at me.

"What was that?"

"The message."

"So, some asshole is calling and leaving heavy breathing messages?"

My stomach sinks. *He didn't hear it.* Is it possible I'm imagining it? First Mel, now him? Maybe I should have let Rainey listen. "It seems that way," I reply. "We've changed the number for the second time, and Rainey offered to put a tracing team on it."

"Which place is this for?" he asks.

"The shelter."

"Assholes. Want me to look into it, too?"

I shake my head. "I can deal with it." I push up from my chair and walk to the window to look down at the club. Owning this place was never a dream of mine, but it became a safety net. A wall of literal supernaturals surrounding me, keeping me safe from those who were merely waiting for an opportunity to grab me.

My biggest regret from my captivity? That I didn't manage to kill all the bastards.

"Eira, what is it?"

Fearghas's voice is so much closer now, but he doesn't touch me. That's been our entire relationship —two people constantly walking on eggshells.

"I'm okay." Turning toward him, I smile. "You up for a drink?"

He doesn't respond right away. The intensity of his stare is something I'm used to, something I long for on those rare nights I don't get to look upon his face. I'm a selfish bitch, that's for damned sure.

"Always," he finally replies. He turns away and retrieves his jacket before heading out through the door. I follow, desperately craving the peace he gives me even as I feel like shit for using him the way I do.

The dining room is packed tonight, though Fearghas's booth is empty and waiting as it always is. I'm not even entirely sure when it became his, but patrons know not to sit there, and if they do, the staff forces them to reconsider.

As he always does, he slides into the side facing the door, and I move into the seat opposite his. Within seconds, Jeanie is at our tableside. She sets cocktail napkins down on the table then greets Fearghas with a smile.

"The usual?"

"You spoil me," he flirts.

Jeanie blushes despite being happily married for the last half-decade.

It really shouldn't make me jealous, but I can't help it. "Thank you, Jeanie."

"Yes, ma'am." On black flats, she rushes away, her footsteps fading into the background.

"How are things going for Delaney's baby shower? It's coming up, right?"

He nods. Ever since appointing himself big brother to the Astor sisters, Fearghas has been a constant form of support for the hunter and the witch. It's absolutely adorable and manages to make him even more endearing than he already is.

"Rainey is going to lose her mind the second that kid comes out," he jokes. "She's already preparing for every possible worst-case scenario."

"That seems appropriate for her." A homicide detective by day, the youngest Astor has likely seen a lot of horrible things she'd rather not mention. Overprotective aunt? That will be an understatement for how I imagine she'll behave.

"With the house being warded now, hopefully, she can breathe easily from now to the birth." When he raises an eyebrow, I add, "I went with her after the council meeting. She had my blood added to it."

Fearghas's brow arches further—almost comically—clearly indicating that he knows me well enough to be surprised I let anyone have even a drop of my blood. For years, I've fought to keep everyone at arm's length. After all, if you have no one close to you, there's no one to betray you. And siren's blood?

"Drop by drop, siren whore. Your blood is almost as addicting as your body."

The memory catches me off guard, and I force myself to take a deep breath, silently wishing the moment would disappear. I want it gone, gone and buried like the bones of that bastard.

When I finally manage to gain control, I'm not surprised to see Fearghas watching me intently. "You're struggling tonight," he says.

"I told you why."

"If I can help—"

"I'll be sure to let you know," I interrupt.

Jeanie approaches our table and sets two whiskey glasses down. The amber liquid inside will do little more than give us a momentary buzz, but it's still comforting. "Any food tonight?"

"No, thanks," Fearghas replies, and Jeanie rushes away, heading to a table with three shifter males. "You ever going to be honest with me?"

I glance up to see Fearghas watching me. “What do you mean?”

“Something’s bothering you,” he replies, pointedly. “Something more than just those phone calls.”

“Why do you say that?”

“I can tell.” His response is quick, curt. He’s frustrated, but I know telling him the truth would only lead to more questions than I’m ready to give.

“I’m pretty exhausted, Fearghas. We’ve had a lot going on lately. Especially with the humans hunting our kind.”

His expression softens almost instantly, and he lifts his glass, though he doesn’t take a drink. “I understand that. We will put a stop to it. Peace will come.”

“We’ve both been around long enough to know that peace rarely lasts long. Especially given the humans that now know of our existence.”

“They’ll forget.”

“Maybe. Things are different now, though. The last time supernaturals were outed, they went after witches. Now, they know about all of us.”

“Most of us,” he corrects. “I doubt anyone suspects sirens to be walking on land.”

I chuckle, my mind automatically drifting to the cartoonish way my kind has been portrayed over the years. They’ve called us all mermaids, not even realizing the two are not one and the same. And mermaids? They'll rip your throat out faster than a rogue wolf will. "True."

Fearghas's glass clinks against the table as he sets it down and leans in. "Everything is going to be okay." The golden flecks in his eyes move through the green, evidence of the powerful fae so easily hidden beneath the human exterior.

My breath hitches, my lips falling apart. I know he sees it, senses the way he makes me feel, and even as I know I can't ever act on it without losing what little sanity I have left, there's a part of me—a sadistic part—that wants his body on mine.

So that for once in my life, I can feel *real* passion.

Except...I can't. Maybe once upon a time, it would have been possible, but now? I'm far too broken to piece back together. "How's Jillian settling in?"

He groans, and I fight a smile. "She asks a lot of questions."

"I can imagine. She's a human in a supernatural world. Things are bound to be confusing."

Leaning in once again, he casts a curious glance to the right before focusing on me. "The thing is, I know she wants to help. But this mental picture she has for a utopia where we all live together peacefully—it's little more than a fairy tale. These humans that are slaughtering our kind need to be dealt with, and I don't mean diplomatically."

"That's what she's pushing for? A diplomatic solution?"

"You heard her at the meeting. She wants everyone to get along. Hold hands. Sing fucking campfire songs. And while it's honorable, it's not going to happen."

"What of Sheelin? She believe you need to hold hands as well?"

His expression darkens, drastically. "Sheelin is another beast entirely."

"No more visits from her, then?"

With a shake of his head, he returns to his whiskey. "She's planning something," he says, returning the glass to the table. "I just can't seem to figure out what it is."

CHAPTER TEN
FEARGHAS

Sheelin, what in the bloody hell are you up to? As it does so often, my thoughts drift to my sister while I cross the street to my car. These days, normal thoughts are a fable. Between my concern for those I care for, tracking Sheelin, and being Jillian's own, personal thesaurus, stress is my fucking middle name.

Add in the debilitating fear that nearly took me to my knees this morning, and now I'm concerned over what's happening with Eira. *Shit, that fear...* My stomach churns as I recall the heart-pounding terror that washed over me through the slight bond between us. I've never run so damned fast in my life as I did racing up the stairs to her office, grateful I'd only been in the dining hall.

Yet, by the time I'd arrived, the fear had scaled

back, and she'd had it mostly under control. I climb behind the wheel of my car and fire it up just before pulling into the flow of traffic.

Is it possible the phone calls are what worried her? But even as I think it, I shove that away. Eira is a woman who has seen the darkest of monsters; some fucking weirdo calling would not bring that level of terror.

No, she's keeping something from me, and while secrets are not exactly foreign between us, she's never outwardly lied to me before. It makes me—uneasy. After all, how in the bloody hell am I supposed to keep her safe if she's not telling me the whole truth?

Nothing I can do about it now, I remind myself. Eira's a private woman, and if I know any damned thing at all, it's that any attempt to force her to reveal something she's not ready to reveal will be met with an ass-kicking.

I, for one, am tired of having my ass kicked.

Forcing myself to think about anything else, I focus on the project that's taking up most of my spare time these days—or was before I became a babysitter. The house I've been steadily remodeling for the last twelve years is still in complete disarray though, thanks to the last couple of months being slow, the living room finally has interior walls. Putting the old Colonial house back to its original condition has been a painstaking process, but with each completed room, I find myself more and more in love with it.

Twenty-two minutes from Eira's club, it sits in the center of a huge grove of old trees. The sprawling grounds are next on my to-do list once I finish the final touches on the inside of the home.

The moment I make the turn down the long drive, a feeling of peace washes over me. This place is my sanctuary. Out here, away from the prying eyes of hunters, wolves, witches, and vampires, I get to be completely normal.

Just a man working his ass off to remodel a house he hopes to one day raise a family in. After purchasing under a fake name, I ensured there was nothing to tie me to the property. My enemies—they are vast. Protecting my heart—my home—is priority number one.

The enormous house comes into view just ahead, and I smile as I type in my code to open the massive rod-iron gate separating it from the rest of the world.

Built half of stone and half dark wood, it stands on the top of a hill overlooking a huge pond and sprawling gardens. Trees rise on both sides, framing the drive in a canopy of delicate shade. I follow the drive down and park in front of the house.

After shutting the engine down, I climb out and take the steps one at a time, stopping on the huge wrap-around porch. Once I've reached the top, I turn and take a deep breath, inhaling the pine-scented air around me.

This is home. Or it will be one day.

Once inside, I shrug out of my jacket and nice shirt, trading both in for a toolbelt. Then, I head upstairs to pick up where I left off. The wooden walls are barren throughout the house, but as soon as I get the stain and lacquer applied, they will gleam as they did once upon a time.

Then, I can start on the decorating, which will absolutely be my least favorite part of this entire process. Why? Because it means that the project is coming to an end, and soon I can put it all on the line; show Eira exactly how much I care.

This house will be my gift to the one I love. A promise to cherish her, to do whatever is necessary to keep her safe. My thoughts darken as I consider the one person who can stand in the way of that dream becoming a reality.

One person who seems set on destroying me. I can only hope I figure out what she wants before she puts me in the ground to join our father.

"The party has arrived!" I announce as I step through the front door of Tarnley's pub. It's already packed wall-to-wall with attendees, though the guest of honor hasn't arrived just yet. Willa offers me a tight smile from where she stands beside the witch who is mated to her beta shifter, Z.

"About time. You hear anything from Eira? She coming?" Rainey asks as she shoves through the bar toward me.

"She will be here," I assure her, more than enjoying the stress painted so painfully on her face. Rainey doesn't give a shit—until she does. And then, she gives more shits than anyone else. I snort to myself. I'm becoming more and more American the longer I hang around her.

The door opens again, and a young woman with dark hair slips into the room alongside a witch and hunter, the three of them all the same age.

The dark-haired woman sees me and grins widely, wasting no time to push through the crowd. "Fearghas!" she squeals and throws her arms around me. I hug her back, so happy she seems happy.

"Bella, how are things? How's life as a boring human?"

She releases me, and I flash a grin. The young succubus came to our aid after her hive wouldn't allow her to refuse the transition from young girl to soul-sucking monster. She'd longed for a normal life, and we'd been more than happy to help her achieve that.

"It's so great. I'm leaving for the University of Florida next week."

"Oh?"

Nodding frantically, she loops an arm through the young witch's. "I can't wait for something other than snow."

"I'm glad to hear it."

"I hate that you're leaving us, though." Magnolia rests her temple on Bella's shoulder momentarily then straightens.

"At least it will just be you and Drexel then." Bella wags her eyebrows as she nods toward the hunter in deep conversation with Tarnley.

"She's coming!" A woman calls out.

"Shit!" Rainey rushes back toward the bartop and, with the training and blood of her hunter line, manages to jump on top without so much as a grunt. "Hey! Everyone!" The room falls silent. "Cole, keep her out for one more second," she adds. Thanks to his shifter hearing, he's likely already heard her, and since Delaney has the senses of a witch...she has not. Rainey clears her throat. "Remember, big, giant surprise."

Murmurs and chuckles break out through the room.

Elijah steps forward, and Rainey jumps down beside him. "Lights, Tarnley!"

The room plunges into darkness, and I hear Rainey whisper, "Ready."

Mere seconds later, the door opens, and Delaney's

voice fills my ears. "I cannot wait to put some onion rings in my—"

"Surprise!"

"What the—!" She jumps back into Cole as lights fill the room once more. Green power sparks at her fingertips as she gapes wide-eyed at everyone in the room. Finally, after a moment of silence, her shock turns to utter appreciation, and her caramel eyes fill with tears. "You guys!" She covers her mouth with both hands.

"Don't get all emotional on us," Rainey says with a smile, as she wraps her arms around her very pregnant sister.

"You already threw me a party."

"Yeah, but that was when I thought we were all going to die." Rainey releases her and steps back.

Delaney turns to me. "Fearghas!"

Chuckling, I wrap an arm around her shoulders and guide her further into the room. "You're looking good, *Máthair*."

She beams up at me. "You guys are too good."

"Nah, just right." I release her and offer her husband a hand. Cole takes it with a grin.

"Good to see you, Fearghas."

"You, too..." I trail off as a shiver of awareness runs up my spine. An uncomfortable buzzing begins beneath my skin, starting near my heart and spanning my chest, before slipping down both arms. It can only mean one thing, and the moment she steps inside, Eira steals every bit of my attention.

Wearing a long navy-blue skirt paired with a white shirt and pale-pink blazer, she's a vision. Her white hair is loose, falling down nearly to her waist in a shimmering waterfall of white silk. Violet eyes find mine, and color invades her milky cheeks.

She's everything. Everything and so damn much more.

"Sorry I'm late," she says, pulling her gaze from mine and shifting to Delaney.

"Nonsense! I'm so glad you're here." Delaney wraps her arms around Eira then steps back. "You look beautiful."

"Please. It's nothing compared to you," Eira replies. "You are positively glowing."

Delaney blushes. "Thank you."

Heat climbs up my spine, my magic reacting to Eira's presence. I turn away, needing distance between us so I can catch my damned breath. Every single moment of every single day, she invades my thoughts.

I want to wait.

To be what she needs.

But right now, surrounded by our closest friends as they get married and have kids—my desperation for the same is at an all-time high. I force my thoughts back to the unfinished house, reminding myself that I have a plan as I slide onto a seat at the bar.

"Fearghas." My name on her lips is the sweetest kind of torture.

"Eira." I turn to face her as she slips onto the stool beside me. "Everything okay?"

"It is. With you?"

"Peachy. That's the phrase Americans use, isn't it?"

She snorts. "Yes, Fearghas. That is a term that is used."

"Can I get you guys anything?" A female vampire stops in front of us and sets two cocktail napkins down. Her red gaze signals her youth, though the thick band of hazel around the inside shows her control. She grins at me.

"Coffee, please. And a shot of whiskey."

"You got it, handsome." She winks and turns to Eira. "And for you?"

"Water." Her tone is sharp, though polite as ever.

"Water, huh? Cutting back?" My attempt at a joke is pathetic, at best.

Eira doesn't immediately reply as she turns around and faces the room. "She looks so happy, doesn't she?"

I follow her gaze, my own landing on Delaney as she throws her head back and laughs, one hand on her swollen belly. She practically glows with joy, and the unselfish side of me is so damned happy for them and their soon-to-arrive son. "She does."

"Do you ever wonder if you'll settle down?"

"Here you go." The vampire sets the cups down behind us, so we turn.

I lift the glass and down the whiskey in a single gulp, really wishing for a change of subject because my answer is not going to be what she's hoping it will.

"Well?"

I glance to my left, not even mildly surprised to see her violet gaze on me. "Well, what?"

"Don't pretend you didn't hear me."

Sighing, I nod. "I suppose I would have liked to settle down one day, but I'm just not sure it's in the cards for me."

"Same." Her reply surprises me. In all the time I've known her—at least, this version of her—she's strayed from conversations about family, about love. After what was done to her, I certainly don't blame her for being afraid of intimacy, even if I wish she'd let me show her what it means to be loved with everything someone has.

"I suppose my invitation must have been lost in the mail."

I jump up from my barstool, but before I can turn around, a hand grips my shoulder, and the room around me vanishes. When I reappear, I'm standing on a cliffside surrounded by massive trees. Snow crunches beneath my shoes as I attempt to figure out who the hell brought me here—wherever this is.

"Shit!" Wind whips past me, damn near knocking

me off the side of the cliff before I manage to catch my balance.

Feminine laughter drifts over me, and my stomach churns with recognition. “Careful, brother, that’s a long way down.”

“Sheelin,” I growl her name, rage and a bit of fear overtaking me.

She appears in front of me, her white hair blowing loosely around her face. Combine that with her dark gaze, and she looks more rabid than ever. “Dear brother, mine, so good to see you.”

“Wish I could say the same. I’m still disappointed that you’re not dead.” *And I’m at a mild disadvantage*, I remind myself. Without the ability to dematerialize, I’m completely at her mercy. There’s no damned telling where she’s taken us now. I can only hope it’s somewhere in the vicinity of Montana. Or, shit—at least in the same world.

“I’m harder to kill than that,” she replies easily. Her white dress trails behind her as she moves, a predator circling would-be prey. But she’s going to be damned disappointed because there’s no way in hell I’m letting her take me out today. “Where’s your little pet these days?”

“Busy.”

“I wonder what your siren would say if she knew you were traipsing around with a human.”

I don't let her false accusations get to me. "What do you want, Sheelin? Where are we?"

"Not in Faerie," she replies smoothly. "If that's what you're wondering."

Good to know. "Where are we?" I ask again.

"Still in Montana. I see the eldest Astor is knocked up. How sweet for you all." She changes the subject quickly then begins to pace the mountainside.

Her mention of Delaney brings about a fresh wave of nerves. Is that why she's brought me here? To separate me from the others? "I'm getting really exhausted with your shit, Sheelin. Start answering my damned questions, or take me back."

She turns to me. "You tried to kill me."

"Are we really doing this again?" I groan, then cross my arms against the bitter cold. My damn nipples could be registered as fucking weapons at this point. "You murdered our father in cold blood; then proceeded to try and kill everyone I care about. I'd say you left me with little choice."

"I'm your sister. Not the Astor bitches," she spits back. "Me! And you chose them!"

It guts me to see her this broken. It shouldn't, but I can't help if a part of me still sees the innocent young girl she'd been. The little sister who'd followed my every move; the same one who'd climb into bed with me when she'd been scared. Sheelin had been my best friend.

In a lot of ways, she'd been my only friend. And I failed her.

"I didn't choose them," I reply. "There was no choice because you made it when you picked the wrong damned side."

A tear slips down her cheek as she glares back at me, nothing but hatred in her golden gaze. "Yes, you did. You picked them over me. Two non-fae to replace the sister you no longer wanted. Why? Because I was a broken toy you could just discard?"

I swallow hard as pain closes around my heart like a vise. "You chose the man who raped you over your own family," I remind her.

She snaps back like I struck her—eyes widening, her horror plain as day. Which is always the way she acts when *he* is brought up. Whether it was a way to cope with what happened or twisted fucking Stockholm's, I don't know. "He loved me," she snaps.

"He *used* you," I shoot back, taking a step closer. "Manipulated you into removing our father from the throne. Then he took you as captive. A prize to be shown around."

She closes her eyes tightly and shakes her head. "No. He *loved* me," she repeats. "And you stole him away from me."

The way she sees the world is so warped, so broken; the crushing guilt I carry over what happened to her smothers me here on this mountain top. I can still hear her screams as he took her, still picture the bruises on her face when she'd been dragged back downstairs and tossed at our feet.

He'd fucking murdered my sister that day.

My Sheelin.

And I hadn't been man enough to kill him then. Nor when his guards threw my family out. And every time I'd tried to break into the castle, I'd failed.

Until he captured Delaney, Cole, and myself. Then, I'd killed him.

But it was already too late.

"I only wish I could have killed him long before that."

She smiles, though there is no humor in the completely alien expression. "But you couldn't because you were too high to do anything, right? Too wrapped up in all the whores you shared your time with. You chose them over me back then, and the Astors over me now."

Her words are a punch to my gut. But not because they lack truth. "Do you not see what he did, Sheelin?" I step forward, moving toward her now. If I can just get her to see—to understand—then maybe I can get my sister back, at least in some capacity.

"I loved him. Loved him more than anyone, and you stole him from me. *Stole* him," she repeats. "Because of that, I will make you pay, Fearghas. I will kill every single person you care for, starting with the two you replaced me with. Tell me, do they know how you treat your sisters? Do they know that when it comes down to it, you will choose yourself every single time?"

Panic sends my pulse racing even faster—so damn quick I can barely catch my breath. "Sheelin." I step forward. "Please, we can get you help. Come back with me. I will find a way to help you." Even as they leave my lips, though, I know my pleas fall on deaf ears.

They always have.

"I don't want your help," she spits back at me, eyes flashing with power. "You will pay for all you've done, Fearghas. You will all fucking pay. And you'll never see me coming."

CHAPTER ELEVEN

FEARGHAS

Ten miles down a snow-covered mountain, and I finally managed to get somewhere I could flag a driver down. The elderly woman who stopped to get me was sweeter than she probably should have been, but I happily accepted her ride and listened to her chatter about her late husband and how similar I look to him.

It was the least I could do.

"Thank you so much, Minnie," I tell her with a smile as I climb out of her car in front of Tarnley's pub.

"You're very welcome, dear, very welcome. Please feel free to phone me up if you ever need anything else."

Here's hoping my crazed sister doesn't abandon me on the top of a mountain ever again. I hold up the slip of paper she slipped me. "Will do, thanks. You should stop picking up random hitchhikers, though," I remind her. "Not all of us are nice."

She laughs and nods. "Deal. I'll do my best, but when I see such a handsome, well-dressed man, I can't help myself."

Dirty bird. No longer faking it, I flash her another smile. "Take care."

"You, too!" she calls out as I shut the door and watch her drive away. The street is empty, and since it's well past five in the morning, I'm assuming the party is over. While I'm in desperate need of a shower, I know calling Rainey and letting her know what happened is priority number one, so I head straight to my car where I'd foolishly left my phone.

My brief ray of sunshine in this shit situation? Since Sheelin took me away from the party—away from them—I'm assuming she knows better than to confront those I care for on their turf. *Hopefully.* I reach into my pocket for my keys, unlock my car, and slip into the driver's seat. Then, I lean back, close my eyes, and take a deep, calming breath.

Sheelin is alive.

She is after my friends.

Fucking great.

Someone slams a fist into my window. "What the fuck!" I jump and shove the door open as Rainey steps back.

"Don't you what the fuck me, asshole! Where the hell have you been?"

Heavy bags line her eyes, and beside her, Elijah looks just as exhausted. My fight is gone in an instant. I lean back against my car and run both hands over my eyes.

"Where have you been?" Rainey repeats. "You just fucking disappeared."

"I was abducted," I snap.

"Abducted? By who?"

"Sheelin."

The hunter falls completely silent, a feat for her. She gapes at me, looks to Elijah, then back to me, again. "Sheelin."

"Did I fucking stutter?" I know I'm being rude, but after the shit day I've had, who the hell can blame me? "Listen. I just hiked ten miles down a mountain and spent the last thirty minutes in the car with a kind woman who talked constantly. Again, kind, but it's been a fucking day."

"Did she—are you okay?" She takes a step toward me.

"I'm fine. But you all need to be on the lookout. She's out for blood. Where's Delaney?"

"With Cole. He took her home a few hours ago."

"She was out that late?"

"We all were. Every single one of us has been looking for you since you disappeared."

New guilt crushes down on me over the fact that I nearly went home and showered before checking in. "I'm sorry. Clearly, I'm fine. Just got a little extra exercise in today."

"Fearghas."

"Rainey."

"Elijah." We both turn to the ex-vamp who shrugs. "I felt left out."

Rainey grins at him then turns back to me. "I will call everyone and let them know you're okay."

"Left my phone here," I tell her, gesturing to the cell sitting in a cupholder. "Didn't want to interfere with the party."

She smiles softly. "Let me know if you need anything. If you want me to kick her fucking ass for you, I can do that."

"We have to find her first."

Fight flares into Rainey's eyes. An expression I would never want to be on the receiving end of. "We will."

Her phone buzzes, so she reaches down and retrieves it from her pocket then presses it to her ear. "We'll check in with you tomorrow. You'll be safe tonight?" she asks me, ignoring whoever is on the other end of the call.

"I am."

"*You found him?*" Delaney's voice echoes through the receiver.

"We did. I'll fill you in when I get there." She ends the call and shoves the phone back into her pocket. "I'm serious, Fearghas. You'll be safe?"

"Yes. But you and Delaney may not be."

Rainey shakes her head. "That bitch isn't getting anywhere near Del. Not with the wards, Cole, and her magic."

"Sheelin is resourceful," I tell her. "And she's pissed."

"Any particular reason you think she's gunning for us?"

"She believes I chose you and Del over her. Apparently, she's quite jealous."

"How nice. I'll warn Del, and we'll watch our backs."

"Great. I'm going to go home and shower, try to sleep for a bit, then I'll give you a call. Deal?"

"Deal. But if I don't hear from you by seven tonight, I'm coming after your ass. That's fourteen hours to shower, shit, eat, and sleep. Not necessarily in that order."

Chuckling, I turn to Elijah. "Make her wait until then, please."

He snorts. "Making Rainey do anything is an impossible request, my friend." His gaze softens. "I'm glad you're okay."

"Thanks. Me, too." I climb into my car and turn it on as Rainey and Elijah head down the street. Before they reach their car, I'm pulling away from the curb and speeding toward my apartment.

Within minutes, I'm already marching toward the elevator that will carry me to the very top of the building. It's nearly completely silent around me, and for that, I'm damned grateful. The fewer people I cross paths with, the less I must fucking pretend that everything's okay.

After climbing into the elevator, I type in the code that will take me to the penthouse suite. As soon as it's moving, I force myself to take a deep breath. Then another. Being pissed the hell off will do me no damned good right now.

But then I feel her. The steady warming of my body that signifies the presence of the one person I can't live without, and that anger—that rage—intensifies.

The doors open, and I step up to my door. Taking a moment, I close my eyes—my futile attempt at catching my breath. The truth is, whenever Eira is around, there's no damned chance of that. She consumes me. Body. Mind. Soul.

And for the first time since we met, I wish like hell my magic had chosen someone else. Anyone else. Because that would mean I have one less thing to worry about.

Before I can reach the handle, the door swings open, and Eira stares up at me. Her violet eyes soften, and she takes a steadying breath.

The air charges around us as we stare at each other. It's where we spend most of our time...this purgatory between love and friendship. Had I not been so exhausted, I might have time for it tonight. But emotionally, I'm worn the fuck down. Physically? Well, I walked over ten damned miles, literally in the fucking snow, so what do you think?

"Eira," I greet as I move past her and into my apartment, trying to pretend her very presence doesn't sear my already aching heart.

The door shuts behind me, and her soft footsteps follow me across my apartment.

"Are you okay? Rainey called and said Sheelin had you? She didn't tell me much else. I just turned around and you were gone."

"Sheelin did." I set my wallet, keys, and phone down on the counter, then head into the kitchen for the bottle of whiskey on top of my fridge. Without even bothering with a glass, I unscrew the top and put it to my lips. After drinking greedily, I lean back against the countertop. "It was quite the family reunion. Even more eventful than the one where Jillian was in attendance."

Her brows draw together. "What happened?"

I take another drink, downing the rest of the bottle before taking a break. My throat burns, the effects of the whiskey only dulling my senses for mere moments before my metabolism shoves it from my system. "She wanted to have a little chat on top of a mountain. Remind me of all my failures, threaten my friends—the usual."

She crosses her arms, and I know she's trying to figure out why I'm being such an ass. "You don't have any past failures."

If I wasn't already so damned raw, I might have laughed. "I've been alive nearly a thousand years longer than you. I assure you, Eira, I have failed plenty."

The tension between us is so damned potent it's intoxicating. My gaze drops to her full mouth, to the way her lips are parted. One heartbeat. That's how long it would take for me to slam my mouth against hers. To push her up against the wall and fucking ravish her the way I've wanted for more time than even I can comprehend. To bury my fingers in her hair, my cock in her—

"You're a good man." Her interruption is damn appreciated, even if her words are utter shit.

I snort. "You don't know the half of it."

"Then tell me. I'm here for you."

That does it. *I'm here for you*, she says. *Here. For. You.* I whirl on her. "What about you? Care to tell me what you're hiding from me? If we're such good friends, Eira, then tell me why you were so terrified yesterday."

She takes a cautious step back. "I don't know what you're talking about."

"You never do, do you? Eira is so fucking powerful she needs nothing and no one else." Normally she calms my storm, the steady racing in my blood—but tonight, she's the eye of it, the reason for the fissures forming in my soul.

"Fearghas." Her hand touches my arm; her palm scalds me through the fabric of my shirt as the contact sends my nerves buzzing, my blood boiling within my veins. My gaze finds hers, and I can picture what would happen if I grab her now. I can see myself crushing her against me and taking her mouth with the force of over a millennia of passion bottled up inside of me.

But doing so would scare her, and even as angry as I am, I'm just not that much of a fucking bastard.

Even though it kills me, I pull away. "I don't have the patience required for this conversation. Please go." I make a move past her, but she reaches out, and slender fingers close around my arm once more. This is the most she's ever touched me. I want to revel in it, appreciate the feel of her hands on me, but the moment is tainted by my memories of the past.

"Please let me help you, Fearghas. Talk to me."

My voice is low, my tone so sharp even I barely recognize it. "Unless you want me to put my hands on you, I suggest you remove yours," I warn, careful not to look into her eyes. "I'm volatile right now, Eira, and you fucking know how I feel about you. Since I imagine you have no need or want of a relationship with me, I suggest you act accordingly. Because if you keep touching me, I'm going to lose what little control I still have."

Her hand tightens around my arm, but within a heartbeat, she's releasing me. "You know where I am if you need to talk."

There it is. *Talk.* It's always talking. Centuries and centuries of conversation. It used to be enough—but not anymore. "I'm tired of fucking talking. See yourself out." I leave her standing in my kitchen as I slam the door to my bedroom and begin stripping out of my dirty clothes. I leave them in a pile, more than happy to burn them later.

Then, I turn on the water and let the steam fill up the bathroom as I stare at myself in the mirror. From the outside, you'd never know the turmoil within my soul. The pain in my chest. I rub my palm against the skin above my heart, hoping to alleviate at least some of the fucking pressure.

"Tell me, do they know how you treat your sisters?" Sheelin's words run through my mind on repeat. Over and over again, I hear the pain in her voice, the screams from the night she was stolen from us. The way my parents cried, their pleas that fell on the deaf ears of soldiers who'd once been loyal to us.

All of it happening while I was too fucking high to do a damned thing about it.

My life ended that day, turning me from the prince I'd been raised to be, into the man who would go on to slaughter an entire platoon of soldiers in an attempt to rid the world of one man.

And I'd still failed.

CHAPTER TWELVE

FEARGHAS

"You're in a foul mood," Jillian comments as soon as we're sitting in my car.

"That's what happens when you don't sleep."

"Anything you want to talk about? I'm an excellent listener."

I turn the key, and my car roars to life. Then, turning to Jillian, I arch an eyebrow. "No offense, Jill, but we just don't know each other that well."

She snorts, taking absolutely no offense. "Fair enough." Then, she faces front and claps her hands together. "Where are we headed?"

"Eira's club," I snap.

"Ohhh, got it."

"What the hell is that supposed to mean?" I demand, while I pull out onto the street.

"Just that I understand the bad mood now."

I open my mouth to respond, but before I can bitch her out, my cell rings. With one hand on the wheel, I reach into the center console where I'd tossed it and answer. "Yeah?"

"Get downtown as soon as possible. The alleyway beside Mooney's. You know it?"

"I do. I've got Jillian with me." I say, making brief eye contact with the human beside me.

"I don't give a fuck, Fearghas. Bring her. Just get here."

The call ends before I have a chance to confirm, though there's no need. Rainey's tone had been more than enough to convince me something is wrong. "We've got a stop to make." The light turns green, so I accelerate faster than normal, my tires screeching against the asphalt in response.

"Everything okay?"

"We're about to find out."

Jillian is quiet a moment before clearly deciding to fill every moment of silence with questions. "So, Eira. Siren, huh?"

"Correct."

"That's insane. The power she puts off... It's incredible." Jillian's amazement is clear enough in her tone, and for some reason, it pisses me off.

"She likes to be left alone. You will not tell anyone of her existence, understand?"

"Yeah, of course. I'm not going to repeat any of this."

"There are people who would use her for her magic. I need you to understand what will happen if word of her gets out." I whip in and out of traffic.

"I won't. I told you, I'm not here to make your lives more difficult."

"Fine. On that same note, telling anyone what you are and what you can do could be a death sentence for you."

"Really? I thought you said the ones that would kill me are dead."

"I said the old council was gone, but the humans out hunting us? If they were to discover you're a damn supernatural divining rod, they would do anything to get their hands on you. As it stands now, they're counting on a heart rate test."

"I hadn't considered that. Shit. Still, I'd never do it."

"You'd be surprised to see the shit someone will do if provided the right kind of motivation." My thoughts drift darker, and I shake it off; I've no time for the past. Not now.

I pull into a parking spot right behind Rainey's car and climb out. Jillian follows suit, and together, we make our way toward the crowd that has gathered near the entrance to an alleyway. I barely take one more step before I smell the blood—a lot of it.

Heart pounding, I move faster. And when I get close enough to hear the sobbing, I sprint, no longer bothering to care whether Jillian is behind me. Is it possible Sheelin got to Rainey? Elijah?

Shoving through the crowd, I emerge into an alleyway splattered with blood. Heavy metal hangs in the air, leaving a tang on my tongue, in my lungs, as I scan the small space for Rainey.

My gaze lands on her standing beside Elijah as they stare down at a petite brunette woman propped against the brick siding of Mooney's. "No," I choke out. "*No.*" We can't have lost another one.

Not now.

But as I move closer, as I get a clear view of eyes I know all too well—something breaks inside of me.

Rainey turns to me. "Bella," she chokes out. Though Elijah's expression is strained, he keeps a hand on her back as she attempts to keep it together.

"I don't...how?"

"Oh, no." Jillian's gasp lets me know she's behind me, but I don't tear my eyes from Rainey. Not until heavy sobbing overwhelms the sound of my own blood hammering in my veins.

Glancing to the left, I take in a blood-splattered Magnolia and Drexel. He's wrapped her in his jacket as her body shivers violently.

"She was supposed to be normal. She just wanted to be normal," she cries out in anguish.

My gaze drifts from her to the dead humans on the asphalt, and then to the one still breathing as he kneels, hands cuffed behind his back. He glares back at me, a challenge that tells me exactly what I need to know. Still, I ask anyway. "What the fuck happened?" I choke out and take a step closer to the young succubus, who just wanted to be human. She'd joined our group and helped us fight back against the council because she wanted a normal life.

A life without killing. Without bloodshed. And yet, she ended up dead in an alleyway, anyway.

Rainey clears her throat. "Mags and Drex met her for some dancing. When they came out, they were attacked by those fuckers." She gestures toward the humans.

My vision turns red, and power sparks through my blood. They'd murdered an innocent girl. A girl who was not even old enough to drink. When tunnel vision begins to take over, I start toward him.

"No."

Jillian's word has me spinning on my heel. "Excuse me?"

"You're going to kill him."

"Do you not see what he did?" I roar at her. "Take a good look at the young girl!" I thunder. "Do you know she turned her back on her entire family because she didn't want to be supernatural? Out of all of us, she was the one who actually had a fucking chance!"

"Violence is not the answer," she says, softly, her expression pained.

I ball my hands into fists. "You going to stop me?" I demand. "Go ahead and fucking try." With rage burning hot through me, I turn back toward the man who is currently grinning at me. "I'm going to give you something to fucking laugh about, asshole."

But before I can reach him, his eyes widen, and he begins to choke. Blood pools from his mouth, his eyes, his nose, as his body shakes violently.

"What are you doing to him?" Jillian yells as she runs forward. "Stop! We need to have peace!"

"I'm done playing by your rules."

We turn toward Magnolia, who snaps her fingers. The man jolts once more and falls to the ground alongside the other two.

"Mags," Drexel whispers.

Tears stream down the young witch's face. Humans who gathered behind us gasp, some scream, and we turn toward them. Their horrified expressions showcase exactly what we've just proven to them we are. Monsters. But that's the harsh reality—if you paint someone as a monster, treat them as one, soon, that's exactly what they'll become.

"Your kind murders mine." Magnolia shoves out of the jacket, turning toward the human spectators that remained. "You will die for it."

They turn and run, scrambling in an attempt to get away from the young witch. As soon as they're gone, she collapses right into Drex. Together, they sink to the pavement. Rainey does nothing.

Elijah does nothing.

I do nothing.

Jillian whirls on Rainey. "You need to arrest her. Now."

"No."

"She just killed a man."

"I don't know what reality you're living in, but that was not a man. That son of a bitch deserved so much more than what he got."

"Bella tried to stop him from coming for us," Drexel says. "Due to her transition, her heart rate was just barely high enough to be considered a super. They killed her to make an example—to show us what they were going to do to us." Eyes hard, the young hunter looks far older than his nineteen years. "I tried," he cries out as Magnolia leans into him, wrapping two slender arms around his neck. "I swear I tried to save her."

My chest burns with anguished rage.

"He was incapacitated," Jillian insists. "Couldn't defend himself. The violence was unnecessary."

"As far as I'm concerned, he attacked her, and she fought back in self-defense." Rainey pulls out her phone. It's then I notice her hands shaking. Elijah reaches forward and takes it.

"I've got it."

Rainey nods and turns toward Bella. Shoulders straight, she looks one breeze away from collapsing.

"That was not self-defense. It was murder." But even as she insists it, I notice her gaze drifting to Bella and then to the man.

I turn toward Jillian. "You are new to this world, so let me fill you in. When someone in our world hurts an innocent—be it human or supernatural—we take care of them. It is quite literally the job of a hunter. Very few instances go before a court, a judge, or a jury. We are the executioners. Period."

"You can't operate like that if you ever want to live alongside the humans peacefully."

"Peacefully?" Rainey chokes out as she turns toward us. "Does it look like she died peacefully?"

"I didn't—she didn't deserve to die."

Rainey grinds her teeth together and moves toward us. "No, she didn't. This is war, Jillian. And they just hit entirely too fucking close to home."

"You can't do this. You are a police captain."

Rainey reaches into her pocket and withdraws her badge. "Not the fuck anymore, I'm not." She slams it against Jillian's chest then reaches in and pulls out her service firearm, which she also shoves into Jillian's hands. Then, she drops her car keys to the ground at Jillian's feet and walks away.

It kills me. Rainey Astor is the strongest person I've ever met. She's unbreakable.

At least...she was.

Jillian turns to me. "She can't do this. You have to talk to her."

"Cleaners are coming in," Elijah tells us. "Tarnley will be here any minute, and we'll take Bella with us."

"Who the hell is Tarnley?" Jillian demands as the vampire blurs into view.

"Fuck. I'd hoped I'd heard her wrong." He moves toward Bella and kneels beside her. With a steady hand, he lowers her eyelids. I move forward, shrug out of my jacket, and cover her torn body with it. Squatting down, I lift her gently, standing as I cradle her against my chest.

"Fearghas, you can't do that. You're tampering with a crime scene."

I move past Jillian and head into the street as Tarnley guides Magnolia and Drexel out.

"She is under arrest!" she calls out. "This is not how things should be done!"

Elijah opens the back door to my car, and I slide in, keeping Bella in my lap. Another car pulls up beside me, and I glance over as Bronywyn rushes out and opens her back passenger door for Drexel and Magnolia. The young supernaturals slide in, and Tarnley climbs into the passenger side. Within seconds, they're speeding off, and we follow.

Elijah reaches over and clutches Rainey's hand. She sniffles, and in the reflection of the window, I see tears rolling down her cheeks.

The mood in Bronywyn's living room is somber. Delaney cries beside Cole, Willa stands in the corner with her beta shifter, Z, and Walker stands in a corner by himself—his eyes red. Bronywyn and Tarnley are seated on the couch, while Rainey and Elijah stand in another corner.

Eira stands beside me, her expression hard, body rigid.

At some point, Magnolia cried herself to sleep in Drexel's arms, but the young hunter has yet to speak since leaving the alleyway.

"I really wanted to handle this the right way," Rainey says, breaking the silence. "I thought I was doing the right thing, letting the system work." She glances around the room. "But this has to stop. By whatever means necessary."

"We need to play by our rules," Cole says. "Hunt them down and kill every last one of them."

"They're humans," Willa says. "We're going to have to take precautions. Make sure we're not caught."

"Old rules apply," Tarnley says. "My cleaners will be on standby before the human police can find anything."

"Jillian already knows how we operate," I tell them. "Which means we're going to have to be extra cautious."

"How much does she know?" Delaney questions with a sniffle.

"Enough," I reply.

"She a threat?" Rainey asks.

"Not yet. I really think she means well, but she's blinded by what she's been trained to believe. She's a *Faic*," I tell them.

"What the fuck is that?"

At Rainey's question, I turn my attention to her. "It means she's a human with the ability to sense supernatural power."

Walker whistles. "They are really fucking rare."

"Says the psychic," Rainey shoots back at her partner. The animosity between them does not go unnoticed. "Who shouldn't even be here."

"Where you go, I go, partner. That's how it works."

"You're not the one who turned in a badge."

He raises his shirt. "I took an extended leave of absence."

"She fired you?"

"No. Actually, she damn near convinced me to stay. Which is why I agree with Fearghas. She's not a threat...yet. As long as it stays that way, I really think she'll do what she can to help. But she will do everything by the book, which means Magnolia is now wanted for murder."

"I'll fucking put a bullet in Jillian before she gets her hands on her."

"We all will," I assure Rainey.

"Do we need to move the council meetings?" Delaney questions.

I know what she's asking—we all do. For months, we hid under the radar, all sharing one house, and I, for one, am not interested in ever going back there.

"No. Mags stays hidden, but for the rest of us—Walker and me excluded—it's business as usual. She shows up, she'll be outmatched."

"Magnolia and Drexel can stay here," Bronywyn offers. "She doesn't know about my clinic yet, right?"

I shake my head.

"Great." Rainey's taut expression becomes harder. "Bella deserved better."

Nods of agreement echo around the room.

"We're going to put these assholes down. There's no way in hell they're ready to go up against all of us."

Silence fills the room, and in it, I recall the first time I met the young succubus. The memory comes flooding back and, with it, the agony of knowing she'll never go on to achieve everything she'd been desperate for.

"Any word on Sheelin?" Rainey questions.

All eyes turn to me.

"Sheelin?" Bronywyn steps forward. "She's back?"

CHAPTER THIRTEEN

EIRA

The already dark mood shifts once more with Fearghas's confirmation.

"Of course, she is. Because why wouldn't she be? It's not like we get one damned minute to breathe!" Bronywyn explodes, a rare show of temper from the normally cool-headed witch.

I certainly can't blame her. We've already lost so much—and here we are, preparing to bury yet another of our group. "She showed up at my apartment the other night then abducted me from the baby shower."

"And what? She deliver a gift basket? Flowers? What did she want?" Delaney whirls on Rainey. "You don't seem surprised."

"Because I knew about it."

"Why the hell didn't you tell me?"

"We have enough to worry about," Rainey replies.

"Adding to your already expansive stressors seemed a horrible idea."

Cole squeezes Delaney's shoulder as new tears stream down her cheeks.

"Fearghas, she tried to kill you."

"She did."

"Why is she back?" Cole questions.

"To fuck with me. Jillian nearly got caught in the crossfire."

"Oh, great. So now she knows there's a sadistic fae after us, too." Delaney shakes her head angrily. "This night can end any moment now."

"I'm going to find her," he assures her. "Sheelin is mine to deal with."

"Any word from Ridley? He was looking for her, right?"

All eyes shift to Elijah.

"None," Fearghas replies. "As far as I know, he and Rachel are still in Faerie. But Sheelin knows he's looking for her now. She'll remain relatively hidden. Likely, she's sent him on a wild goose chase."

"Any way we can get a message to him?" Bronywyn asks.

"Not without another fae who can go between the worlds."

"Perfect." Delaney shakes her head then closes her eyes and takes a deep breath. I've never seen her this wired, this overwhelmed. "So we stay the course; continue looking for the humans. We cross paths with Sheelin, then we'll just take her out as well."

Fearghas doesn't reply, but I can feel the shift in his mood as a heavy weight settles in my stomach. His relationship with his sister is more than complicated, and even I don't fully understand what led the siblings to be at life-or-death odds.

What I do know is that Fearghas is too good of a man to see that Sheelin's decisions are not his to carry; they're hers. Because of that, he will feel every ounce of the pain rained down upon her from any one of us.

"We meet back here tomorrow for the funeral," Rainey says, before she turns to Bronywyn.

Fearghas turns away and heads for the door without saying goodbye, so I follow. "Fearghas?"

He doesn't stop until we're out in the cold. "What is it?"

"Where are you going?"

"To find Sheelin."

"Alone?"

"She's broken, Eira. And if I can convince her—"

"You can't save everyone," I urge him to hear me, to believe what I'm saying, because it could very well mean the difference between him surviving this or making a decision that leads to him being stolen from me.

"I have to try," he replies.

Sensing his conviction, I move to stand in front of him. "Then I'm coming with you."

"No."

"Yes." Swallowing hard, I stare up at him, trying like hell to not recall the all too recent memory of his breath fanning over my face.

"Eira—"

"Listen, the world is full of snow and ice right now, which means water is at my disposal everywhere I turn around. Don't make me freeze you."

"Fine." The corner of his mouth lifts in a grin that makes my heart flutter. How I wish I could simply surrender to what I feel for him. Before I fully realize what I'm doing, I reach forward and press the tips of my fingers to his cheek.

He stills beneath my touch, and I force my unease back down. This is Fearghas. *My* Fearghas. He would never hurt me. Even if he'd been out of sorts the other night, he still gave me a choice. I slide my fingers down over his clean-shaven jaw, and his eyes close as his mouth falls open, just slightly.

I let my gaze drop to his hands. Clenched into fists, they remain firmly at his side.

"Thank you for trusting me," I whisper.

His eyes flutter open, and for a moment, I lose the ability to breathe. "I always want you with me."

The door behind us opens, and I step back.

Fearghas clears his throat and shifts his attention to those leaving the house.

"Are you okay?" he asks.

"I will be once we catch these fuckers. Where are you two going?" Rainey questions.

"I'm heading home. Eira?" he asks, looking to me.

Even though I despise lying, I swallow hard and say, "Heading home as well."

"Be careful," she says as she climbs into the passenger seat of Bronywwyn's car. Elijah climbs into the driver's side, and soon, they're pulling away.

"I'll meet you at your house." Fearghas turns away, and I watch as he retreats to his car. So many times over the years our relationship has shifted, but lately, it feels as though we're teetering upon the edge of a cliff.

One small gesture away from falling.

Dressed in jeans, boots, and a pale-blue sweatshirt, I'm just closing up my house for the night when headlights illuminate my drive. Fearghas's car comes to a stop, and he climbs out, wearing dark jeans, black boots, and a navy-blue shirt covered by a leather jacket.

And damn it if he doesn't look perfect. It's so rare

for me to see him out of his suits, but the grim look on his face keeps my lust at bay.

His eyes narrow on my face. “You okay?”

It’s then I realize I’m staring. “Yes, sorry, lost in thought.”

With a nod, he moves around to the passenger seat and opens the car door so I can climb in. Ever the gentleman, he waits until I’m inside before closing it and moving around to get back in behind the wheel.

“Where are we going first?” I ask, fidgeting with the hem of my sweatshirt.

“Lucy’s old place.”

“The house you guys hid out in?”

He nods. “It’s a start, though I’ll be surprised if she’s there.” Tires crunch against the gravel of my drive as he pulls out and hits the smooth asphalt of the highway taking us out of town. “She’s either that arrogant or not that stupid.”

A haunting melody plays through the speakers, barely loud enough for me to make out the words. My gaze drifts to the hand resting on his knee. For a moment, I imagine reaching over and taking it, threading my fingers through his. How nice and normal that would be.

The very fact that I’m thinking about initiating that type of contact is a surprise—even to me.

Forcing my gaze out the window, I stare at the

steady city lights in the distance. "How are you doing?"

"Fine. You? Any more calls to the shelter?"

"Not that I know of," I lie. "I'm headed over there tomorrow to meet with Mel."

If he noticed my mistruth, he doesn't say anything. "You're not concerned about a possible threat?" he asks as he exits and hits the road that will take us toward Lucy's hideout.

"Not one I can't handle." Oh, how I hope those words are the truth. Now is when he'd usually make a joke—something along the lines of 'Eira the badass'. The fact that he doesn't, that he remains silent and serious, is evidence enough of his nerves. "Fearghas?"

"What?" he glances over, and for a brief moment, our gazes meet.

"Why did you not want to include the others in looking for Sheelin? Is it truly because you're worried about putting too much on their plates?"

He sighs. "Honestly? I'm worried about Rainey shooting first, asking questions later."

"Fearghas—"

"Sheelin and I have a complicated history," he interrupts me, but I don't take offense. "She blames me for what happened to her."

The steady ache in my chest blossoms into something akin to heartbreak. For him; for what she went through. "That's not on you," I insist. "What happened to her, the guilty party there is the one that carried it out. The ones that stood idly by, allowing it to happen. Not you."

He purses his lips but doesn't respond as he directs the car onto a long gravel road. Trees line the drive, their canopies hanging over the top of us and blocking out even the faintest moonlight. "Either way, she blames me. If I can reason with her, I might be able to make her see that I never left her."

"Fearghas, some people cannot be saved."

"You were." He glances at me as he puts the car into park. "What you went through was a nightmare, and you're sitting here with me, right now. That's evidence enough that she's not condemned."

I didn't mate the man who raped me. While I don't dare speak those words out loud, they are the first ones that come to mind. Sheelin may not have deserved what happened to her, but she chose where she went from there. Instead of trying to move past the pain, she embraced it, turning it into rage directed at the one person who would have done anything to help her. I can feel horrible for her, but still see her for what she is: a murderer. There's not a doubt in my mind that, if she gets the chance to take out Fearghas, she will.

Which is why I'm here. I won't let that happen.

I can't let that happen.

"Just promise me you won't do anything reckless."

He grins at me now—though it doesn't fully reach his eyes. "Reckless is my specialty."

I shake my head and open the car door while he does the same. As we meet around the front of the car, he holds out a silver blade. When I take it from him, our fingers brush momentarily; the light contact is exhilarating. For so long, I couldn't stand a single touch, but the last couple of months, as I've spent more and more time with him, I've grown accustomed to the occasional contact.

Even crave it.

My mind briefly drifts back to his apartment where I'd initiated it. What would have happened had I not removed my hand?

Pain. Dark. Chains. Laughter.

I shake my head and pull my hand back. "Thank you."

He palms another blade. "We stay together."

Nodding in agreement, we head toward the looming house. The massive structure is completely dark, and while I was only here a few times, I can feel the negative energy surrounding the place. It seeps into my bones, and my magic urges me to push it out.

"I'll be happy to never have to come here again," Fearghas comments as we move up the wooden steps and onto the wraparound porch. He stops in front of the door and takes a deep breath before shoving it open.

It creaks as it swings open. He moves inside and flips on a switch. Soft light bathes the foyer, illuminating the sheet-covered furniture in the corner of the sunroom. Silently, we move farther inside, and I glance into the living room where we hosted Bronywyn's wedding shower and Delaney's mini baby celebration.

A smile stretches across my face as I picture them sitting there, all of us laughing as though there was not a care in the world. As though Odette wasn't in the process of marching an army here to take us all out.

Those stretches of normalcy have been so damned welcome over the year of war. While I stayed out of most of the fights—at Fearghas's request—there wasn't a day—or night—that went by without my staying up and pacing my living room, awaiting a text from Fearghas to let me know he'd survived another day.

I glance at him now as he checks the hall closet. Soft light casts shadows over his face, accentuating his sharp nose and strong jaw. He deserves so much better than what I can give him. Yet, even as I can admit it, I hope he never figures it out. Because without him, I'm not sure I can maintain as I have all these years.

Like paper in water, I'll dissolve beneath the pressure, I'm sure of it.

"Upstairs?" he asks, turning to me.

Quickly, I avert my gaze. "Following you."

He takes the first step moments before something

crashes in the kitchen. We both whirl and race down the hall, heading through the door, blades drawn.

Only to find—nothing.

"What the—" Fearghas trails off as he moves around the island. He kneels, disappearing from sight, so I move around and find him squatting in front of a pile of shattered porcelain.

"What is that?"

He reaches down and lifts a pale-yellow piece to show it to me. "It was a bird." The color from his face is gone, his cheeks pale, though I cannot imagine why.

"A bird?"

"Sheelin was here." He drops the piece and stands. "Son of a bitch!"

I jump with the adrenaline and power surging, but I force myself to stand still even as my fear wants to force me to take a few steps back. It sizzles along my skin—a magic, unlike anything I've felt. Staring down at my skin, I see tiny sparks flaring to life, and I'm awestruck.

What the—I...

"I'm sorry."

Looking back at Fearghas, I feel the magic begin to die down. "How do you know it was her? Maybe an animal—"

"The bird tells me it was her," he replies, though he doesn't elaborate further, and I don't press. Fearghas pissed off is one thing, but the charge of power that rolled off him? It was... I look back down at my arms, noting my magic is back to normal. There are no sparks, no surges of static electricity, just pale-blue fabric.

"We need to check upstairs." Fearghas abandons the bird and moves past me, leaving me standing in the kitchen. As I stare down at the porcelain bird—the shattered pieces broken apart on the floor—I can only hope Fearghas will not break, too.

CHAPTER FOURTEEN
FEARGHAS

The stench of stale cigarettes very nearly sends my stomach hurling as I step into the third antique shop of the day. Situated on the edge of the city, this place is damn near my last hope that my sister is lingering—and apparently shopping—locally. From what I know of her, I'd be willing to bet money she is—but who knows.

So, armed with a plastic bag full of porcelain shards, I make my way to the countertop where an elderly woman with curly white hair is gently polishing an old clock.

"Excuse me?"

She turns and stares at me for a moment, expressionless—almost as if she thought I was simply a part of her antiques. Then, she smiles. "Well, hello, dear. What can I do for you?"

"I am looking for something and was hoping you can help me." Reaching into my pocket, I pull out the bag of broken pieces.

Her brow furrows. "Oh, no! You poor dear. Is this an heirloom?" She sets the polish rag down and moves over to a velvet-lined tray sitting on top of the counter. When she reaches for the bag, I hand it over and watch as she opens the top and dumps the contents onto the tray.

"No. I actually just got it, but the man who runs an antique store I visited earlier says it's quite rare."

She hums. "I'll say, this is from my personal collection. Such a shame. The sparrow was my favorite." Clicking her tongue, she shakes her head.

Meanwhile, my heart lifts with hope. "Your collection? Do you remember who bought it?"

"I do. Peculiar girl, that one. It was my sister who dealt with her."

"Is she here? Your sister?" I add at her questioning look.

She shakes her head. "She isn't feeling well. The flu. Called in this morning."

"Any chance I can see the rest of the collection?"

"Of course. Right this way." She gestures for me to follow as she moves around the counter and toward the back of the shop. The place is piled high, floor to ceiling, with shelves that are covered in old items. The energy here is strong enough to make me believe they might inadvertently have a few magical ones as well.

Though those pose no actual threat to any humans who may purchase one unknowingly. You have to be supernatural in order to get any real use out of a spelled item.

The woman comes to a stop just before a huge cherry wood cabinet. She reaches into her pockets and withdraws a set of keys, unlocks the cabinet, and opens it. The inside is completely full of porcelain birds.

Dozens upon dozens of them.

"Why did you sell her this one if it was your personal collection?"

The woman's brow furrows again as though she's searching for the memory. "I don't actually know why," she replies. "How did you get it?"

"My sister gave it to me."

"I am so sorry it's broken."

I stare at the black eyes of a porcelain cardinal. Sheelin was here. How she found this place, I don't know, but there's no doubt she got it from here which means she's staying local. Otherwise, why shop here in Billings?

"I would love to talk to your sister, if possible."

"No. I'm afraid it's not. She's sick."

"Can I have her number?"

"Absolutely not," the woman replies as she locks

the cabinet and heads toward the front of the store. As soon as she's back behind the counter, I make eye contact with her and let my power surge to the surface.

"You are going to write your sister's address down for me," I tell her, using magic to influence her mind. It's a trick only fae possess. Light fae can only influence non-supernaturals, and most of us hate doing it. It's a perversion I reject on all counts, but this is literally life or death for everyone who's ever meant anything to me.

"Yes. Okay. Right away." She pulls out a piece of paper and a pen and quickly scrawls the address down. As soon as it's done, she hands it to me.

"You will forget I was ever here," I say, and release the hold.

"Who are you?"

"Just a customer who wanted to see your clocks."

"We have this one," she says, gesturing to the one she'd been polishing upon my arrival.

"Thank you. I'll take it." Reaching into my pocket, I withdraw my wallet and hand the woman a hundred-dollar bill. "Keep the change." Armed with my new clock and the address, I head toward the door and out into my car.

As soon as I'm behind the wheel, I pull up her sister's address on my GPS. The place is literally right down the street, so I abandon my car, clock inside, and opt for a walk instead. Fresh air never killed anyone, right?

As I move alongside humans traveling to and from their destinations, I allow myself to imagine what it must be like to simply go along with the monotony of the day. Wake up, work out, eat breakfast, go to work, love on family, eat dinner, go to bed.

Damn, what I'd give to wake up and do that all over again.

The stark white apartment building just ahead looks to have been built in the late eighties, but it's been well-cared for. Balconies overflow with green plants while cheerful red doors shine beneath the bright sun.

After re-checking the address, I note the place I'm looking for is on the second story, so I head for the exterior concrete steps.

Overhead, a door closes, and an older woman shuffles down toward me. As soon as she realizes she's not alone on the steps, she stops and smiles. "Hello, what's a young man like you doing here?"

"Visiting a friend," I reply. Magic sings along my skin in response to this woman. Why? I've no clue, but something is off. "Do you live here?"

She grins. "No, as it happens, I was visiting a friend, too." She moves past me. "Have a good day, birdie."

I stop in place and turn. "Sheelin."

Before my eyes, she transforms from the old woman into the sadistic woman I know her as. Quickly, I look around to see if anyone noticed, but if they did, they're doing a damn good job at hiding it.

Smart.

"What the hell are you doing here?"

"Visiting a friend," she repeats. "Say hello to yours for me." With a wave, she dematerializes. Wasting no more time, I bound up the stairs, heart in my throat. If she hurt an innocent, if she killed a—the door is locked, but I kick it in, boot planted firmly on the red.

A second later, the copper tang hits my lungs.

I rush into the tiny apartment. It doesn't take me long to find who I'm looking for. Blood stains her white sweatshirt, and the elderly woman I was looking for is lying face-up on her kitchen floor surrounded by shattered porcelain teacups on the floor around her.

As horrific as the sight is, it's still nothing compared to the realization that I've met this woman before. Rage suffocates me as I gather her into my arms and hold her against my chest. Since her body is still warm, I urge my power into her, trying like hell to use the life force of the topiary around me to reanimate her.

But as always, I'm too late.

"Fearghas? Is that you?"

I glance up as Jillian lowers her weapon and three uniformed officers file in behind her. I hadn't even heard them approach—something completely unusual for me.

"It is."

"What the hell happened?" She moves into the kitchen, cautious steps bringing her closer to where I still sit propped against a counter, Minnie in my lap.

"Sheelin," I manage.

"Your sister?"

"Yes."

"She killed this woman?"

"Yes."

"Then why are you here?"

"Because I fell into her trap," I tell Jillian, honestly. Had I not gone after her, had I not tracked down the bird, would Minnie still have been killed? Since Sheelin waited until I arrived to carry out the heinous act, my best guess is no.

Minnie died because I wanted to embark on some twisted redemption mission for a woman who's been dead for over a thousand years.

Jillian kneels before me then glances back over her shoulder. "Get the place taped off, and find me next of kin," she orders.

For the first time since she arrived, I meet her eyes. Red hair pulled back from her face, she's wearing a black leather jacket and dark jeans—nearly the same type of attire she'd been in when I left her in that alley.

"I need to know what your connection is with this woman, and I need you to step away so the crime scene investigators can do their job."

"No need. I can tell you who killed her."

"How do you know it was Sheelin?"

I glare at her. "I will not be interrogated by a human," I snap.

Her expression hardens. "You will because I am the acting police captain, and you were just found in an active crime scene." Reaching behind her, she withdraws cuffs. It takes me no energy to discern they're made of iron.

"Going to arrest me, then?"

"If I have to. By the book, Fearghas. Please don't make me do it."

Gently, I set Minnie's body aside and get to my feet. Then, I hold out both wrists. "If you don't arrest me, I'm likely to kill a lot of people," I tell her, honestly.

"Fearghas—"

"No. I can feel the restraints on my temper already waning." Gesturing to the dead plants around me, I lock gazes with her. "I will kill however many supernaturals I need to in order to find my sister, and the only way you're going to stop me is with those iron cuffs."

She swallows hard, and I watch the battle play out on her face. In this moment, though, I don't trust myself not to do exactly what it is I'm threatening.

With an angry sigh, she slaps one cuff on my wrist, twists it around my back, and cuffs the other one. "I can't believe you're making me do this."

I don't say anything. Not a single word—not a sound—as she marches me outside and down the steps. Humans watch, some with tears in their eyes, others looking like they're ready to rip out my throat.

As she forces me into the back of what was once Rainey's service vehicle, I notice two people watching me from the crowd, their mouths set in a grim line because they know exactly what this means.

CHAPTER FIFTEEN

FEARGHAS

"Are you fucking kidding me?" Rainey slams into the cell block, but I don't bother sitting up. "You got arrested? What the hell is wrong with you?"

"I have a plan," I tell her.

"Was your plan to be arrested and tossed into a cell reinforced with iron? Because if so, great fucking job."

"It was, actually."

When she doesn't say a word, I sit up and stare at her. Cheeks flushed with color, eyes shooting daggers, she looks about ready to march in here and put me out of my misery. How sad is it I'm honestly hoping she does?

"Why?"

"If I'm in here and Sheelin shows up to taunt me—

which she likely will—I'm literally surrounded by iron."

Her eyes narrow on me. Then she sighs. "You're using yourself as bait to trap your sister in a cell."

"Yes."

"She's going to sense the iron."

"Probably, but since there are cameras in here, I'm counting on Jillian showing up right on time and pumping her full of iron bullets."

"Did you tell her about this plan of yours?"

"No. But you can."

"Because you just knew that I'd march down here?"

"There's no way in hell you'd miss an opportunity to hand my ass to me, Rainey. I took a gamble...and here you are."

A muscle in her jaw tightens. "This is bullshit."

"She killed an innocent woman today, Rainey. Murdered her in cold blood because she picked me up on the side of the road."

"What?"

"After Delaney's baby shower, the victim—Minnie—picked me up and gave me a ride back to my car."

Her cheeks flush again, and her hands tighten into fists. I see the moment she comes around to my plan, though, because her expression softens just enough that I know she won't push back anymore. "Fine. But Jillian will not be the one who comes to your aid." She turns away. "I don't trust her to hit the broadside of a bull's ass with a potato gun."

Just as she's about to reach the door, it opens again, and the aforementioned untrustworthy backup strolls in. "I heard you were here."

"Still have those who support me." Rainey crosses her arms.

"I never wanted to be enemies."

"You sure have a funny way of showing that. Trying to arrest—and actually arresting—my friends and all."

Jillian moves around her and comes to a stop before the bars. "I told him I didn't want to arrest him, but he wouldn't leave the scene."

"He didn't kill that woman."

"I never thought he did," Jillian replies, coolly. "But I have laws to follow, and he was being difficult. Add to that the threats—"

"Threats?" Rainey turns to me, almost looking proud.

"I may have threatened a supernatural rampage."

"It's what's needed nowadays."

"No, it's not." Jillian pinches the bridge of her nose in frustration. "Why can't you people see that violence isn't the answer?"

"Because in our world, it is."

"Maybe it was once upon a time, Astor, but now?

Now that humans know about you guys? There have to be laws that apply to both sides."

"And how do you plan to contain a bunch of supernaturals?"

"You had the cells reinforced with iron."

"I did. What of the humans that are out slaughtering innocents? You think they deserve to be reformed and re-released?"

"The justice system is there for a reason."

"The justice system is fucking flawed. Pedophiles released after serving only a few years? Murderers? Rapists? They all deserve to fucking burn for their crimes, and yet, I've consistently arrested the same fucking assholes year after year because your justice system lets them go. Here's a hard truth, Jillian. Psychopaths. Do. Not. Change. They just find more creative ways of getting away with it."

"Vigilantes have no place in this world."

Rainey snorts. "Yeah, sure they don't." She glances my way, and I see the exhaustion in her dark eyes. "Fearghas let you arrest him because he has a plan to catch Sheelin."

"*Let* me arrest him? After what he said, he really had no choice."

"He always had a choice," Rainey shoots back as though I'm not here.

Jillian doesn't press further. Instead, she turns to me and crosses her arms. "What plan?"

By the time Jillian and Rainey both leave, we'd managed to come to an agreement. A feat that, in itself, was far more exhausting than it should have been. Both women clearly want to take the lead, and neither is willing to compromise.

Rainey sleeps a few cells down from me, the door unlocked and ready for her to leave the moment Sheelin appears. I have a sneaking suspicion Jillian enjoyed arresting her far more than she should have.

"Stop thinking about it," Rainey groans. "I can practically hear your thoughts all the way over here."

"I thought you were sleeping."

"Not with your erratic heartrate sending my adrenaline spiking." Groaning, she sits up and leans against the wall to stare at me through the bars. "What's on your mind?"

Arching a brow, I turn to face her. "You want to talk feelings with me?"

"Why the hell not? It's not as though there's much else to do."

"What do you want to talk about?"

"Why have you been avoiding me?"

Straight to the point, Rainey Astor-style. "Because it seemed the safest thing to do, given the current circumstances."

"Right." She snaps. "I typically avoid those I care about when shit hits the fan, too."

"Rainey, Sheelin is gunning for you and Del. If I continued to be around you—"

"I hate to break it to you, dumbass, but if your crazy-ass sister wants to come for me, she's going to come whether or not you're around. That's the way it works."

"Sheelin is easily distracted," I explain. "She'll get bored if there's nothing to see."

"Which is why you went out hunting for her without me?" At my curious expression, she adds, "I have security cameras up at Lucy's old place."

"You saw Eira and me."

"I did."

Not seeing a point in lying about it, I sigh and lay back against the cot. "I wanted to reason with her."

"Sheelin? That's a tall fucking order."

"She's my sister. I thought that maybe I could find a way to reach the shred of innocence still in her."

"I hate to be the one to break it to you, Fearghas, but Sheelin proved who she was the day she killed your father."

The moment that will be branded in my mind for eternity comes forward. The sight of my father falling to the ground; my mother's screams; Sheelin's dark laugh—it will all haunt me. Rainey is right—that much I know—but the idea of losing her, of failing her a second time, was too damn much to carry.

"Why is she so hell-bent on coming after you? Because you killed her mate?"

"That and more."

"Care to elaborate?"

"Sheelin and I have a twisted past, Rainey. She blames me for a lot of what she's been through because I hadn't been there to protect her."

"That's a shit way to look at things."

I don't point out how wrong she is—how Sheelin has every right to hate me for what happened to her. If I'd have been there, if I'd have been lucid, I could have protected her. Or, at the very least, saved her as soon as they threw us out of the castle.

But I hadn't, and Sheelin paid for it.

"How did you know to go to that antique shop?"

"I'd gone to two others before that one, looking for whoever sold that bird Sheelin left at Lucy's."

"I didn't realize you saw her that night. She wasn't on any of the cameras."

"We didn't see her. We just found the bird."

"And you knew it was Sheelin?"

"It's an inside thing between us. When we were kids, she found a baby bird that had fallen out of the nest." The thing had been barely larger than my thumb, its wings bent at an unnatural angle. Tears streamed down Sheelin's face; the very idea of an innocent creature suffering tormented her. “She wanted to save it. I told her it needed to be put out of its misery.”

“Harsh.”

“It was the truth. I tried to convince her that letting the bird live in pain was heartless since it was unlikely to be able to survive.”

“I thought you fae could heal.”

“Not in our world. We cannot heal other fae or any creatures from Faerie. That magic only works in this world.”

She’s quiet for a moment. “Did you kill it?”

“No. Sheelin would have been heartbroken, so she took it inside and kept it in a teacup as she tried to nurse it back to life. It didn’t survive,” I add quickly. “When she took me to that mountaintop, she reminded me of that story.”

“She’s fucking with your head.”

“She is,” I agree. “But in her mind, I’m going to let you all down. She is using that logic to save you the pain by putting you out of your misery, like we should have done the bird.”

I can see it, the twisted logic in her thought process. It’s almost innocent in its simplicity, and unfortunately, understanding it means I also realize now that she cannot be reasoned with. Sheelin must be stopped by any means necessary.

"I'm sorry it's you, Fearghas," Rainey says. "But you have to see that none of this is your fault."

I don't respond. Partially because my throat is constricted and doing so would cause the onslaught of tears I'm holding in to fall. But mainly, it's because Rainey is wrong, and I don't have the courage to explain to her exactly how far off she is.

CHAPTER SIXTEEN

EIRA

"Eira?"

I glance up from my desk to the woman peering into the room. "Yes?"

"You have someone here to see you."

My heart warms, my first thought on Fearghas. It's been two days since I've seen him—the longest I've gone without him—and to say I miss him is a massive understatement. I shut my laptop and stand. "Send them in."

She smiles softly and steps out of the way. Instead of Fearghas, though, I'm greeted with the sight of one of my oldest friends.

"Elijah."

"Eira, you're looking spectacular, as always." He crosses the floor but doesn't touch me right away. It's not until I go in for a quick hug that the ex-vampire puts his arms around me.

"You, too. Marriage suits you." I gesture to the chair across from my desk then slide down behind it. "What can I do for you?"

He hesitates a moment, finally meeting my gaze. "I'm actually here about Fearghas."

My brows draw together in confusion, even as I fear what he's about to say. It's been two days since that night at the house, two days since I've seen or heard from the fae. "I thought he and Rainey were close."

"They are. He's..." Elijah trails off, which is never a good sign. It means he's choosing his words carefully. And if I've learned anything about him since the day he rescued me, it's that Elijah rarely pulls punches.

I sit up straighter, mentally kicking myself for not checking in with Fearghas the day after he dropped me off at home. "What is it, Elijah?"

"He's in jail."

"Jail?" My stomach plunges. "What the hell is he doing in jail?"

"After you went to the house with him and found that bird, he went searching for the shop where it was purchased."

"Sheelin could have gotten it anywhere."

"Yes," he agrees, "but apparently, she got it from a local shop. The sisters that owned it had a full set."

"Okay." I lean onto my desk.

"When he went to talk to the sister who sold it to Sheelin, he found her dead."

"Oh no." Leaning back in my seat, I cover my mouth. "Sheelin?"

He nods. "He told Rainey he ran into her as he was arriving. The neighbors heard him kick the door in and called the police. When Jillian showed up—"

"Jillian?" Growling, I get to my feet. "She arrested him for the murder?"

"Calm down," Elijah orders. "Fearghas instigated it. He forced her hand because he thinks Sheelin will come after him, and then they can trap her. The cells are iron," he adds.

"It was a plan, then?"

"Yes."

"He has to realize he's a sitting duck in there, though. She'll kill him if she corners him."

"Rainey is there to back him up."

"Jillian arrested her, too?" My mind reels as anger-induced adrenaline brings my magic to the surface. If both Rainey and Fearghas are in jail—if Sheelin catches on—they are literally sitting ducks. No way in, no way out.

"Rainey got herself arrested to aid Fearghas."

"When did this happen?" I demand. Elijah remains silent. "Elijah, when did they get arrested?"

"The day before yesterday."

"Are you kidding me? Why didn't anyone tell me?"

"Fearghas asked us not to."

"I'm going to kill him," I growl as I stand and begin to pace. I've got enough on my plate and now this? I'm just supposed to sit idly by while he uses himself as bait? And not just him! The dumbass convinced Rainey to go along with it, too!

"I'm telling you because I am not one to keep secrets from my friends. And also because I fear you a bit more than him." He winks, his way of disarming me, and dammit if it doesn't work—just a little.

Plopping back down in my seat, I force myself to take a deep breath. "Rainey is there to put her down when this plan inevitably goes sideways?"

"Yes."

"That's good. Okay, maybe I won't kill him."

Elijah chuckles. "I would avoid it if possible." His expression grows serious once more. "How are you doing?"

"Why do you ask?"

"Rainey mentioned prank phone calls. You look exhausted."

"I thought I looked 'spectacular, as always?'" I joke back.

Elijah grins. "Spectacularly exhausted."

"Stress will do that to you," I counter as I run both hands over my face. "It's not just the phone calls, or even them and Sheelin." My admission is a difficult one, made even more so by the new stress piled upon my shoulders.

Still, Elijah is my oldest friend. And out of everyone, he'll understand the most. So, I get to my feet and cross the room. After sliding a painting of the *Cliffs of Moher* aside, I enter a code and swing open my safe. Nestled inside is the tiny tape from the recorder at the shelter.

Elijah's curious gaze follows me back to my seat where I slide the tape into the recorder on my desk.

"What's that?"

"A recording of the last phone call."

"The voice you heard? Rainey said neither she nor your security could hear it."

"They couldn't." It can't just be in my imagination, though I can't even begin to understand why no one else can hear it. My thought is that perhaps it's spelled and only people who knew him are able to hear. It's a long shot, but I don't know what else to do.

I take a seat back at my desk and stare down at it.

"What's that?"

"What I am about to tell you must stay between us." I meet his gaze. "I wouldn't ever ask you to withhold anything from Rainey, but if you do tell her, she must also agree to confidence."

"Eira, what's going on?" He leans forward in his chair.

Before I can change my mind, I reach down and hit play.

The heavy breathing fills my office, but I don't watch the recorder. Instead, all of my attention is on Elijah and his expression. *Coming for you, my whore.*

The recorder shuts off as my heart falls.

He didn't hear it, either; I know from the lack of reaction to the words.

"That's strange."

"You don't hear the voice?" I ask, again.

Dark brows draw together in confusion. "No."

"There's a robotic voice, Elijah. Buried within the breathing and the crackling, it's there. I've listened to it dozens of times, timed it, and it's always there. Thirty-two seconds in."

"What does it say?"

I fall silent. If I say these words—if I utter them out loud—it makes it real.

"Eira? What does it say?"

Closing my eyes, I take a deep breath, then open them again as I repeat, "'Coming for you, my whore.'"

He sits up straight now, his mouth falling partially open, eyes widening in shock. Of everyone I know, he's the only person who ever saw me at my darkest. He's the only person alive who knows exactly what I went through, because he was there to pick me up after I'd had my vengeance.

He faced my demons with me. Saw them shackled.

“It can’t be.”

“I don’t know who else it could be.”

“He’s dead, Eira.” Elijah pushes to his feet and begins to pace. “You have to tell Rainey about what the voice said—about what it means.”

“I don’t want Fearghas finding out.”

“Why the hell not?” he demands. “If that bastard is back—”

“Fearghas has enough going on with Sheelin. Hell, he’s stressed enough to get both him and Rainey locked in iron boxes. If he’s distracted by anything else it could mean that bitch gets the upper hand. Besides, you’ve seen him. If he thinks I’m in danger, too, he’ll lose it.” My hope is that he will see reason, that he will understand my need for keeping this just between us.

“That man is the only one who poses a serious threat to you,” he reminds me. “Because he knows how to keep you powerless. You realize that, right?”

My throat constricts. “Trust me, Elijah, I know. I’ve taken every possible precaution to protect myself.”

“Your house being surrounded by water will do nothing if he manages to capture you.”

“He won’t.” I move around my desk to stand before him. “Besides, as you said, he’s dead. Chances are it’s someone completely unaware of what they are actually saying.”

A muscle in his jaw ticks. “As soon as I get the chance, I’m telling Rainey what the voice said, and I will be letting her know what it means. But I will ask her to keep it from Fearghas."

I nod in understanding. "Thank you."

Elijah is quiet a moment before running a hand through his long hair. "Eira, you really should tell him."

"I can't. Not yet. Other than the fact that he's in jail, things have been weird between us."

This revelation seems to genuinely surprise him. "Since when?"

"Since I went to his apartment to check on him after Delaney's baby shower."

"You two have an argument? That has to be a first."

"It's difficult to have an argument when you rarely talk about anything heavy," I tell him. "Though, it's not the first time. We did get into it a time or two when he was trying to sideline me through the fight with Lucy."

"That's true, I suppose." He arches a brow at me. "Are you okay?"

"I'm not as delicate as I look," I remind him. "I'll be fine."

"What are you going to do about the calls?"

"As I told Rainey, we changed our number after the first few, and since this one, we've had no further contact. My hope is that the sadistic asshole has moved on to harassing someone else, though I am taking the tape over to Bronywyn today. I want to see if she can tell me whether or not it's somehow been spelled."

"Someone can spell a phone call?"

I shrug. "I don't know. But I figure if anyone does, it'll be Bronywyn."

"Fair assessment."

"I also talked to Willa this morning. She offered to send some of her shifters into the woods just outside the shelter. They'll keep an eye on things until we're sure the danger has passed."

"Smart."

"Seemed the best private security I could buy. Trust is hard to come by these days."

"Isn't that the damned truth?" He steps toward me, but keeps his hands at his sides. "You're not alone in this, Eira. Never again. If any of them come anywhere near you, I will fucking murder them. We all will."

I smile despite the ache in my chest at the memory of the weak woman he'd pulled from the bottom of that dry well. "I know I'm not alone," I assure him. "But if he comes for me again, I'll be ready."

With a bag full of fresh on the shelf Valentine's candy, I step into the shelter. Maribel is waiting for me, holding a steaming mug of coffee in her hand. "Right on time, as always." She smiles softly at me as I hold up the canvas bag. "And with gifts, I see. Given the time of year, I'm going to assume you have Valentine's candies in there."

"You know me so well." I offer her the bag, and she takes it with her free hand then slings it over her shoulder as we begin to walk. "Anything new?"

"No. Just the usual. No new tenants in the last couple of days, though we did have a family move out."

"Who?"

"Ashleigh and her son, Josh. They left to go live with her parents in Utah."

"Oh, okay. That's good." I make it my mission to know the name and backstory of everyone who comes in and out of this place. They are my people—my charges—and knowing everything about them helps me keep them safe even after they leave.

Ashleigh's ex-husband was a senator for Washington State. She'd fled here after he attacked her one night, and when he tracked her down, she ended up on our doorstep. Being that I am as well connected as I am old, I managed to handle him swiftly and with little trouble.

It's amazing the things money and status can buy. Which, in this case, was the freedom of a sweet woman and her seven-year-old son.

"I'm glad they're getting their lives started."

"Me, too," she adds, sadly. "Though I will miss her. Woman made the best hot toddies in the state."

Chuckling, I follow her around the corner. We're just about to make another turn when a small, dark-haired girl skids to a stop in front of me.

"Did you bring her?" she asks, hopefully.

Chuckling, I shake my head. "I'm sorry, Olive. Rainey couldn't come with me today."

Her face falls for a moment, but then she's nodding. "I bet she's super busy beating up bad guys."

"Most definitely."

The little girl's face completely lights up. She reaches behind her back and withdraws a folded piece of paper. "Can you give this to her?"

"Absolutely." Taking the paper, I place it carefully into my pocket.

"Thank you."

"Anytime."

"Olive!"

The little girl glances over her shoulder where her mother is waving at her. "Gotta go, see you later!" she adds, before bounding off.

"That child has more energy than any of the others combined. You sure she's not one of you?" Maribel asks with a sly smile my way.

"I'm sure," I reply. "I need to stop in and see Mel. You okay?"

"I am. Left a few things for you on my desk, so just come by when you're done."

"Will do." Leaving Maribel in the entrance to the dining hall, I head off to the right and walk into Mel's office. Feet propped onto the desk, she has her nose in a book, not even bothering to set it down as I take a seat across from her.

"One sec," she says as her eyes flicker across the page.

I'm about ready to douse her—not the book—in water when she finally closes it and looks up at me. "Sorry, it was just getting good."

"Anything new?"

Mel shakes her head. "We've had no phone calls, no threatening letters, nothing. It's really strange. My guess is someone was just prank calling us."

"I'm taking the message to a friend of mine; going to see if she can track it."

"A cop?"

"A witch. Figured you had the detective work down."

"It never hurts for a second opinion," Mel says. "Especially given the sensitive nature of our work here. Could be an ex of one of our people, a family member of an ex—anyone who would have anything to gain by screwing with us."

"I have a feeling it has little to nothing to do with the people here," I tell her. And since I don't see the harm in a half-truth, I clear my throat and add, "There was a voice embedded in the message."

Mel sits up straighter in her seat then leans in. "What do you mean a voice?"

"It sounded almost robotic."

Color floods her otherwise pale cheeks. "What did it say?"

"It said, 'Coming for you, my whore.'"

"How did I not hear it?"

"No one can hear it but me. That's why I'm taking it to the witch."

"So someone is trying to get at you. Either that, or they didn't realize you'd be the only one who could hear it." Her tone is distant, as though she's processing the information even as she says it aloud. She snaps her fingers. "Which is why you freaked out."

"Yes."

"Shit. So it could be an ex, then. 'My whore' could mean anyone."

Except it likely doesn't. "It's possible."

"If the message was, in fact, meant for you—which we can safely assume since you're the only one who could hear it—then who is the caller, and how did they find this place? The club is supernatural community public knowledge. Everyone knows you run it. But the shelter has always been under the radar."

"I don't know," I admit. "But I'm aiming to find out."

"This puts a bit of a different spin on it. You really shouldn't be going anywhere without protection," Mel warns me.

"I'll be fine. I've taken precautions to protect myself, and while I don't want to make any of our residents uncomfortable, I will be upping the security on the exterior. The guards will stay out of sight, but they'll be around, should anything happen."

"Okay. As long as they don't come into the shelter, that should be fine."

"I'm going to give them your number. They'll report directly to you and *only* to you. I won't even have any direct contact with them, and I'm going through an outside source for the hire."

"Who?"

"A local pack. Their alpha is an acquaintance of mine."

"Akacheta's?"

I nod, honestly surprised she knows about Willa and her family. As much as the humans would like to believe it, their rumor about all supernaturals being connected? It's about as true as the belief that all humans know each other. There are so many of us it's nearly impossible to know everyone.

"I've run into a few of her wolves here and there. Since I'm nosy and prefer to know who's around me, I've asked."

Which makes complete sense. "Keep an eye out for

a call later, and let me know if you notice anything out of whack."

"You, too, Eira. Watch your back." Her gaze softens, concern etched in her expression.

"Will do."

CHAPTER SEVENTEEN

FEARGHAS

"Have to say this is something I never expected."

I jump up from the cot the moment Sheelin's magic permeates the air. She stands just outside the bars of my cell, grinning from ear to ear. "You're the one who caused it."

"Rainey. So nice to see you."

"Wish I could say the same," Rainey replies, darkly.

Sheelin leans in toward the bars, though she doesn't touch them. "I don't suppose this is in response to your sweet friend, Minnie, is it? Such a shame." She clicks her tongue, and rage burns through my veins.

"She was innocent."

"She was pathetic. Do you know how excited she

was to have a visitor? Her sister and her did not get along, either. It was difficult to get that sparrow from them when good ol' Andrea got in the way."

"Do you get off on hurting those who can't protect themselves?"

Sheelin turns to me. "I don't know, Fearghas. Do you?"

"Hey, asshole, I was talking to you."

On heeled boots, she turns toward Rainey, taking careful steps to avoid actually touching the bars. "You know I find you quite interesting, hunter. You're quite the mystery."

"Oh? You're easy enough to figure out." Rainey takes a step back from the bars.

"One minute, you don't care; one minute, you do. You and Fearghas might as well be the same person. After all, you let your sister down, too, didn't you?" Rainey doesn't reply, and Sheelin laughs. "Lucy told me all about it. About how Delaney's blood splattered the alleyway, her body growing cold while you were out and about, living that normal life you'd craved. The same one you murdered your sister for."

Rainey's hands clench into fists. "I didn't murder my sister."

"Don't let her get into your head, Rainey."

"Yeah, there's no telling what I'll find if I were to take a peek, is there?" She kicks the unlocked door open and grins. "You weren't trying to trap me, were you?"

Rainey takes a step farther inside, and I move toward my bars.

"I'd stay where you are, brother. I sure would hate to snap Rainey's pretty little neck."

"You're outta luck on that one, bitch." Rainey whips out her gun the moment Sheelin is within the confines of the cell. She fires—no hesitation.

One shot.

Two.

Three.

Four.

But Sheelin is gone. I whirl, scanning for her, and Rainey grunts. When I turn back toward her, adrenaline surging, I see that my sister is behind her, pressing a blade to Rainey's throat.

"Sheelin! No!" Gripping my own bars, I yank the unlocked door open and rush down the hall toward Rainey's cell.

"Let's see what's inside, shall we?"

Rainey groans as her eyes roll back in her head. Teeth clenched together, she begins to shiver violently in response to the assault on her mind. All the while, Sheelin watches me as the blade steadily bites in. Crimson beads on the surface of her skin.

I know I'm screwed.

There's no way in hell I can move fast enough to get to her. "Please, stop, Sheelin."

"No. This is far too delicious. Tell me, Fearghas, did you know your little sister here still has nightmares about her sister dying?" She laughs, the maniacal sound utterly terrifying. "I suppose a trip to the Veil will calm her anxiety, wouldn't you say?"

I lunge forward.

A gunshot echoes through the room, and Sheelin stumbles back.

Rainey falls forward, head slamming into the concrete before I can reach her.

Another gunshot has Sheelin's body jerking violently. Without bothering to look to see who pulled the trigger, I race forward, dropping my shoulder as I prepare to knock Sheelin to the ground. But before I reach her, she glares my way and disappears.

Shoulder slamming into the concrete, the bones crack, and it's all I can do not to howl in pain and rage.

"Rainey, wake up."

Clutching my shoulder, I stumble toward Rainey, who's unconscious on the ground with Jillian beside her. "She's breathing," she tells me.

"Call Elijah and Bronywyn. Now." I reach into my pocket with my good arm and toss my phone her way.

She doesn't argue, just does as she's told as I wrap my uninjured arm around Rainey and pull her into my lap. Her eyelids flutter, compliments of Sheelin's mind assault. "I'm sorry," I whisper as I press my fingertips to her temple.

Magic flutters to the surface, slipping from me to Rainey as I aim to soothe the pain keeping her unconscious.

That's what happens when fae force their way into your mind. Some come out okay—barely noticing that anything happened. Others will begin to lose pieces of their memory, and an unfortunate few lose their minds, altogether.

It all depends on what damage the fae chooses to leave behind.

And we won't know what Sheelin did until Rainey wakes up.

"Have I mentioned that you both are morons?" Delaney roars, one hand on her swollen belly. "No, not you two, you *three*," she growls, looking to Elijah.

"It was a good plan," Rainey insists from her place in the hospital bed, deep within Bronywyn's clinic. Thanks to her hunter abilities, the gash on her forehead is already healed, though her vision is still a little off, given what Sheelin did to her mind.

"A good plan?" Delaney whirls on Cole, who shrugs. "A good plan she says!" She turns back to Rainey, much faster than a woman as far along as she is should be able to move. “If it were a good plan, you wouldn’t have ended up in the hospital, and Fearghas wouldn’t have ended up with a broken arm!”

“Dislocated shoulder,” I correct her, gesturing to the sling on my arm.

Delaney narrows her eyes at me. “You should have known better. Her I expect it from, but you should have known better. You, too,” she adds to Elijah.

Rainey snorts. “Pot, kettle? Less than a year ago, you went off by yourself.”

“Yes. And you made me swear I wouldn’t ever do it again.” Delaney’s bottom lip quivers, and my heart all but breaks in response.

“You couldn’t have helped,” Rainey insists as she swings her legs over the side of the bed. Elijah is right beside her, offering a hand to steady her.

“I could have,” Bronywyn snaps. She’s been silent since Rainey woke, watching and listening to Delaney rip us new ones. “You could have come to me.”

“The more supernaturals there, the easier it would have been for Sheelin to sense a trap.”

“And speaking of traps,” Delaney says, turning to me. “How did she dematerialize inside an iron cell?”

I swallow hard, focusing on a speck against the pale-pink painted walls. “Light fae are the only ones affected by iron,” I tell her. “Our magic has boundaries—lines that cannot be crossed—which is why the dark fae posed such a great risk to us. They were banished because they could not be killed."

"Do you think that was a dark fae pretending to be Sheelin?"

I shake my head and meet Bronywyn's blue gaze. "No. I think Sheelin is becoming a dark fae."

Her eyes widen. "That's possible?"

"It is if she stole the magic from a dark fae," I reply as the weight of that accusation sinks in.

"The same way a witch steals power?" Delaney questions, and I shake my head.

"Not entirely. In order to obtain that magic, she would have had to capture and immobilize a dark fae, then rip the power from the creature by absorbing its soul matter."

"Hold the fucking phone. Soul-matter?" Rainey questions.

"Dark fae have no soul tethering them. What they do have is a form of energy that keeps them alive. We call that soul-matter. When one dies, that matter is re-absorbed into the Veil, reinforcing the prison keeping them in place. It's why they were imprisoned there; murdering each other literally results in their prison growing more secure."

"What happens to her now?"

"It varies, depending on the fae. Most lose their heads; some seek out death. As far as I know, there's only one fae who's ever managed to successfully absorb dark fae soul-matter and remain mostly intact."

"Who?"

At Rainey's question, I meet her gaze. "Rafferty."

"Ridley's brother?" Her jaw drops open, and based on the other shocked gazes, they feel the same.

"As in the same one who rescued us when we were trapped in Faerie?" Cole questions.

"One and the same."

"He seemed normal. Well, normal for a fae," Delaney adds.

"But that means he murdered a dark fae, too."

"He did. The one who murdered their sister."

"Oh my gosh. I didn't know." Delaney shakes her head, sadly.

"He inadvertently absorbed the dark fae's abilities, though he doesn't allow himself to be driven by it."

"All of this means we need to assume Sheelin has even more power?"

"No. But she is no longer constrained by the same rules as we're used to."

"Fantastic." Rainey releases Elijah, clearly steadier on her feet now. "I need to shoot something."

"You need to rest," Bronywyn scolds. "You can get back to the shooting tomorrow. Sheelin did you no favors screwing with your head the way she did."

"Sleep, my love," Elijah whispers as he presses a kiss to her temple.

"Fine." She lets him steer her toward the door, but before she steps through, she grips my arm. "Thank you for not letting her kill me."

"Jillian saved you," I tell her, honestly. "If it weren't for her—"

Rainey groans. "Fine, I guess I owe her a thank you, too."

"And a damned parade," Elijah adds.

Delaney wraps her arms around me, and I offer her my free one in a brief hug. "Dinner tomorrow, asshat."

I don't respond, just offer a tight nod as she and Cole move out into the hall with Bronywyn right behind them.

One by one, those I care for file out of the room until, finally, I'm left standing alone. As soon as I am, I slip the sling off my arm and stretch, glad the vampire blood Bronywyn gave me has already healed the worst of my injury.

Resolution settling in, I toss the sling to the table.

Sheelin stealing the power of a dark fae changes things. Massively. It makes her even more unpredictable—and I was struggling before.

I'm done playing the game she is. Done waiting for her to show up, only to be a step ahead of us—again. Tonight she could have stolen the life of one of the most important people in my life. Being near them makes them targets. Her showing up at Minnie's apartment proved just how desperate she is for a production.

She doesn't want to just make me pay.

She doesn't just want revenge.

No, Sheelin wants me to watch as she tears my life apart. But no more. It's well past time I start playing by my own fucking rules.

Well past time I changed the game.

CHAPTER EIGHTEEN
FEARGHAS

"Son of a bitch." My head might as well have been split open by a damned axe for the pain shooting through it right now. Surprisingly, though, when I reach up, there's no blood, no gore, just unbroken skin and immense agony.

I roll out of bed, trying to remember exactly what got me to where I am right now. And then it all comes running back.

A pack of stray wolves somewhere between here and Shepherd. They'd been attacking a campsite of terrified human teenagers, and I'd taken them on with nothing but a smile. My throbbing hip is proof of the bite I received for my trouble, which is precisely the reason for the headache.

You've got to love wolf venom.

I cover both eyes with my hands, pressing my

palms into the orbital bones in hopes of alleviating even a little of the pain. After a few moments of attempting that, nothing happens. *Lovely.*

Cue a fist beating on my door, and I'm wishing I'd died last night. "Go away," I groan.

"Fearghas, I know you're in there!" She slams her fist onto my door again. "Open up!"

Grumbling the entire damned way, I begrudgingly climb out of bed and make my way to answer it, yelling, "I'm coming, you bloody impatient woman." I grip the handle and yank open the door to a very pregnant and red-faced Delaney Astor.

She doesn't even bother greeting me before shoving into my apartment.

"Please, come in." After shutting the door behind her, I turn.

"You are an asshole, you know that?"

"What have I done now?"

"Oh, I don't know, avoiding me, ignoring my phone calls, standing me up for dinner two nights ago, then again last night. Ring a bell?" Then her gaze drops to the hip still bared due to my lack of shirt, and she snarls. "What the shit is that! Were you out hunting? Alone? And I know you were alone because everyone else was at my house last night for a meeting!" She screams the final word, making her cheeks turn a shade of crimson I didn't even know was possible.

It's adorable even as I have to pretend it's not. "I'm sorry I missed dinner. I had other things to tend to."

"Other things. Other things! Like getting yourself bitten by a shifter!" She steps forward and reaches out to touch me.

I jump back. "It hurts, so you want to poke it?"

Delaney rolls her eyes. "I'm not going to poke it, you dumbass." Warm fingers touch the tender flesh just above the wound. A warmth spreads through my side, and the pain vanishes within an instant. Not just from my side, but my head as well.

"What did you do?"

"Healed you."

"You can't heal."

She beams at me. "I can now. Which you would have known if you'd bothered to show up last night."

I stare down at her. Typically, witch powers don't evolve that hastily in a matter of months, which is about how long she's been a witch. But then my gaze lands on her pregnant belly. "The ley line magic your baby is holding onto."

"We think so." Her caramel gaze narrows on me. "Now, what the hell is wrong with you?"

"I was out for a joy run last night and came across a campsite being attacked. What was I supposed to do? Let those teens be puppy chow?"

"No. Of course, not. But you could have called."

"And you all would have not made it in time. With

Ridley in Faerie, there's no instant travel available anymore."

"I guess." She chews on her bottom lip, something entirely Delaney. It makes my chest ache because I also know that being near me is the least safe place for her right now.

"Besides, you're supposed to be keeping your distance, remember? Bloodthirsty sister on the loose and all?" I turn away and head into the kitchen for coffee.

"I'm not scared of Sheelin."

All joking gone, I turn toward Delaney. "You really should be."

Her eyes widen a bit, and I can see she's pondering what to say next. "You beat her last time."

"Barely. And only because I got the drop on her as she was fighting Bronywyn." After filling the water canister, I pop it down onto the coffee pot and scoop fresh grinds into the basket. Then, I hit brew and turn toward Delaney. "Sheelin is dangerous because she's unhinged. There's no logic to her strategy, no way to know what's coming next. With Heather and Lucy, we always knew their end game. With Sheelin, there's no telling."

"We know what she wants, though: to make you suffer."

"That is a part of it, sure. But Sheelin wants *revenge*, Delaney. Seeing me in pain, it's not going to be enough for her. She will come after all of us, and we'll never see it coming. She's that damned good."

"You sound a little impressed."

"Sheelin is my sister, Delaney. There are things there, things that happened none of you can even begin to comprehend. Impressed? No. But I sure as hell know when to admit I'm matched. More than even, seeing as how she can dematerialize and I cannot."

Her eyes flash with power. "Sheelin is alone; you have us. I'd say that more than tips the scales in your favor."

I appreciate what she's saying—the sentiment in the kindness—but it's nothing but false security. For whatever reason, that pisses me off. "You don't get it, do you?"

"Get what?"

"Sheelin has no boundaries. *Nothing* is off-limits to her. A pregnant woman?" I gesture to her swollen belly, and she instinctively rests a hand on it. "Rainey would hesitate, Tarnley, too...but Sheelin? She sees an opportunity to up the game, and she will take it."

Delaney's eyes widen with fear even as they fill with tears. I scared her. Which is exactly what I was aiming to do. "I am not inept," she snaps back.

"I never said you were. But you have to stay the hell away from me. If you don't come near me, it's harder for her to find you."

"And how are you trying to find her, Fearghas? By going out and trying to get yourself killed?"

"If I'm dead, she has no reason to come after any of you, does she?" The words are out of my mouth before I can stop them.

Delaney takes a step back and gapes at me. "If you think for a second I'm going to let you get yourself killed over this, you're a damned moron."

"Understatement of the millennia," I retort as I turn to grab my coffee. The dark liquid fills my porcelain cup, and I take a moment of solace in watching the steam rise above the cup.

"You'd leave Eira, then?"

"First of all, I'm not out sacrificing myself, Delaney. I'm far too arrogant for that." Leaning back on the counter once more, I face her with my coffee in hand. "And second, Eira wants nothing to do with me. She's made that painfully clear."

"I'm sure she just needs time."

"Time?" I snort. "That's what I do, though, right? Fearghas is always around for everyone whenever they need him. I risked my neck to pull Rainey out of Heather's grasp, right? Then, risked it again for a man who claimed to have the power to rescue my sister. And, well, we know how that one worked out. And how about the time I sacrificed my abilities to go into the Veil and rip out your mate?" Tears spill down her cheeks. "Let us not forget the fact that Bronywyn nearly killed me only a few months ago, and I had to drive a blade into my sister's chest in order to keep her from being skewered."

Her bottom lip quivers. "You did what was right."

"You have your happy ending," I tell her. "Rainey, Bronywyn—all of you are happy, so stop looking for another fucking fight. Sheelin is mine to deal with, and until I get her taken care of, all of you need to stay the hell away from me."

"Shutting us out won't work."

"Then you're all going to die. It's as simple as that."

She swallows hard, and I yearn to reach for her, to hug her and tell her that everything will be all right. But doing so would lead to her remaining here longer than she needs to. I need her gone because that's the only way I can keep her and her baby safe.

Sheelin wants to hurt me. Delaney would be one hell of a way to start.

"What happened to you asking me to run away?" she chokes out.

My chest tightens.

"You told me that we could leave Billings, take Rainey, and be happy."

"You would have never been happy with me, Delaney." My tone is soft, and I do my best to keep my own pain out of it. My demons are not hers to bear. They never have been, and asking her to abandon

Billings, her mate—it was fucked. I see that now. Hell, I saw it then.

"We could go now, though. We could take Cole, Rainey, Elijah—and we can run. She won't find us."

Swallowing hard, I set my coffee down and step toward my best friend. Then, I reach out and take both of her soft hands in mine. "Did we run when Heather was up against Rainey? When Lucy was out for blood?"

"No," she chokes out as tears spill down her cheeks.

"And we definitely didn't run when the council was after all of us, did we?"

She shakes her head.

I release a hand to cup her cheek, then use my thumb to brush the tears away. "Sheelin is my fault, Del. And it's well past time I set it right. Running is just not an option for me anymore."

Her shoulders shake so I pull her against me and wrap both arms around her. "You don't have to do it alone, though."

"I really do, Del. This time, I really do."

CHAPTER NINETEEN

FEARGHAS

Watching the world move as though nothing is wrong fucks with your head. Inside, I'm a mixing bowl of emotions—fear, anger, longing—all vying for control over my mood. The last three days have passed relatively silently, save for the supernaturals who I've killed in my Sheelin pursuit.

Apparently, being pumped full of iron-laced bullets put a damper on Sheelin's 'torment Fearghas' plan. I'm not hopeful enough to think she actually succumbed to her wounds—especially not given her new power boost.

If, she has, in fact, taken in the dark fae power.

"Hey there, handsome."

I glance up from my brood session to find Jackie

beaming down at me from beside the table. "Hey, Jackie."

"Haven't seen you around in a while." She slides into the booth across from me. "Everything good?"

"Peachy. Can I get a glass of whiskey?"

"Absolutely." She starts to get up, but pauses. "You sure you're all right?"

Forcing a smile, I nod, more than appreciating her interest. I've no doubt, if I were to lay all my secrets out for her, she'd listen, if only to run for the hills the moment I stopped speaking. "Just been a long day."

"Okay. Whiskey coming up." As she passes, she squeezes my shoulder then disappears into the back.

Eira is somewhere nearby if the magic buzzing beneath my skin is any indication, though I haven't seen her. In fact, I've made it a point to not see her ever since the night we were at Lucy's house. But tonight, I couldn't help myself. The need to be near her is far too strong to be able to resist when I'm already so damned strained.

As though my thoughts called her, she steps into the room, stealing the breath from my lungs. Dressed head to toe in shimmering navy blue, she's a fucking dream. Hair loose around her face, it moves as she does, gliding across the floor toward me.

"Fearghas." She slides into the booth, taking the same spot Jackie vacated only a few minutes ago.

"Eira."

Leaning back in the booth, she turns her head to study those around us. "Haven't seen you in a while."

"Been busy."

"Oh yes," she replies. "I heard. Jail can be a nasty place." Her eyes flash with power and irritation.

"It was. Especially since Rainey nearly died and I fucked up my shoulder."

Her expression hardens further. "I wish I could say I felt bad for either of you."

"Here you go," Jackie sets a glass of whiskey in front of me then looks to Eira. "Want anything, boss?"

"No. Thank you."

With a nod, Jackie leaves, and I turn up the glass, downing the contents easily.

"What the hell is up your ass?"

She glares at me. "You keep making foolish decisions that are going to get you killed."

"Didn't realize you cared that much. Do I need to start running every decision I make by you before I make it?"

She doesn't immediately reply, though she does turn away and shake her head. Frustration assaults me through this twisted one-sided bond we share, making my skin crawl. "I just want to ensure you're making smart decisions and not jumping every time Sheelin leaves you a ceramic bird."

"A woman died," I tell her. "An innocent human woman."

Eira's expression softens. "I heard."

"Then you know why I needed to try something—anything—to get her."

"And it nearly resulted in your death."

"What would you have me do? I had an opportunity to try to trap her."

"Which failed."

"Not entirely."

"How so? She got away, didn't she?"

"Not before Jillian pumped her full of iron."

Eira's mouth falls slack, her eyes widening. "She what?"

"Jillian shot her four times just before she was going to slit Rainey's throat. We haven't seen her since."

Her silence makes me uneasy as she processes what I've said. "How did she get away if she had iron in her body?"

"I believe she's taken on dark fae soul-matter."

"Shit, Fearghas." Eira shakes her head in disbelief. "That's—"

"Really fucking bad, I know. Except, maybe not. Perhaps she'll go insane and implode all on her own." I lift my glass only to find it's empty.

Jackie reappears at the table with a bottle in hand. "I can refill it."

"Leave the bottle," Eira orders.

"Yes ma'am." Jackie sets the whiskey down and

retreats.

With the wave of her hand, Eira brings the whiskey out of the bottle in a steady stream until my glass is near-full. Then, she pops the pour spout off and drinks directly from the bottle. Her nerves are potent, making me wonder if maybe something else isn't going on, too.

"What is it?"

"There's something you need to know."

"What?"

"Come with me." Without waiting for my response, she slides out of the seat and heads toward the back. I follow, aware of the heavy drumming in my ears from my pounding pulse. She's nervous, scared, and that can't mean anything good.

Together we make our way to her office in complete silence. It's not until she's shut the door behind me that she takes a deep breath.

"What is it, Eira?"

Still not speaking, she moves toward the painting on her wall that shields her safe. After opening it, she heads toward her desk and puts a small tape into a recorder that's already sitting out. "I told you about the phone calls."

"Yes."

"You heard the message."

"The heavy breathing, yes. Has the bastard called again?"

"There's a voice in the message."

My brows draw together as I narrow my gaze on her. "A voice? I didn't hear one."

"I know. No one can hear it but me."

"What does it say?"

"'Coming for you, my whore.'"

Coming for you, my whore. I repeat the words in my head, already thinking of a dozen different ways to murder whoever the hell left the message. "You believe it was meant for you." It's not a question because that's the only thing that could account for her fear.

A tear slips from her eye. "Back when I'd been held captive, when he'd—when what happened to me was carried out, that was his nickname for me." She meets my gaze. "'Swallow it down, my whore.' 'Take it all in, my whore.'"

Her voice cracks, and I move toward her. She throws up a hand, stopping me in my tracks. We've never discussed what happened to her—not the details, anyway. I'd wanted to know so I could help her, heal her—though I honestly hoped never to find out all of it.

Mainly because I knew I'd want to kill those who are already dead.

"He branded me," she chokes out as she turns around. Her fingers shake as she struggles with her zipper.

Swallowing hard, I step forward. "May I?" I ask before I touch her.

She nods.

With shaking fingers of my own, I reach up and touch her back right between her shoulder blades. She stills and lets out a breath; the bond between us grows stronger as I steadily lower the zipper just enough to see the start of a scar on the left side of her upper back.

I hook the shimmery fabric with a finger and pull it to the side, revealing a brand in the shape of a W. I want to yell. To pummel everything in my path. My blood hammers, adrenaline sending my magic to the surface.

Though I let none of it show.

Here, in the privacy of Eira's office, I swallow down my rage and trace the corner of the W with the tip of my finger. She sighs, sending my pulse racing. My cock hardens in response to the lust coming off of her body.

It's a fucking aphrodisiac and sends all rational thought out the window.

I continue tracing the scar, her skin warm beneath my tender touch. Flexing the fingers of my other hand, I force myself to keep it firmly at my side instead of snaking it around her waist and yanking her against me.

No speaking.

Nothing but the heavy beating of our hearts.

Logically, I know I should stop. That I might be pushing her too far.

We have boundaries between us, lines that cannot be crossed.

Leaving the tips of my fingers against her skin, I lean in closer and breathe her in. Eira gasps but doesn't move, so I move closer and press my lips to the marred skin of her brand.

"Fearghas," my name, a plea on her lips, is the sweetest melody to my frayed heart.

"Your skin is exquisite," I tell her as I steadily raise the zipper, letting my fingers trail over her skin as I move it up. Still, when it's fully zipped, I don't move my hand. It's not until she turns toward me, meeting my eyes with violet ones illuminated with power, that I remove my hand.

Tears stream down her cheeks...but it's not sadness coming from her now.

It's longing.

I've always known we had a connection, but I never realized—or allowed myself to believe—she felt the same as me—until now.

Which is even more heartbreaking than her choosing not to be any more than friends. I drop to my knees before her, and she stares down at me. "I will protect you, Eira. I fucking swear it."

"Fearghas, stand."

I shake my head. "I vow to protect you, Eira. To

shield your body with mine, your heart with mine, my life for yours." As I speak the words, the bond between us intensifies, fae magic swirling around the both of us as it seals my oath. The oath of a bonded man.

"Fearghas."

"Please just let me protect you. If anything were to happen—I won't fucking survive it."

"I'm scared," she chokes out, this powerful woman with the strength of an ocean at her back. "Every time I close my eyes, I'm back there, broken, my body used. I can't go through that again."

"You won't." I move in closer, a man on his knees. "Let me protect you."

"I don't know if anyone can. It should be impossible for him to even make that call, Fearghas. He's dead. I killed him."

Except people in our lives rarely stay dead these days. "Even if it's not, let me help you."

She swallows hard. "Will you stay with me tonight? I—I don't understand it, but you being near me, it helps." Reaching up, she brushes her tears away. "I know you have a lot on your plate, and I feel so pathetic asking. But I'm so tired. The stress is breaking me apart—the waiting for another phone call that may or may never come."

Standing, I lean forward with one finger and gently wipe a stray tear from her cheek. "I am anything you need me to be, Eira."

CHAPTER TWENTY
EIRA

Nerves frayed, I unlock the front door to my house and move inside. I only have about an hour before Fearghas's arrival. Once the door is locked behind me, the alarm activated, I take a deep breath and lean against the door, my legs still shaking from the vulnerability of showing Fearghas a piece of my past.

For so long, I fought to keep him away from it. Even while I'd been down there, plunged in darkness, I rarely let my thoughts drift to him. The idea of tainting my memory of the kind man I'd met with what was my present then seemed wrong.

Just as bringing him into my memories of the past has always felt. Opening my eyes, I study the foyer of my house; the décor I'd painstakingly chosen to bring a bit of joy into my life.

"Okay, Eira, this is happening," I say aloud, before pushing off the door and heading through my house. The curtain of water parts for me, and I toss my jacket onto the back of my couch before heading into my bedroom, finally stepping into the adjoining bathroom where I stare at myself in the mirror.

Surely I'm crazy. Something must have snapped within me. But from the moment I felt him step into the club tonight, I'd fought the very idea of asking him to come here, to stay beside me while I try and get even an hour of uninterrupted sleep—something that's been completely alien to me ever since I heard that voice.

And after showing him my scar—I shake my head and slip out of my dress. The only other person who's seen it is Elijah. That's only because he pulled my naked body out of the hole. He'd tried to help me get rid of it; spent years trying to find a way.

Magic didn't work, though. Spells, healers, herbs—nothing would erase the last physical reminder of what happened to me all those years ago. Reaching into the shower, I turn the knob, and spray falls from the rain shower mounted to the ceiling.

Then, I stand naked in front of the mirror. With a deep breath, I turn to the side to study the scar. Just like the memory, the W hasn't faded at all since the day I received it nearly four hundred years ago.

At least, now I can look at it without wanting to vomit.

When the steam begins to fog the mirror, I turn away and step into the shower, letting the hot spray wash over my body. It wets my hair, flattening the strands down my back as it turns my skin pink, the heat bordering between pain and pleasure while my body adjusts to it.

Was it foolish to ask him to stay? Possibly. I've always kept these boundaries when it comes to Fearghas, never letting him move in too close, yet keeping him just close enough.

This crosses over into uncharted territory between us, though. Yet, even as I fear it, there's an exhilarating part to having him so close. A part of me that wonders if maybe I keep pushing myself to the brink of discomfort, I'll be able to take that plunge I so desperately crave with him.

To feel his body against mine, his hands on my skin.

He's the only man I've ever craved in that way. Sex doesn't scare me because it's not the act of two people coming together that is so debilitating. Rather, it's the vulnerability I feel by letting myself want him. The power he holds over me as a man—a fae—even as I trust him implicitly.

After adding soap to my washcloth, I run the fragrant lavender over my skin. I move faster than I usually do, both excited and terrified for Fearghas's arrival.

My hand brushes over the scar again, and I stiffen because, for a brief moment—I feel Fearghas's fingers on it, a gentle caress that soothed even as it aroused.

It's the first time he's touched me that way, and even now I can feel him; feel his lips pressing against my skin, his warm breath washing over me. I drop the washcloth and run my fingers over the raised ridges again as I close my eyes and imagine that he hadn't stopped there.

That he'd let his lips trail up my shoulder, to the side of my neck. The hollow of my throat.

My breasts.

My stomach.

The insides of my thighs.

Warmth pools in my belly—lust potent enough to have me bracing a hand on the cool tile of the shower. The throbbing between my legs grows even stronger as I trail my free hand down, letting it slowly caress my skin.

Lower.

Lower.

All while I imagine him. *"I will protect you, Eira. I fucking swear it."*

I rub the tip of my finger over my clit, and arousal pummels me. A soft moan leaves my lips as I begin stroking myself, all the while letting my mind play tricks on me. Allowing it to convince me it's Fearghas's hand, not my own, bringing me to the edge of complete bliss.

"If anything were to happen—I won't fucking survive it."

What would his hot body feel like pressed against mine as water falls on the both of us? As though he really were here, I can feel the press of his lips to the side of my throat as my orgasm builds.

"Eira."

Legs heavy, I work faster, faster, picturing his other hand reaching around to cup my breast, to run his thumb over my nipple.

My orgasm rockets through me, and I throw my head back, crying out as I come, and for the first time, I can all but see him flipping me around, pinning me against the tile, driving into me—our bodies coming together for the first time.

Vision swimming, it takes me a moment to get my bearings, and even though I know I'm likely running short on time, I slide down the tile and sit on the bench against the wall I'd been bracing myself on.

Thoughts of Fearghas continue, though, even in my sated state of mind.

If fiction is as good as this, as incredible...then what would it feel like if I were no longer pretending?

CHAPTER TWENTY-ONE

FEARGHAS

This is a horrible fucking idea. I step up onto the stoop of Eira's house, too damned afraid to ring the bell. Forehead still coated in sweat from the lust that had me taking a long, cold shower before heading over here, I know I look like—what would Rainey call it?—a hot mess.

Had Eira not confided in me, had she not told me how badly she needed me, the chances I'd be standing right here are slim to fucking none. Because when I'm strained like this, I try to avoid her.

She pulls the door open, and I'm awestruck.

For the first time since I met her, she's wearing no makeup.

Nothing.

Not a lip color or mascara.

Baby-blue glasses are perched on her nose, and

she's wearing fuzzy pajama pants the same color, paired with a white t-shirt that makes my fucking mouth water.

This really was a horrible fucking idea.

"Thank you for coming." She smiles, and even though it doesn't reach her eyes, it melts my resistance.

"Of course."

She steps to the side, and I move into her house, inhaling the heavy scent of jasmine as I do. My cock hardens despite the near-freezing temperatures I exposed it to in that damn cool-off shower, so I reach down and rearrange myself before she's walking around me.

"Tea?"

"Sure." I follow her into the kitchen, trying like hell not to stare at her perfect ass that somehow looks even more appetizing in fuzzy pajamas than the glittery gown she'd been in before. "You sure you're comfortable with this?" Setting my jacket down on the back of a barstool, I watch as she pulls a mug out of the cabinet and sets it on the counter.

"Honestly? No. But I don't know what else to do."

She seems relaxed, and the joy coming off of her is refreshing.

After placing a tea bag inside the mug, she fills it with steaming water from a kettle then turns to face me. "Are you okay with it?"

"I'm fine," I assure her.

"Good. I typically read, but I do have a TV, so we can watch that, too."

"I like to read."

"Really?" She arches a blonde eyebrow, and it's another shot of fuck-this-idea to my cock. It's a damned good thing I'm hiding behind the countertop because whatever the fuck is going on would likely terrify the woman in front of me.

"Sure." Reaching into my bag, I withdraw a book and show it to her. "Even brought my own."

"What is that?" She leans in and barks out a laugh. "Tell me you are not reading a self-help book."

"Listen, this one is particularly interesting."

"You're well over two thousand years old, Fearghas. I highly doubt now is the time you're going to start developing new *Atomic Habits*."

Grinning, I shrug. "You never know. What are you reading?"

She reaches behind her and shows me a book boasting a young girl sitting on the cover, wearing a long, blue shirt.

"*Defiant*, huh?"

Her grin warms my blood. "It's a good book. Just started it yesterday." A timer I hadn't realized she'd set goes off, so she removes the tea bag, stirs, and hands me a mug.

"Where do you usually read?"

Color flushes her cheeks. "Bedroom."

"You want me to sleep on the couch?"

Eira swallows hard, looking nervous in a rare show of vulnerability. "I'd rather you be with me if that's okay. But if it's too much—"

"It's fine," I interrupt. The ability to sleep beside her? I'll jump on that shit even if it means needing to purchase an iron chastity belt. I shove my book back into the gym bag I brought with me, sling it over my shoulder, and follow her down the hall, tea in hand.

The curtain of water surrounding the main part of her house is hardly a distraction from the hammering of my own heart. We step into her bedroom, and that hammering intensifies, sending my lust skyrocketing. It's all I can do to maintain my composure as I set the gym bag down on the bench at the foot of her bed.

She moves to the left side of the bed and sets her tea down. "The bathroom is through there if you need to change."

I don't speak—mainly because I'm terrified of what will come out should I open my mouth. So, silently, I unzip my bag and pull out the charcoal sweatpants I brought with me. The instant I step foot into her bathroom, though, I'm slammed with need.

Fuck. Taking a deep breath, I steady both hands on the sides of her sink in an attempt to curb the appetite steadily building well-past innocent sleepover. *Base-*

ball. Baseball. Baseball. After far longer than it should have taken me, I finally manage to get control.

By the time I'm stepping out into her bedroom, though, I'm struck with a sight so utterly beautiful that it steals my thoughts. Tucked beneath the puffy white blanket is Eira, hair loose around her shoulders, eyes on the book in her hands.

I want to cry.

To thank whatever brought me here to this moment.

And when she looks at me, I become increasingly aware of just what I will do to get her to love me the way I love her.

Pale-pink lips fall open as she stares at me, the tension between us stronger than it's ever been. "I, uh, don't typically sleep in a shirt, but if you need me to put one on—"

"No." Eira clears her throat. "However you typically sleep is fine."

I don't bother to let her know that I usually sleep naked—mainly because that might be crossing right on over her comfort line, and I desperately want to remain right where I am. So, with a raging hard-on I'm trying hard to hide behind the pile of clothes in my hands, I move across the room and toward the bed, not dropping my pile until my back is turned toward her.

Then, I retrieve my book and carefully climb into

bed. The covers are soft, the sheets smooth, enveloping me in the scent of her as I settle against plush pillows. Eira glances my way again and smiles. "Thank you."

"You're welcome. How are you doing?" I can't imagine it's easy, given her past, to have a man in her bed.

"It's you," she says, simply. "So I'm fine."

I don't think she realizes just how badly I needed to hear those words.

"Do you need to talk about—"

"Not tonight. Tonight, we are normal, just friends, having a sleepover. You know, I've never had a friend sleepover before," I tell her, my attempt at lightening a heavy mood. Maybe if I approach this as friends, the near-painful hard-on I'm sporting will go away.

"Me neither."

"Then we're each other's firsts. Fantastic." I grin at her and open my book as she chuckles softly.

"I'm glad it's you," she replies, returning to her book with a smile on her face.

Soft sobbing pulls me from sleep.

"No," Eira whimpers. "Not again."

I sit up, reaching for my phone so I can turn on the light. Her eyes are shut tightly, expression strained, body dripping with sweat. "Eira," I whisper, not wanting to touch her just in case that makes it worse.

"Not again."

Glistening catches the corner of my eye, and I glance up, swallowing hard when I realize the entire bed is surrounded by shimmering liquid. Eira jerks, and the water moves with her, a liquid shadow.

I turn back to her. "Eira, love, wake up."

Her breathing turns ragged, and it's not until the liquid moves closer that I decide to take the risk. With gentle fingers, I touch her cheek. "Eira," I whisper. "You're safe." My heart pounds as I trace her soft skin with the tips of my fingers.

She stills. My gaze returns to the water above us, and I watch in awe as it steadily recedes. It's nearly silent in its return to the fountain in the corner, and the moment the final drop falls, I turn my attention back to Eira. The dim light of my phone casts soft shadows on her now-smooth expression.

With a deep breath that is partly me being grateful I didn't drown and partly because I long to keep touching her, I remove my hand. But the second I do, she whimpers, her expression tightening again. Brushing my fingertips against her cheek once more, I watch her relax into my touch.

It should thrill me, the fact that my very touch soothes in her sleep, but all it does is cause the ache in my chest to grow tenfold. How many nights has she been terrified in her sleep? How often does she wake with a liquid shield surrounding her bed, her subconscious attempt to shield her from the demons lurking within her mind?

Keeping contact with her, I scoot up and lean back against the plush headboard. I know that when she wakes, she'll likely panic, but for now, in the quiet of her room, the only sound being our combined soft breathing, I pretend this is normal. That the chaos of our life is little more than a nightmare we'll one day wake up from.

If only I believed it.

CHAPTER TWENTY-TWO
EIRA

The mouthwatering scent of cooking pulls me delicately from sleep. After slipping a robe on, I head toward the kitchen, feeling a hell of a lot more rested than I have in weeks. Months even. I step into the kitchen and freeze in the doorway as I take in the sight of Fearghas standing in front of my stove.

His back is to me, giving me an amazing view of his broad shoulders covered in tight black fabric. *Damn. That's something a girl could get used to.*

"Coffee?" he asks over his shoulder.

I don't ask how he knew I was here because I imagine it's the same way I sense him before he arrives. While I may not understand the connection between us, I do know it's something I never want to lose.

"Great, thanks." Crossing toward the pour-over carafe full of steaming dark liquid, I take a peek in the skillet. "Are those—"

"Bangers." His wicked grin gives me an energy boost caffeine would envy.

My stomach growls as I stare down at the Irish sausages currently cooking in the skillet. "Where did you get bangers?" I haven't had a traditional Irish breakfast in—well—since before I was stolen away.

"I have my connections."

"You have a banger connection?"

He snorts. "How do you think I've survived all this time without an Irish breakfast? I used to go back weekly when my travel plans were little more than thinking of the pub I wanted to visit."

Sadness weighs me down enough to have me abandoning my coffee and leaning back against the counter. "How are you handling that? Not being able to dematerialize?"

"It was hard, at first." He flips the sausages. "Though now it's merely frustrating at times."

"I imagine."

Fearghas clears his throat and transfers the cooked sausages to a plate. "How did you sleep?" I watch as he cracks four eggs into the hot skillet.

"Better than I have in a long time."

"Any nightmares?"

"I don't think so. None that I recall, anyway, which

is a nice change."

He smiles at me. "Good."

"How about you?"

"Great. Slept all night. You don't snore too much."

Without thinking about it, I reach out and lightly smack his arm. "I don't snore at all."

His grin softens slightly, and my cheeks flush. The contact between us has always been strained, but here lately, I'm feeling more—inclined. "Fine. You don't snore. Much," he adds, quietly, as he plates the eggs.

Plates in hand, we take seats at my bar and begin to eat in silence. The idea that our night is about to end and we're going to be forced apart by events of the day puts a somber mood on a delicious breakfast.

"Whoever your connection is, he's amazing."

"I'll be sure and let Ridley know."

"They're back?"

He shakes his head, disappointment written all over his face. "He brings them to me in bulk, and I freeze them. So while you were sleeping, I ran to my apartment and grabbed some."

"Thank you very much. It's delicious."

Our eyes meet, his soft green gaze locking on mine. "I will happily cook you breakfast, anytime."

"Then, maybe tonight, you can come back over?" The invitation is out of my mouth before I can stop it. Not that I would have. Restful sleep beside a handsome man is well worth the anxiety of asking.

His grin spreads. "Absolutely."

"You are supposed to stay in the tree line." Mel's voice carries down the hall from her office, loud enough that I can hear it the moment I step into the shelter.

"They've been going at it all morning." Maribel shakes her head in frustration.

"What happened?"

She sighs. "He stepped far enough out of the shadows to send Mel into a tizzy."

"Did anyone see him?"

Maribel shakes her head again. "Mel only saw him because she was looking for him. The pack has done a fantastic job at remaining scarce."

This is the one thing I was worried about. Since her husband killed her, Mel has an innate distrust for the male species—not that I blame her, of course. But we need the pack's help, at least until we find out who the caller is and why they're harassing the clinic.

Picking up the pace, I round the corner toward Mel's office.

"Good luck," she whispers, right before ducking into her own office.

"We were in the treeline," a man snarls, his deep tone agitated.

"Then how did I see you?"

"Because you're a control freak who can't allow us to do our job without your constant hovering!"

"*My* constant hovering? Listen, that thing between your legs doesn't give you the right to—"

"Hey, guys, what's going on?" I breeze into the office as though I wasn't just power walking down the hall. Mel glares at me as one of the largest men I've ever seen crosses his arms. He's shirtless, his tan skin stretched over taut muscle. Dark eyes level on me a moment before he nods toward Mel.

"Captain Mel over here can't seem to keep her eyes off me."

To my complete surprise, Mel's cheeks actually flush with color. "That is *not* it, at all. You can't seem to stay your ass in the tree line where you belong. If any of these women were to see a man of your—of your—"

"Size?" he asks with a wicked grin. "Girth? Go on, say it."

Mel huffs, her nostrils flaring in anger, while I try like hell not to laugh. I imagine it's been far too long since Mel had a spat with a handsome man. And this one—definitely handsome.

Before she completely loses it, I step further inside the office. "I'm Eira."

"Nyle," he responds, without looking away from Mel. "We take the security of your residences very seriously. I can assure you, stepping out and frightening anyone is not our intention."

"Don't let it happen again," Mel snaps. "Sneak out the back."

"Something I'm used to." He winks at her, then moves past me and out into the hall.

I wait until I hear the back door shut before cocking my head to the side and saying, "Little tension there, huh?"

"He's an arrogant prick who needed to be put in his place."

"You seem to have done a decent job."

She growls—as in actually *growls*. "He better keep his ass hidden from now on, or I'm going to feed him his balls."

"Kinda seems to me like he might actually enjoy that if it comes from you."

"Is this why you're here? To harass me about doing my job?" Her words lack heat and only further my amusement. I've never seen her this flustered before.

"Just checking in. Wanted to make sure we had no issues now that the pack is here."

"That question was likely answered the moment you walked in the door."

I chuckle and take a seat across from her. "Fearghas stayed with me last night."

Mel's eyes widen so damned far they might as well have popped out of their sockets. "Wait a damned minute. As in *the* Fearghas? The incredibly sexy fae I might throw my 'No men for eternity' policy out the window for?"

"How many Fearghases do you think I know?"

"Shit." Mel leans back and props her feet up on the corner of her desk. "I don't want to be crass, but how was the sex?"

Had I been drinking anything, it would have spewed all over her. "We didn't have sex."

"Am I hearing you right? He slept over, and there was no sex? Was there pre-game?"

"Pre-game? What? No!" Covering my face with both hands, I shake my head. "I told you about our weird connection; he just stayed over so I could sleep."

"So he watched you sleep? Creepy Edward style?"

"Creepy Edward—what the hell is that?"

"How do you not know who Edward is? I thought you read!"

"I do read."

"Then let me help you out." Mel gets to her feet and reaches into a bookshelf where she withdraws five hardbacks. They hit the desk with a heavy thud. "Read these. Thank me later."

Lifting the first book, I study the apple on the cover, then flip open to the blurb. "You want me to read a book about vampires?"

Mel's eyes practically glitter with excitement. "Not just any vampires. These are Forks vampires."

"Am I supposed to know what that means?"

"You will."

Knowing this battle is lost, as it consistently is when it comes to Mel recommending me books, I close the flap and pull them into my lap.

"So he watched you sleep. Did anything happen?"

"He made me breakfast this morning."

Mel lets out a low whistle. "The guy doesn't get laid and still makes you breakfast. Damn, Eira, that's something."

"I wish I could be what he wants," I say. This is the most open I've been to Mel, but for whatever reason, the words just keep tumbling out.

"What he wants?"

"A relationship. A future."

"And why are those things bad? Not all relationships end up like mine did, you know."

"I'm not made for relationships. Not anymore. I can barely stand to be touched. How am I supposed to manage hugs, kisses...sex?"

"First of all—" She throws up a hand. "Get creative enough, and you can have sex with limited touching."

"Mel—"

She chuckles. "Look, I get it. Being murdered by the one who promised to love me 'til death do us part' was a bit of a head-fuck. It took me years in the afterlife before I managed to be interested in men. Now, casual sex is how I remain this constant ray of sunshine." With a sigh, she meets my gaze. "What happened to you was much, much worse than my situation, so I get needing time to process, to heal. But don't you deserve to be happy? Don't you deserve for that bastard to have not also stolen your future away?"

"I wish it were that easy."

"There's nothing easy about it," she tells me. "No matter which way you look at it. The best thing you can do for yourself, though, is to at least try and see the benefits of a happy ending. Pun intended." She winks, and I can't help but laugh.

"We need to figure out who that caller is, and then I can breathe a bit easier. Maybe then, I'll think about seeing if we can move forward."

"Glad to hear it." She leans forward and presses a button on her computer. The screen illuminates. "As far as calls go, there've been no more messages. Just calls every day from unknown phone numbers. It could be some kind of auto-call program? I'm still looking into it."

Mel continues, describing different ways whoever is calling could be automating the action, but my mind is back in my house. The truth is, having Fearghas beside me last night—in my kitchen this morning—I'm far more open to the idea than I've ever been.

Who knows? Perhaps Mel is right and the caller is little more than an asshole playing a prank. Perhaps it's not my past trying to come back and haunt me.

Literally.

CHAPTER TWENTY-THREE

FEARGHAS

"It's cold as shit tonight," I complain as I pull my jacket more tightly around my shoulders.

"Stop being a pansy. You hear anything?"

Elijah shakes his head as he returns to the binoculars draped around his neck.

"You're sure this is where they've been coming?" I question, peering down into the alleyway next to a nightclub downtown.

"Positive. Every asshole I've interviewed says this is the place they get their information."

"And by 'interviewed,' you mean removing pieces of them until they talk?"

Her dark eyes narrow on me. "I don't question your methods; don't question mine."

I put up both hands in mock surrender. "Fair enough."

"What are you so interested in getting back to? Your sitcom reruns?"

"First of all, I've moved onto *Yellowstone*, and second, I do have somewhere to be."

"Stalking to do?"

"Actually, I'm spending the night with her."

I could have heard a pin drop with the shocked silence that sentence elicited from both Rainey and Elijah.

"Sorry...what? You're sleeping together? Since when?"

"We're not sleeping together," I tell Rainey. "Not in that way, anyway."

"But you're staying the night?" Elijah questions.

"I am."

"Sounds like you're sleeping together to me," Rainey comments, returning to the edge of the building we're perched on.

"She just didn't want to be alone."

"I think it's great she called you," Elijah tells me. "She needs you, even if she won't admit it."

"Well, I need the two of you to pay attention because we're about to have some company."

The doors open, and a handful of humans stumble out, all laughing and joking as though they don't have a care in the world. One would think they are merely companions leaving the bar if it wasn't for the crude nature of the things they are saying.

"Yeah, man, huge fucking tits. If she weren't supernatural scum, I might have let her suck my cock before I killed her."

"Fucking supernaturals."

Rainey's hands tighten into fists as she steps onto the ledge. Elijah moves up beside her with me on the other side. After nodding briefly, she jumps down, landing on her feet.

The men whirl.

"Hey, boys."

"Supernatural," they growl.

"Hunter, actually." She reaches behind her and withdraws a dagger. "I'm assuming from your conversations you're the group I'm looking for, but I have some questions I want answered before we get to the fun part of the evening."

The men are silent a moment. They exchange looks then burst out laughing.

Rainey's demeanor doesn't change.

"You're the cop. The fucking detective. You can't do shit because we ain't broke no laws."

"So you didn't just admit to murdering a supernatural? A woman? You said something about her tits—did you not?"

The man in the middle, boasting a short, black mohawk, grins at her. "Your word against mine, sweetheart."

"No. It's not." In a blur of movement, she sends a

dagger flying. It whirs through the air and buries in the man's chest, straight to the hilt. His eyes widen, and he stumbles backward, all the while staring down at the dagger in disbelief.

When he finally falls to the ground, the thump rips his friends from their stupor, and they pull out firearms.

Cue Elijah and me.

We jump down right behind them, immediately ripping the weapons from their hands. I snake an arm around the throat of the fucker in front of me, and he fights against me as Rainey strolls forward. One glance at Elijah proves the human is trying to escape his grasp as well.

Good fucking luck on that one.

"You cunt! You're going to fucking pay for it!"

"Possibly."

"You're a cop, and you murdered him!" the one I'm holding yells.

"I'm not a cop anymore. But I am a hunter. And you know what my job description is?" She steps forward, and both Elijah and I tighten our grips. "Killing those who hunt innocents." She drives her blade up into the chin of the man Elijah is holding.

Elijah's jaw tightens, his displeasure apparent even from where I'm standing. She rips her blade free, and her husband releases his hold, sending the man's body to the ground beside his friend.

"And then there was one." She moves toward the man I'm holding, who seems to have raised his IQ by ten points if his silence is any indication. "Tell me where to find the rest of you."

The man's head turns toward his dead friends then back to her. "Sacrifice is necessary in war." He spits on her face, and I rip him backward, tightening my arm around his throat.

"You're dumber than you look." She looks up at me. "Let him go."

I do as she asked and release the fucker. He glares at her, hands tightening into fists.

"I'm going to hunt and kill every single one of you. It's what I'm good at—literally in my blood. So, while you may not want to tell me where to find your buddies, you can count on one solid truth." Rainey takes a step toward the man. "Any supernatural deaths will be carried out tenfold on your friends. Family. Anyone who condones or looks the other way will pay."

"Bring it, bitch."

"I'll give you a five-second head start." She steps back, and the man turns to run.

"Five. Four. Three. Two. One." She sends her dagger flying with the full force of the supernatural energy in her blood. He falls to the ground, silver sticking out of his back, before he ever had a chance to leave the alleyway.

"Killing is not the way to bring peace," Elijah says softly, as Rainey retrieves her dagger.

"No? Does punishment not keep human nature at bay?"

"Punishment is not killing."

"Sometimes, it is. I'm simply speeding up the supernatural judicial system." After sheathing her dagger, she turns to us. "The bottom line is they won't stop hunting us until they fear the consequences. Death is a pretty damned good consequence."

"This isn't you," he insists.

She snorts. "This is me, Elijah. This is who I was before we met and who I will be from now on. Peace is no longer an option. It just took me way too damned long to realize it." She turns and leaves the alleyway, heading back down toward where we left our cars.

"You worried about her?" I ask, keeping my voice low in case she's still in hearing distance.

Elijah sighs. "I am. I've never seen her this—"

"Unhinged?"

He runs a hand over the back of his head. "Unpredictable. Turning in her badge? Never thought she'd do that. And now, killing humans?" Reaching into his pocket, he withdraws his cell and fires off a text.

"Tarnley?" I ask, and he nods.

"He'll come clean this up; keep Rainey off of Jillian's radar as long as she can be."

"Supernaturals being outed changed the game," I tell him. "You remember what it was like in Salem."

"I do. And think of all the lives that were lost on both sides."

"Let's hope it doesn't get that far."

He meets my gaze. "If it does, we've already lost."

One hour. That's exactly how long I have before Eira is expecting me. Plenty of time for a quick nap, which I desperately need after not sleeping much last night. I have a sneaking suspicion tonight will be no different.

After pulling out my keys, I step off the elevator. My gaze locks on Jillian's as she pushes off my door.

"I'm fucking tired."

"This can't wait," Jillian insists as I unlock my door.

"I'm assuming it can." I open my door and push into the apartment. By the time I'm prepping to shut my door, Jillian's red-tipped fingers wrap around it, preventing me from shutting it.

"This can't wait," she repeats. The dark expression on her face has me pulling open the door and stepping to the side so she can move into my place.

After shutting the door softly, I turn toward her and cross my arms. "What is it?"

Jillian faces me, and I can already see a difference

between the woman I left standing in that alleyway and the woman before me now. "We've had half a dozen more murders in a matter of days."

"Supernaturals?"

She nods. "Brutally killed. One was a doctor, worked at a hospital downtown."

"Name?"

"Max Dollins."

"Son of a fucking bitch." My magic flares to life, and a bottle on my counter shatters at the energy around me charged with power.

Jillian flinches but doesn't jump. "I'm assuming you knew him?"

"Yes. He worked with our friend, Rachel. We rescued him from a dark fae a few months ago."

"Rachel. She is on an extended vacation?"

"Something like that. When was he killed?"

"Tonight. In the parking garage of the hospital."

"Humans?"

"I don't know. This murder was different than the others, he was—disfigured. Tortured."

My jaw tightens as anger pummels me. Now, Rainey killing those three men seems a small price to pay for the lives of my kind. "I want to see the body."

"Fearghas."

"No. As much as you don't want to admit it, Jillian, we're all in this fight. Every single-damned one of us." I move toward my door and gesture for her to leave. "I want to see the body. Either you show me now, or I'll break in later—your choice."

Jillian hesitates a moment, but I see the second she realizes escorting me is in her best interest. With a nod, she moves toward my door. I open it, and together, we step outside into the hall.

"What was Max Dollins?" she asks as the elevator doors close in front of us.

"A shifter."

"They have packs, right? People to notify?"

"Not him. He was alone. As far as I know, Rachel was his only friend." And she's not even here to bury him. Why does that make his death even harder to swallow?

"I never said we weren't in this together," she says, softly. "But peace cannot be had in the midst of war."

My reply is instant and a truth I know all too well. "You're wrong. Peace exists because of war."

CHAPTER TWENTY-FOUR

FEARGHAS

"What the hell is she doing here?" Jillian demands as Rainey's car pulls in moments after I reach the front door.

"I called her."

"I didn't say she could come."

"Then you can take it up with her." Moving past Jillian, I step into the hallway of the morgue. It's cold —colder than I would have expected, given we're not actually where they keep the bodies.

Above that, though, is the stench. Pungent death clings to the air; my enhanced senses pick up on it when Jillian likely notices nothing but the cleaning solution used to mop the floors.

"Jillian," Rainey's greeting is sharp. "Enjoying my job?"

"Hardly. Want it back?"

"Not a fucking chance." Rainey moves past her and into the hall.

"Where's Elijah?"

"He and Cole had to do some security checks on the council chambers."

Jillian shoves past us and heads down the hall. "So it's a party, then. Too bad I forgot balloons."

"No worries. I'm not high maintenance," Rainey shoots back.

Jillian enters a code on a keypad mounted to the wall beside double doors. They swing open slowly, the motorized humming practically elevator music at this point. "As I told Fearghas, his body was discovered in the parking garage of the hospital."

"Was he killed there?" Rainey asks.

"No. We're pretty sure he was dropped there after he was killed."

"What evidence supports that?"

At Rainey's question, Jillian stops in her tracks and faces her. "You'll see when you get a look at the body." She swallows hard, her nerves making my stomach churn in preparation for what we're about to see.

She grips a silver handle and pulls the door open. With a heave, the tray opens all the way, revealing a white-sheet-covered body.

The hesitation is apparent. But after one more deep breath, Jillian grips the sheet and pulls it back.

"Motherfucker." Rainey's snarl matches one of my own as we take in the disfigured face of Max Dollins.

Or, at least, what was Max Dollins.

Now, his face is caved in on one side, every bone shattered, with some sticking through grey flesh. Blood crusts his hair and nearly all of his exposed skin.

Jillian pulls the sheet down further, revealing a chest covered in lacerations. Slices, some chunks of skin missing...he was absolutely tortured.

Brutally.

Rainey's shoulders begin to shake with the rage vibrating through her like a damned train. I wrap an arm around her shoulders, and she calms—but not much.

I know she's a ticking time bomb; I just hope we're out of here before she goes off.

"We don't know that it was the humans this time," she says. "There was no silver, no iron, nothing that would have incapacitated him."

"Defense wounds?" I question.

She shakes her head. "Nothing. His hands were completely unmarred, and there are no binding marks around his wrists." She lifts his arm to show us.

"What else could have done this?" Rainey demands. "If not those fucking humans?"

"I don't know," Jillian replies, sadly. "But if it were them, I don't know why he didn't fight back."

"Did you run a blood panel? They could have injected him with silver."

"We did. He was clean."

It's then I notice a black line on the inside of his left arm. Releasing Rainey, I step forward. "What's this?"

"Fresh tattoo. Looks maybe a few hours before he was killed."

"And you didn't think to mention that?" Rainey snaps.

"I didn't see how it was relevant."

I reach forward and raise his arm. There, on the inside of his left bicep is a small, tattooed bird.

"What is it?" Jillian moves in closer to get a look.

"A bird." I replace his arm. "Why would a feline shifter get a tattoo of a bird?"

"Keep your enemies close?" Rainey snaps. "I don't know."

"Step back."

Both women do as I ask, and I place both hands on either side of Max's head.

"What the hell are you doing?"

I glance back at Rainey. "Since magic is tied to the soul, he's little more than a human shell at this point. I should be able to see his last few moments."

"You can see who killed him?"

"Yes." Closing my eyes, I call to my power. My

wings open, their constant presence taking form now as they stretch around me. I push my magic into Max's body and focus on my need to see what he saw, to access his memories.

This is something that can only be done on a *live* supernatural by a dark fae. Being light fae, I may not have the ability to read the mind of a living supernatural, but a recently departed one? That I can unfortunately do.

It takes me a few moments since he's been dead a while, but soon, it takes form, and I'm plunged into his final seconds.

"Please. Stop," he groans. Body bloody, he sits in a chair, untied but still as a rod.

Feminine laughter drifts over me, chilling my bones. I turn toward the sound, my gaze landing on Sheelin. Dressed in all black, she looks nothing like the woman I knew as my sister. And when she steps into the light, my heart shatters for the final time.

As I witness her golden eyes laced with black smoke, it confirms my fears.

Sheelin has taken in the power of a dark fae. "As soon as you tell me what I want to know, I'll end your pain." She kneels before him, holding a silver blade that glints in the fluorescent lights above.

"I don't know where she is. Last I heard, they were going to Faerie."

"Well, they don't seem to be there anymore."

"I promise, that's all I know," he chokes out.

She slices the blade over his pectoral muscle, and he screams. I stumble backward. Seeing the monstrous grin that spreads over her face is more than I can handle.

"Tell me!" she screams in his face.

"I don't know!"

"Fine." She grips him, and they disappear, taking me along with them. When the memory continues, we're hovering over the hospital parking garage, Sheelin's massive black wings keeping both her and Max suspended. "Let's try something else, shall we? Do not scream." Then, she turns in my direction, something that should have been impossible.

"I hope you enjoyed the show, big brother."

She drops him.

He plummets down.

I rip my hands away and fall backward. Metal crashes, and I suck in breath after ragged breath as I attempt to hear the words coming out of Rainey's mouth while she kneels before me.

All I can hear, though, is the sound of my own blood hammering.

"It was Sheelin."

Walking into Eira's house right now feels wrong.

I'm far too dark to bask in her light, but here I am as promised.

She answers the door within seconds, removing my ability to change my mind and go home. Her smile fades instantly.

"What happened?"

"You have any whiskey?" I ask.

"Yes." She shuts the door and heads into her kitchen with me following. After retrieving her decanter, she pours two fingers into a glass and offers it to me.

I down it, not noticing the burn through my numbness.

"Fearghas, what happened?"

"Sheelin killed Max Dollins."

"Max Dollins?"

"The shifter who was the Chief of Medicine at Rachel's hospital."

Eira gasps and covers her mouth with the hand not clutching the whiskey. "You know it was her?"

I nod as hot tears sting the corners of my eyes. I've only cried a handful of times in my life; that type of weakness is not something I typically care to demonstrate, especially in front of others.

But the darkness in Sheelin's gaze.

The pain in Max's as he was frozen, unable to fight back.

That shit is going to fucking haunt me forever.

"Fearghas." Eira sets the decanter down and moves toward me. She hesitates a moment as I look away, but a heartbeat later, her arms are wrapping around my waist.

The tears stream faster now, and the ache in my chest expands painfully, despite the fact that this is what I've wanted forever.

I don't touch her with my hands, but I lean down and rest my cheek atop her head, breathing in the scents of jasmine and vanilla as I do.

"I'm so sorry, Fearghas," she says softly, pulling back.

"I saw what she did to him...relived the memory. She tortured him, Eira. Tortured him while he was unable to move."

Her expression darkens further. "Then she did take in the power of the dark fae."

"She did. And she used it to kill Max. I have to find her. Stop her. If she can force supernaturals to do her bidding, there's no telling what kind of damage she can do."

I start to turn away, but Eira stops me by placing a hand on my wrist. "Not tonight, Fearghas. Start tomorrow."

"Tomorrow might be too late."

"Tonight you are too raw. Take the evening, rest, and tomorrow, track the bitch."

The need to be near her again is so great that I

don't argue or dare mention tonight will bring me no rest.

No peace.

And based on her expression, she knows it, but pulls me toward her room, anyway.

CHAPTER TWENTY-FIVE

FEARGHAS

Crimson wells on my palm. The pain is there, a sting that radiates up my forearm—but it's barely notable compared to the burning ache in my gut. Sheelin's absence since murdering Max a week ago should have been comforting, but it only sends my anxiousness into a tailspin.

She's up to something. And with the powers of the dark fae at her disposal, I know we're simply standing in the eye of the storm. Sooner or later, the world is going to implode. Unless I stop her first.

Blood droplets hit the parchment stretched out over my table. The aged paper is yellowing, but the magic embedded within the fibers is active as ever. From the center of the droplet, a map appears, inky lines spreading out to all sides. The map comes to life

—thanks to my blood—and I eagerly wait for it to show me what I seek.

Or rather *who* I seek.

Heart in my throat, I watch for the location of my sister to be revealed. Since we're blood, finding her shouldn't be difficult. She could be anywhere in this world, Faerie, or the Veil, and this will, at the very least, narrow it down.

But when the map should have finished filling out, the lines stop, disappearing back into the droplet of blood before it, too, vanishes. "Son of a bitch!" I roar into my empty apartment. Rage and frustration burn through my veins as I shove everything to the floor with one sweep of my arm.

She *has* to be lurking somewhere.

Outside, rain hammers the roof of my balcony. Lightning splits the sky, and I pull out my phone to check the time. I have an hour before I need to head to Eira's for yet another night of no sleep. At least, today I managed a good two hours before waking to a phone call from a very pissed-off Jillian demanding to know the location of three human men who were reported missing.

A knock on my door pulls my attention from the mess on the floor.

I reach it and yank it open, expecting to see an Astor on the other side.

Instead, my heart jumps into my throat when I

take in the soaking wet siren on the other side. Violet eyes meet mine. "What's wrong? Is everything okay?"

"I miss you," she chokes out.

Alarm bells go off in my head. Her magic feels *wrong* somehow. That, or I'm simply that caught off guard. "I just saw you last night."

"Yes." She steps inside. "And already it's been too long."

"Eira—" I hadn't sensed her. Was it because I'd been focused on the map?

Her bottom lip quivers. "I still don't understand." Eira takes a step closer.

"Understand what?"

"How you can spend night after night with me and not move it forward. I'm tired of waiting, Fearghas."

"Waiting..." I repeat the word cautiously, scanning her energy for the source of whatever is off.

"Yes. I want this. You. Me." She takes a step closer. "I love the way you look at me."

She's right in front of me now, so close I can see the specks of color in her irises—and close enough to notice the colors missing.

That combines with the power signature, and I have my answer.

I lean down until my lips are a breath from hers, and she doesn't pull back. With her breath hot on my face, I reach up and wrap a palm around the back of her neck. Lust hammers through my veins, a jackhammer of need that's telling me to ignore the obvious changes.

This is all I've wanted for years. So why the hell shouldn't I take advantage of it?

The answer is easy. It's not really her.

I back her up until she's against the door. "You want me?"

"I do." Her tongue darts out and wets her lower lip.

My hand splays over her milky skin, and I drop it down to her sternum. The heart beneath it is steady. Lust turns to burning rage as I slide my hand up her chest and wrap it around her throat.

I tighten. She coughs and grasps at my wrist, sharp nails clawing at my skin. "Who the fuck are you?" I demand as I slam her into the wall.

"Fearghas, what are you doing?" she chokes out.

"I know you're not Eira, so tell me who you are, where Sheelin is, and I might make your death relatively painless."

She claws at me again. "I'm Eira," she chokes out. But even as she says it, white hair turns ebony, and violet eyes shift to red.

"Succubus," I growl. "I should have known."

"I thought I was the murderer of the family."

The succubus remains in my grip as I whirl on Sheelin. She's perched on top of my countertop, legs crossed at the knees. "This your pet?" I demand as unease unfurls in my belly. One word from her, and she could force me to do anything.

"Yes. So I'd appreciate it if you put her down. Please."

I could do exactly as she asks, but then, once again, Sheelin will have what she wants. And I've no tolerance for anyone who tries to use Eira against me. Keeping all of that in mind, I tighten my grip. Sheelin doesn't appear even the least bit worried, and I can't tell if it's because she doesn't think I'll kill the succubus, or because she has zero attachment. Honestly? I'm betting on it being both of those. "I'll decide that when you tell me where the hell you've been."

"You saw the present I left you?"

"If you mean the man you slaughtered, yes."

"He was so much fun at first. We had the best time on our date. Pathetic kitty wanted nothing more than to be loved." She pushes her lips together in a pout. "Guess it wasn't in the cards for him."

"You fucking tortured him," I snarl back at her, tightening my grip on her succubus.

"He should have told me what I wanted to know. Then, I would have simply killed him."

"And how the fuck was he supposed to know where Rachel was? Huh? They barely know each other!"

"Wrong. They've grown quite close ever since she

became a fae. Quite close, indeed." Her gaze travels from me to the succubus then back to me again. "You could have fucked her, you know. I'll bet she feels just like Eira."

A growl escapes my lips, and Sheelin laughs as she reaches behind her back and withdraws a blade. As she sits there, she slides the tip beneath her fingernails. "Do you remember that baby bird we found outside of the house when we were kids?" She grins and looks up at me. "I begged you to save it, but you believed it was too far gone and that we should just put it out of its misery."

"It's back was broken," I remind her.

"And you still scooped it up and carried it into the house for me to take care of."

"It mattered to you."

"And then it died, anyway." Blade still in hand, she hops down off my counter. "I think about it often. How many times do we scoop the broken off the ground in an attempt to try and save them?"

"It's never foolish to try and save a life." Reasoning with her is pointless; I know that after what I saw her do to Max. After what she did to our father. But I need time to get to the weapon at my back. Time to end her.

"Oh, Fearghas." She moves closer to me, but with the succubus between us, I'm not overly concerned with the blade in her hand. That is until she materializes right behind the succubus and drives the blade into her back. The succubus gasps for air as her eyes widen so far all I can see is white.

Then, she falls slack. I drop her, and she falls to the ground with a heavy thud. Sheelin raises the blade and runs the blood-slicked silver over her tongue. "Delicious."

"What the hell is wrong with you?" I demand as I take a step forward, and bile churns in my gut.

She's deranged.

"Where were we?" She taps the blade to her chin. "Oh, yes, broken things. See, it took me a while to realize you were right. We should have ended that bird's suffering right there. It was broken, damaged, irrevocably flawed by whatever moment drove it from that tree."

I swallow hard, trying like hell to picture the innocent little girl who'd cried for days when the bird passed on. "What the hell are you getting at? Telling me, yet again, how I failed you?"

"Not this time. See, I realized last night that little bird is the perfect analogy for what I'm going to do to your life. Did you not see Max's new tattoo?"

The bird. "You put that on him."

She grins. "I did. He was broken by his loneliness, crushed by the weight of his need for love, much like you are. And your little pet is likely the most broken of them all."

"What little pet would you be referring to?" I demand, despite already knowing the answer.

"Your siren is beyond broken. You think what happened to me was bad?" She snorts and drags her blade over the wall. Painted sheetrock dust falls to the carpet. "Do you know what they did to her, Fearghas?" Her grin spreads, and she turns to face me. "Because I do. And let me be the first to tell you, brother, your little bird needs to be put down. It really is the only humane thing to do."

"You had better stay the fuck away from Eira, Sheelin. Nothing—and I mean *nothing*—will be able to save you if you lay even a single—"

"Shut up." The order is laced with magic, making me helpless to deny it.

"Yes," she chuckles. "Do you know I could send you to Eira's house right now? I could force you to show her the monster you really are—right before you drive a dagger into her heart."

Panic races through my veins, sending my heart rate skyrocketing as my mind travels over all the ways that would kill me.

"I could then make you go to Rainey. To Delaney. To kill them both, too, right alongside their pathetic, love-sick husbands."

Unable to speak, I try to force myself to focus on something—anything—other than the words coming out of her mouth. If she tries to make me do anything, I'll walk off a fucking bridge.

Step into traffic.

Put a bullet in my own head.

But even as I think those things, I refute them. The horrible truth is that when it comes to Sheelin right now—to her dark magic—I am helpless.

She throws a hand up to stop me. "I tell you what. Let's play a fun game." Sheelin claps. "I'll give you a chance to scoop her up and carry her to safety. Ready? Set? Go." With a smile, she disappears from view.

The moment her magic releases me, I turn and sprint for the door, not bothering to pay any more attention to the dead creature on my floor.

There is only one person in the world whose death will literally kill me.

And she's just become my sister's twisted trophy.

CHAPTER TWENTY-SIX

EIRA

"Eira! How good to see you, come in." Bronywyn smiles widely at me and steps to the side so I can move through her front door. She's dressed more casually than I think I've ever seen her, wearing a pink tank top and loose white pants, her blonde hair piled high on top of her head.

"How are you?" I ask as I slip out of my jacket. I've put this off for over a week now, hoping that I could just forget about it somehow. But even with Fearghas pretending to be asleep beside me, I'm finding rest more and more difficult to come by.

I need sleep. He needs sleep. And perhaps getting closure is the best way to obtain both.

Her grin spreads before she moves past me and heads down the hall toward her kitchen. "Doing great."

"Tarnley here?"

She shakes her head and offers me a cup of steaming coffee. "He's at his pub." Her gaze lands on my face and narrows. "Is everything okay?"

"I need to talk to you about something."

"Okay," she says hesitantly, as she sets her mug down. "Is everything okay?"

"I received a strange voicemail." Reaching into the pocket of my jacket, I withdraw the recorder and hit play.

Bronywyn's eyes narrow further as she listens to the crackling and heavy breathing—but just like everyone else, she doesn't hear the voice that comes on after. And then the recording ends. "That's strange."

"You didn't hear anything?"

She shakes her head. "Just the breathing. Why?"

"There's a voice."

"A voice?" She straightens.

"It plays the exact same time on the recording, every single time I listen to it. As though—"

"It's a part of it?"

I nod. "I don't know if it's possible, but I want to see if maybe someone spelled it somehow?" But even as the words leave my lips, I can see the answer on her face. "There's no way to tell, is there?"

Lips pursed, she doesn't immediately respond.

"I'm not entirely sure it's possible to spell a voice. Though, you can glamour someone, so it might be a fae thing. Have you told Fearghas?"

I nod. "He can't hear it either, and for all he knows, there's no way to do it."

"Hmmm. I bet he hasn't left your side since you got this, has he?"

"Something like that. I haven't brought it up again, though, and I want to keep him out of it until I know for sure what I'm dealing with."

Bronywyn arches a blonde eyebrow. "Any particular reason?"

"He's got enough on his plate with Sheelin. Taking on this will distract him when he needs to be focused."

"You do realize that, to Fearghas, you are always going to be a distraction, right?"

I swallow hard. Discussing Fearghas is not something I'm ever ready for, especially when I'm not getting any sleep without nightmares of the past or the passion I long for. Want to know what's more awkward than carrying feelings you know you can never act on?

Having a sex dream about the man lying beside you. The past week has been great, and I'm so appreciative of Fearghas being there, but I need normalcy again.

Mainly because I'm getting dangerously close to

needing to face the feelings I carry for the fae I can't seem to live without. My weakness is what put me in the position I was in before, and there's no damn way I want another.

People discover what you need, and they exploit it to control you. That was one hard lesson for me to learn.

"Fearghas and I are friends," I reply, finally. "It's what works for the both of us."

"Eira—"

"Is there any possible way to check if it's been spelled?"

She stares back at me for a moment. I'm about to grab it and go when she takes a deep breath and nods. "I can try a few things."

"That would be great. Thank you."

"It'll take some time."

"I understand. Keep that copy. I have another."

Bronywyn purses her lips in a tight smile. "I'll give you a call if I find something."

"Perfect." I turn to leave but can't bring myself to take another step. "Fearghas and I can never be anything more, Bronywyn. We're not like you and Tarnley, or even the others. Our past is far too dark for any kind of affection."

"Then I feel very sorry for you both," she replies. "I'll let you know if I find anything."

The roaring of water obliterates any other sound. This is the only time I ever feel at peace. Crystal water pours from the ceiling, falling to the cutouts in the floor where it will be funneled back up, ready to fall again.

Cool spray reaches me even here, the gentle mist wetting my cheeks and washing away the tears that have long since dried.

Panic is not an unfamiliar state for me. Though lately, the attacks are far more frequent than they have been in over two hundred years. Fearghas coming back into my life calmed the storm raging inside of me. For whatever reason, when he's near, I feel safe.

Just as I did that first time we met. Even now, after all the ugliness, I can still picture that day clear as though it were yesterday and not nearly a thousand years ago.

He'd been so handsome, but there'd always been an edge to him, a darkness I'd wanted to push out. My throat constricts as I recall the memory, so I draw my knees up closer and wrap both arms around them.

How many nights have I dreamt of that night on the *Cliffs of Moher*? How many times have I imagined we were back there, and instead of letting him leave, I found a way to make him stay? My life would have been completely different, I'm sure. But he'd had a mission. A reason for coming to this world, and I'd been young—naïve enough to believe I could change the world for the better.

Now, here we are. Both broken. Scarred by what we cannot unsee.

Alarms screech. Heart in my throat, I jump to my feet, my magic already pulling as much water toward me as it can. I rush toward the entrance, heart in my throat. But when I get closer, my body warms, the panic in my chest receding.

"Fearghas," I whisper his name as I turn the alarm off and head for the door.

"Eira! Open up!" he pounds on the door again, his voice raw. I don't hesitate any longer before yanking it open.

His relief is instant. Shoulders sagging, he pushes into my house. "Are you okay?"

"Yes, why—what are you doing here?" I shut the door and cross my arms. "I wasn't expecting you yet."

"No one else has come here tonight?" He looks around as if searching for someone. Even from where I'm standing, I can feel his frayed nerves, the panic keeping his heart racing.

"What is going on?"

He focuses his attention on me with forest green eyes that bore through me in only the way he can. "You're alone here?"

"I was."

He lets out a breath.

"Fearghas, what the hell is going on?"

"Sheelin is coming for you."

I stiffen. "You've seen her?"

He nods. "She came to my apartment."

My stomach churns, but not out of fear. Sheelin is not a threat to me, not with the steps I've taken—but to Fearghas, she's a damned bomb prepared to blow him wide open. "Come on, and let's have a drink." I turn away and head farther into my house. The curtain of water parts as we move through it then falls again, closing us into my bubble. As Fearghas stares blankly ahead, I pour whiskey into two cups before crossing the floor to offer him one.

"Thanks." He turns it up and downs the liquid. The darkness in his eyes, it's worrisome, and I find myself recoiling despite our closeness over the past week. This version of him—the madness in his gaze—it's unnerving.

"What did she say to you?"

He shakes his head. "Doesn't matter." His gaze lands on mine, and the air around us charges with so much left unsaid. "I just needed to make sure you were okay."

"Sheelin is likely telling you what she knows will upset you."

"You lot keep underestimating her," he growls.

Turning away from me, he moves closer to the water. My magic buzzes along my skin; a reaction to our close proximity. "It's going to get you killed."

I don't tell him that death is not among the things I fear, nor do I mention that the woman he's in love with died nearly a millennia ago. "In case you've forgotten, I'm not completely helpless."

Fearghas takes a step toward me, and I hold my ground even though my first instinct is to turn and run. As he stares down at me, a muscle in his jaw ticks. My fingers twitch with the urge to reach up and touch him so damned strong it's making my knees weak.

"Your life is the single most valuable thing to me." His tone is sharp, voice gravelly.

"I don't understand why."

He cocks his head to the side. "Do I really need to clarify further? Fuck, Eira. I've spent the last damned week here beside you, hoping you'll get at least a few hours of sleep, even if it means I stay awake all night."

"I know. I appreciate it."

"You appreciate it."

"I do."

"Tell me, Eira. Is this ever going to happen? Will you ever be interested in more from me?"

The anguish in his eyes, it guts me, but lying to him is just not an option. Not when I'm inches away and already dying to touch him. "Thank you for the warning. I want to try to sleep alone tonight. Thank you for everything you've done."

"Thank you? I have fought to prove myself to you over and over again, and you say fucking thank you!"

I swallow hard, and the cavity where my heart should be fractures beneath the weight of my anguish. "Yes. I'm sorry you believed something else was happening here."

He stares at me, his eyes widening—with shock or rage, who knows at this point—but I do know that my soul is breaking alongside his own.

"It was wrong of me to lead you on when I've known how you felt about me."

"You've known. This entire time."

"You weren't exactly subtle," I retort. "I let you keep coming around because it made me feel better."

"You used me, and now you're tossing me to the curb?"

"You served your purpose," I say, the words killing me. "And I no longer need you. Bronywyn is working on the tape, so that will be wrapped up soon enough."

His lips part, pupils dilating, and power surges through the air around us. It's so potent I retreat a step. Around me, plants I've arranged begin to die; one by one, they shrivel into nothing but black carcasses.

I hold my breath and wait for him to respond. To say anything. But instead, he turns and leaves my house, slamming the door behind him.

"I knew he'd come for you."

I whirl, magic at the ready as I face off with a woman I've only ever seen a handful of times. "Sheelin," I growl her name, anger burning through my veins turning the liquid of my magic molten.

"Hello, siren."

"Tell me why I shouldn't drown you right now."

"Because if you do, your mouse won't be able to play any longer."

"Excuse me?"

Sheelin laughs then continues to stalk a circle around me. "See, you're the bird, but Fearghas is the mouse. The creature you enjoy tormenting before you finally get around to the inevitable and destroy him."

I always knew she was insane. But the words coming out of her mouth make absolutely no sense to me. "I'm not following."

"No?" she arches an eyebrow and runs slender fingers over the back of my couch. "Must be a different conversation, then." The savage grin she gives me has no warmth in it, no humor.

"Why are you here?"

"Because I want to punish my brother."

"Fearghas doesn't care about me. Not that way." *At least, not anymore.*

Sheelin clicks her tongue as she continues to peruse my space. Power blazes down my arms, already causing the water surrounding us to arch toward me. If she makes a move, I'll bring the entire damn pool crashing down on top of us.

"You are a horrid liar, siren. But if that's what you need to tell yourself, I get it. After all, you and I had very similar paths carved for us."

"We are *nothing* alike," I snap back.

"No? Were you not fucked into submission, too? Over and over again until, finally, you gave in?"

I swallow hard at the memories slamming into me, even as I fight to block them out. "I never gave in."

She laughs. "That makes you stupid, then. I took that pain, that fear, and turned it into power. I became what I'd spent my life fearing."

"A monster?"

"A queen," she snarls. "There was nothing else to be afraid of. The worst had already happened and not a single person raised a finger to help me. Honestly, it's better they didn't. Otherwise, we wouldn't be here."

"Fearghas—"

"Fearghas was too high, too busy with his dick buried in whatever fae would bend over for him."

I don't respond, unable to get the image of him a few seconds ago out of my head. Sheelin uses my distraction and moves closer.

"Has my brother not told you? He was quite the whore, you know. Fucking everything he could. Girl after girl, they lined up for him because he gave them the attention they desperately craved. And when the king came for me, when he raped me, do you know Fearghas was too high to even stand?"

A tear slips down my cheek. I didn't even realize I was crying.

"Want to see?"

"No."

"Oh, I think you should see." Sheelin disappears. Moments later, cold fingers press against my temple, but before I can pull away, the room around me becomes somewhere else entirely. I feel cool marble floors beneath my feet. I'm surrounded by white. White walls, white floor, white ceiling—the only color belonging to the golden adornments on the two thrones directly in front of me.

"Please," a woman chokes out. I turn to see two people on their knees. A man and a woman, both wearing elegant garments, stare up at three more men in battle armor.

"Shut your mouth, fae whore."

"Leave my family out of this," the man growls. "Your problem is with me."

The man kneels before him. "Your entire family is a threat to me. As you well know, I deal with threats accordingly."

A door opens somewhere, and the man stands. Between the two guards, whose footsteps echo against the marble, is a shirtless, groaning man.

"Oh, Fearghas," the woman whispers as he's thrown at their feet.

"What did you do!" the kneeling man roars.

"Your son did this to himself. Quite proud you must be to have such a useless heir. He didn't even put up a fight."

I take a cautious step forward, trying to get a glimpse at him. Eyes glazed over and half-open, he stares up at his parents. His bare chest is covered in red marks left behind by someone sucking on his skin.

"What's happening?" he manages.

But before anyone can answer, a woman lets out a blood-curdling scream.

"This is where it gets good."

Afraid to miss anything, but terrified of seeing too much, I don't look back at Sheelin as she appears behind me.

"No! Let me go! Don't you know who I am?"

A man wearing a long black robe strides into the room, gripping a younger Sheelin in his grasp. She yanks against his hold, but he doesn't budge as he throws her to the floor. "Mom, what's happening?" she asks, scrambling toward her family.

"You can have whatever you want," the kneeling man promises. "Just leave my family alone."

"Fearghas?" Sheelin kneels before him. His head lolls to the side toward her, but when he opens his mouth to speak, nothing comes out. "What's wrong with him?" When her parents don't answer, she turns to the one glowering over

them, wearing a savage grin on his face. "What did you do to my brother!" she screams.

"You are delicious."

"No. Leave her alone." Fearghas's mother tries to reach for Sheelin and drag her back, but a hand slammed into her back forces her back to her knees.

"Anything I want, huh? How about you then, treat? You'll be absolutely delicious."

Sheelin's eyes widen with the realization of what's about to happen. My gaze doesn't leave Fearghas, though. He simply lies there, staring at his sister.

"Get up!" I scream at him, so wrapped up in the moment I don't recall that it's merely a memory.

"Spoiler…he doesn't," Sheelin whispers in my ear.

"Let's go have a taste, shall we?" He grips Sheelin by the arm and drags her away.

"No! No!" Fearghas's parents scream and fight against the hold, but they're of no use. Fearghas, however, has no one holding him, and yet he makes no move.

"I don't want to see anymore." I whirl on Sheelin. "Get me the fuck out of here!"

The older Sheelin grins savagely, and before my next heartbeat, I'm standing in my living room once again.

"My brother is not the hero you all have made him out to be," she says. "He's selfish, and sooner or later, you're all going to see it."

She disappears, and I crumble to the floor, chest so

tight I can barely breathe. Over and over again, I replay the memory in my head, the terrified screams, the lack of fight in one of the people who should have protected her.

And then, it all makes sense. Heartbreaking sense.

Fearghas is broken, too.

CHAPTER TWENTY-SEVEN

FEARGHAS

"Remind me again why I'm doing this?"

I glance over at Rainey. "Because if I die, your life will be horribly boring."

"Uh-huh." She draws back the slide of her firearm, loading a silver round in the chamber, before putting it back into her holster and rolling her shoulders. Then, she withdraws a silver blade and looks up at me.

I don't bother adding how I'm so fucking wound up after my conversation with Eira last night that I need to kill something. Though, I'd be willing to bet Rainey might understand and appreciate that perfectly. "Since Sheelin brought one to my house last night, I have to assume she's working with a local den. Given that we wiped most of them out, it stands to reason it could be this one."

"Elijah is making spaghetti tonight, so we'd better

get this wrapped up ASAP. I'm looking forward to marinara smothered noodles. It'll be a nice break from the shit that has been my days—and nights—lately."

"At least it's not Skittles."

Rainey chuckles. "I've been trying to eat better."

That stops me. "You. Eating better."

"Delaney being pregnant got me thinking that maybe I'd like to have a family someday. Maybe. When all of this is over."

I gape at her, so shocked and delighted that one of my closest friends is looking to move forward with her life. And then that delight turns to guilt when I realize she's out here, risking that very future to help me track the sister I let down.

What a fucking hero I am, right?

"Don't get all weird on me. I said I was thinking about it."

We continue walking. "For what it's worth, I think you'd be a great mom."

"Maybe. Delaney's kid is a good way to test that out."

Snorting, I shake my head. This is the first time since Sheelin showed back up at my apartment that I haven't felt like total shit. A Rainey quality, to be sure. She has this innate ability to ease any mood. Her blunt attitude, smart-ass tendencies, and kind heart make for one hell of a loyal friend.

I quietly ease the door open, and Rainey leans

inside. I follow suit, listening for anything out of the ordinary. Rainey is the first to hear them. “Basement,” she whispers.

We move farther into the house. Aged wooden floors creak beneath our boots, and the tin-foil-covered windows block out all sunlight, despite the high position of the sun. Crimson wallpaper is peeling all around us, and what furniture is left—pieces of it, really—is covered in a thick layer of dust.

“So, how are things going?”

“You’re shit at small talk.”

“Good. Then I’ll stop trying. Have you talked to Eira?”

“Not since last night.”

“What did you guys talk about?”

“Do you really want to know?” I stop and glance at her. “Aren’t you the one who doesn’t want to talk?”

She shrugs. “I’m curious. Believe it or not, I’d really like to see you happy, for once. Since you guys were bunking together, I thought you might be getting closer to that.”

We begin moving again, clearing rooms as we go. “I am happy,” I lie.

“Yeah, okay, and I’m going to sprout wings one day.”

“Hey, in this group, you just might. We have a hunter who used to be a vampire, a witch who used to be a hunter, a fae who used to be a human, and a fae who can't dematerialize. Shit changes daily."

She chuckles as she peeks in a doorway. "Fair point. Basement is this way."

Her loud whispers cease as soon as we hit the top of the stairs. The crumbling kitchen behind us is evidence of the death and decay. Succubae are demons, and because of that, they poison any area they spend more than a few minutes in.

Their stench—the putrid odor of death—lingers in the air around us, and it's all I can do to not hurl.

Slowly, we descend the stairs, careful to take them one at a time. Both of us ready for what may come next. With Rainey in front of me, I do my best to keep my thoughts away from all the ways this plan could go horribly wrong.

With the force of a wrecking ball, Rainey slams the sole of her boot into the door, and it splinters. Feminine screams fill the air, and we rush inside, blades at the ready.

"Which one of you bitches is in charge?" Rainey demands.

I keep my back pressed to hers to watch our back, and my gaze travels around my half of the room. At least three succubae in various states of dress are standing against one wall with two human men between them. The poor bastards have their cocks out as they pant up at the demons.

"That would be me." A woman steps forward, wearing chains. Head to toe, the thin metal drapes over her body. It clinks together as she walks, and her red eyes travel over Rainey and to me. "Don't you look delicious?"

Power pulsates in the air around me, and I grin, sending up a silent thank you to Del for her wards. "Nice try, but I'm afraid you're not my type."

"He's more into sirens."

Rainey and I both glance to the left as Sheelin makes her presence known. "Hello, Astor. So nice to see you again."

"The feeling is not fucking mutual." Rainey reaches in with her free hand and draws her pistol. "Breathe wrong and I'm going to pump you so full of silver you'll be shitting coins."

Sheelin laughs. "Iron is the only thing that will hurt me."

"I'm prepared for that, too," Rainey snarls.

"Lurking with the trash these days?" I demand as I step around to Rainey's side. "Looks like you truly have lost sight of your status, sister. Must be all that dark fae magic."

Sheelin chuckles. "Why are you here, brother? Did you get my message?"

My brows draw together in confusion—something that makes her grin spread. "You haven't spoken to your siren today?"

"What the fuck did you do?"

"Easy, Fearghas. Place is still crawling with succubae."

Rainey's reminder falls on deaf ears, though. "Where is she?"

"I have no idea. Left her where I found her, though I'd be surprised if she didn't take off running the moment I showed her who you truly are."

"What the—" My blood ices. "What do you mean?"

"I simply filled her in on the part of you you're so keen on hiding. I mean, she should be prepared for what she's getting into, right?" She glances around at Rainey. "Be ready, hunter. The moment you need him most, your hero won't be there." She glances at the succubus queen. "Feel free to try and kill them both."

The moment she's gone, the succubae charge. I drop my shoulder and slam it into the gut of one, then bring up my blade into her chin. She sputters and falls backward the moment I rip it out. Blood spills down the sleeve of my shirt, but I barely have time to notice before another is attacking.

I spin, slashing out and dropping the succubus to her knees just as Rainey is firing a bullet into the last one standing.

The den queen stumbles to the floor, and Rainey takes aim, firing another two rounds right into her chest. One would think she'd take pause, give herself a moment before jumping right on to the next thing.

But that's just not Rainey. She whirls on me. "Now that that's done... What the actual shit was all that about?"

Rage burns through my veins, turning the blood within molten. "You know enough about Sheelin's past that I don't need to fill in the blanks."

"No, you don't." She sheathes her firearm. "But you can tell me what part of your life she's about outing and why she seems to think you're going to let me down."

I lift my gaze from the blood-splattered floor to Rainey's face. "When Sheelin needed me the most—when it really counted that I be present—I was so fucking high I simply stood by as she was raped. As she was stolen."

Rainey's eyes harden at the same time the muscles in her jaw tighten as she clenches her teeth together. "That wasn't your fault."

Chuckling darkly, I turn away from her. "That's the problem with all of you. You view me as some fucking hero, and why? Because I pulled Cole from the Veil? One good deed does not a hero make, Rainey Astor."

"First, let's cover the hero thing." A hand touches my shoulder, so I turn toward her. "In no way, shape, or form do I idolize you. However, you were there for us when we'd lost hope. You pulled me from Heather's grasp, helped me get back to Elijah; you were there for Del when no one else was—do I need to keep going?"

"I failed my sister, Rainey. I was high and far too busy fucking every fae woman who would have me to even notice there was a threat."

"You didn't fail her," she says, softly. "But you're failing yourself, now. You know me well enough to realize that I don't dwell on the past. Shit fucking happens, Fearghas. But you move on because, unless you have a time travel device in your asshole, there's no way to fix it. Dwelling on the past does nothing but bring that pain forward and make you unable to learn from it. You fucked up? Fine. But her decisions from that moment on are *hers*, not yours."

"I am the reason she is this way," I insist.

"Oh, I'm sorry, did you feed her the crazy bitch pills?"

"Rainey—" I start.

"No. I won't apologize. Sheelin is off her fucking rocker. You want to look at true strength in tragedy? Look at Eira. Her situation is arguably the most horrific thing I've ever seen, and she's a damned badass."

My throat constricts, making it difficult to breathe. Logically, I know she's right. That Sheelin had a chance to pick up and move forward. Hell, even my mother tried for so long to make me see it wasn't my fault. That they'd both been sober and still unable to help.

The bastard had wanted my sister. My father's throne. And three of us couldn't have stopped him even if I had been sober enough to try.

But logic rarely belongs in sibling relationships, and as long as I live, I will never forget the little girl who'd counted on me...and the young woman I'd let down.

CHAPTER TWENTY-EIGHT

EIRA

The silence of my office surrounds me, sealing me into a world where I have complete control. Or, at least, the illusion of control.

My eyes are heavy from a night plagued with nightmares about the past, and it's all I can do to keep them open and attempt to focus on the ledgers I'm attempting to balance. Even as I try to focus, though, all I can see is Fearghas lying on that floor in Sheelin's memory.

He'd been out of his mind; that much was clear. Otherwise, how could he have just laid there? A tear rolls down my cheek, and I try to take a deep breath.

Someone knocks on the door, and I jump, my heart erratic.

"Eira?"

Elijah's voice is a more than welcome distraction. "Come in."

He opens the door slowly and moves into my office, eyes narrowed on my face. "Your heart is pounding. What's wrong? Another voicemail?"

I shake my head. Elijah is my oldest friend; the only person I truly trust completely. And it's in his presence that I lose the fight I'm waging against my steadily unraveling emotions.

"Shit, Eira." He moves toward me, and I stand.

As soon as he stops in front of me, I wrap my arms around his waist. I hate being touched by damn near everyone, but my relationship with Elijah is so innocent, it's the only time I don't cringe.

"What is it?" His hand runs down my hair as he holds me while I cry. More than once, he's eased a panic—an older brother who sits with me in my darkest moments.

After a few seconds, I take a deep breath and pull back. He releases me, though he doesn't move away. "Sheelin came to see me."

"Fearghas's sister?"

I nod. "She showed me something—a memory."

My friend leans back on my desk, his massive form still dwarfing me even though he's half-sitting. "A memory," he repeats.

Looking down at my feet, I swipe both hands over my cheeks then look back up into Elijah's blue eyes.

"She told me that Fearghas is not who we think he is. That he's selfish, and one day he will let us down."

"That's bullshit. Fearghas is honorable."

My throat tightens because the past I share with the fae tells me just that. A past that Sheelin is trying to corrupt by showing me Fearghas's mistakes. I know her reason for coming last night. She said as much when she told me she wanted to make Fearghas pay. But that single memory cannot undo centuries of the man I know. "She thinks he let her down."

"How?"

"When she was—" Swallowing hard, I shut my eyes tightly. Her past collides with memories of my own.

"Attacked," Elijah finishes.

I nod, grateful he knew where I was going without me having to say it. "He laid there, Elijah. He was high, and he didn't even try to stop them. I think about what she went through—about her anger—and I can't help but be mad at him, too. Even as I know he's not like that, I can't stop the questions. Did he know? Did he realize they were coming for her and got high, anyway?"

Sweat beads on my skin as my heart continues to race, the panic attack blindsiding me.

"Breathe, *piuthar bheag*."

Fixing on the sound of the waterfall in the corner, I

take a deep breath—then another and another until, finally, my heart begins to slow.

"The attacks are coming more frequently, aren't they?"

I nod.

"Fearghas is older than both of us combined," Elijah reminds me. "The fact that he's made mistakes is not a surprise. You didn't know me before I pulled you from that well, Eira. But I've killed more people—humans and supernaturals, alike—than you can count. He never harmed his sister. He's not the reason for her pain. Have you tried to talk to him?"

"No. Not since we got into it last night."

"You told him what she showed you?"

I shake my head. "It was before that. She followed him to my place."

"Because he was staying there?"

"He was. Not anymore. He'd come to check on me, and we got into it."

"Why?"

"I can't be what he needs me to be."

"Can't or won't? Don't you think he might be suffering, too?"

"Absolutely." Despite what Sheelin showed me, I know Fearghas to be a good man. A solid man. And likely, he blames himself for what happened to his sister. "But I'm too broken to piece us both together."

“Perhaps you’re both broken in such a way the jaggedness of your sides will fit perfectly.”

I gape up at him, then snort. “You did not just say that.”

He grins, pleased to have boosted my dark mood. “I did. And as corny as it was, I mean every word.”

Shaking my head, I cross the room toward the large windows overlooking my club. It’s packed tonight, both with the residents staying with me for fear over their lives and regulars. “They’re all so afraid, Elijah.”

“We’re working to find the humans.”

“Do you think it’s possible all of this is related?”

“All of what? The humans?”

“The humans, Sheelin, and the voicemail.” It’s something I’ve briefly considered but brushed off. After all, how would Sheelin have known about my past? But since she now has the powers of a dark fae, there’s no telling how she could have gotten that information.

I know a few out there who know what happened to me because they allowed it to be carried out. She could have gotten to any one of them.

“It would be rather coincidental if it wasn’t.”

“What if Sheelin is the one controlling the humans? What if she’s the one who left the voicemail?”

The plan comes together in my mind—everything

from start to finish—and it pieces together with perfect clarity. "Shit, Elijah. I'd bet money she's been playing us this entire fucking time."

"From what I've heard, she's pretty damn off her rocker. That's a rather elaborate plan."

"Yes. But how else are the humans getting their information about supernaturals?"

"They hate our kind. Why work with one of us?"

"The enemy of my enemy is my friend," I say, repeating an old phrase. "If you really think about it, it makes perfect sense. All of this started the month after Rachel and Ridley left for Faerie."

He considers my words carefully, expression unreadable. "If that's the case, if it really is all tied to Sheelin, we'll never find the humans. Not until she wants us to."

"Exactly. This is her game, Elijah. And we're little more than pawns." My cell rings, so I head over and answer it before checking the screen. "Hello?"

Music hammers through the receiver, but even it can't drown out the words. "Ding, ding, ding, little birdie."

My blood runs cold, the muscles of my body freezing from the chill in her words. "Sheelin."

"So smart. I see what Fearghas enjoys about you."

"How the hell do you know what I'm saying?"

"Look down," she says, and I do. There, in the

center of the dance floor, is Sheelin. She raises a hand and waves.

"If you hurt anyone down there, I will drown you in a droplet of your own saliva," I snarl.

She chuckles. "I fear nothing you can do to me, Eira, because I have already been to hell and back." Dropping the phone, she raises both hands and claps, disappearing as the vacant area she'd once occupied fills with supernaturals who don't even realize how close they came to death.

"What did she say?"

"How the hell did she hear us?" I look around, scanning my office for anything out of the ordinary. The entire place is warded to the teeth. She never should have been able to— And then I see it.

A crystal mouse that was not on my shelf before.

As I get closer to it, my anger intensifies. "She heard everything we said," I tell Elijah, as I palm the small figurine.

"How?"

"This." I slam it to the ground, and it shatters, scattering glass in every direction. "We have to tell Fearghas and Rainey." I rush toward the door with Elijah right on my heels.

All of it.

From the very first phone call.

Has been Sheelin. How the hell did it take me so long to see her pulling the strings?

CHAPTER TWENTY-NINE

FEARGHAS

The whiskey in my hand is nothing but a temporary mute button for the ache in my chest. As I turn up the bottle, downing what is now number two of the evening, I revel in the brief moment of dizzied bliss before my full thoughts come crashing back into me.

Sheelin's going to destroy every part of my life.

She tried to get Rainey to turn on me, and thankfully, that failed. But I've yet to hear anything from Eira, and thanks to my darling sister, I know she's aware of the type of person I am.

So, here I sit, hoping to drown myself in whiskey and failing miserably. At least, the angry mob had been dealt with easily enough.

One stern promise from Jillian that she was doing

everything in her power to find the missing humans, and they'd backed right the hell off.

Rainey and I had shown up right as they were leaving. Mild win right there. Something I can hang my hat on.

I open another bottle and turn it up, drinking deeply.

"Brother, brother. How sad it must be for you."

I lunge to my feet, sloshing whiskey, and whirl on my sister, who is currently perched on my countertop —yet again. She tilts her head to the side, somehow looking innocent despite the bloodlust in her shadowy golden gaze.

"What the fuck are you doing here?"

She grins. "Coming to see my little mouse."

Her words are razor blades against my skin. "Haven't you done enough?"

Snorting, she jumps down from my countertop, and her black boots hit the ground with a heavy thud. "I have yet to even begin." She circles me, and I stiffen, even when her sharp nails bite into the flesh of my back. "I won't stop until you're as broken as you think I am." Sheelin comes to a halt in front of me. "When you beg me for mercy, your pleas will fall on deaf ears."

"Spreading rumors is certainly the way to do it," I retort. Taunting her? Likely not a good move. But I'm exhausted.

"Rumors?" She clicks her tongue. "Don't you mean

harsh truths? Besides, I have far more planned for you."

With my free hand, I reach behind my back for the blade sheathed there. I grip the hilt and draw it, sending the iron-infused silver end-over-end toward my sister.

She disappears.

Before I can even think to turn around, fire burns through my back. Blazing agony brings me to my knees, and the bottle that was in my hand shatters beside me.

Sheelin leans down. "I'm going to make you wish for death."

Whatever she shoved in my back twists, and I yell, the excruciating pain lighting my veins on fire.

"How does that feel, big brother? Good? Here, let's try this way." My muscles jerk, and more pain spreads through my entire body.

"What the hell are you—"

"Doing?" she finishes. "Giving you a little gift. Something to ensure your entire world goes up in flame. But don't worry." She drops her face to the side of mine so her breath is hot on my cheek. "I've every intention of being there the moment it's reduced to ash."

My door splinters open. "Get the fuck away from him!"

Vision blurry, I can barely make out who's at the

door. But her voice is branded into my very soul. A tattoo that will forever remain. *Eira.*

"Why look who we have here. I'm surprised." She jerks the object in my spine, and I suck in a breath as my heart steadily slows.

"Let him go, Sheelin," she snarls. My eyes are so full of tears I can barely make out the form standing beside the demolished front door.

"Kill her," I choke out.

"The moment you do and I fall, his heart comes right out of his body. Not that you care, though, right? You've been stomping on it for—what is it now—a couple thousand years?" Her fist tightens, and I gasp.

"He's your brother."

"You've seen what he did. How can you blame me for being angry?"

Eira moves closer, giving me a clearer view of her face. Expression tight, she doesn't even look at me, and somehow that's far more painful than this. "Fearghas is not responsible for what happened to you. He made a mistake, and you've more than punished him for that."

"I've barely begun," she snarls. "But since we're chatting about our pasts, how about we bring someone else to this party? After all, the more the merrier, right?"

Sheelin disappears, and I gasp as burning relief spreads through me like fire while I brace myself against the floor. Blood drips onto the floor, but Eira ignores it as she falls to her knees. "Get up, Fearghas. We need to go."

"I—"

"Stop talking. Get up." She tries to pull me to my feet, barely managing to get me up before I nearly fall back down again. "Dammit, Fearghas."

With her help, I manage to wrap an arm around her petite shoulders, and together we make it to the door.

"Hello, little whore."

Eira stiffens. Fear and anguish fill my body thanks to the bond my magic has made with her. "No. No." Her whispered plea is barely loud enough for me to hear.

"What? Don't you want to say hello to an old friend?" Sheelin questions. "Seems rude to ignore the one man who knows you better than all the rest. Conrad has missed you, Eira. Haven't you, Conrad?"

I look down at my siren, noting her tightly shut eyes, the tremors running through her—and I know all I need to know. Releasing her, I turn and brace a hand on the door jamb, blocking Eira from Sheelin and the mystery man.

He stands beside my sister, wearing a black cloak that falls to the floor, covering most of his body. His head is shaved bald, his dark eyes trained on the woman behind me. “Little whore, how I’ve missed you.”

“Get the fuck away,” I growl.

“Tell me, how does it feel to once again be unable to protect the one you love?”

“Fearghas!” Eira screams, loudly. My heart hammers in my chest, and I turn, but she’s gone.

“Eira!” I whirl back on Sheelin, but thanks to whatever she did to me, I’m unable to move any closer. “Where is she? What the hell did you do?”

Sheelin grins and looks to the man.

“She is my whore. I control who touches her.” He runs a tongue over his lips and disappears. Sheelin follows, and I stumble forward, my vision fading with every passing moment. Pain surges through my head the moment it impacts with the floor, and then everything fades away.

“Fearghas!”

Groaning, I struggle to open my eyes.

Something cracks against my face, and pain blossoms on my cheek. “What the bloody hell?”

Someone breathes a sigh of relief. “What the hell happened to you?”

I crack open an eye, only to be assaulted by bright

light streaming in through the window. "What time is it?"

"It's two in the afternoon."

"I thought fae couldn't get drunk." Elijah's deep brogue comes from somewhere on my left.

"You really hurt yourself, dumbass."

"Rainey?"

"Who the hell else would I be?"

Now I open both eyes and try to focus on the room around me. Glass shattered all over my floor is thankfully the worst of the damage.

Elijah reaches down and yanks me to my feet. The room spins, but other than that and an ache in my back, I feel normal. "I don't—" My gaze lands on a dried stain in my carpet near the bottle. "What's that?"

"Blood."

"Why—" And then it all comes rushing back to me.

Sheelin.

Eira.

A man.

I spin on my heel, breathing ragged as I take in the sight of my intact door. "How did you—did you fix that?"

Rainey's watching me, brows drawn together. "The door?"

"Yes. Was it broken?"

"No."

"Eira. I need to get to Eira." I race out into the hall and toward the elevator at a sprint.

"Fearghas! Stop! Wait!" Rainey calls behind me, but I don't do either. I need to get to Eira, and my panic is overtaking all logic.

"Eira is fine!" Elijah's words stop me just as I'm pushing the button to go down.

I turn as Elijah comes to a stop beside Rainey.

"What the fuck is going on?" Rainey demands. "What happened last night?"

"Sheelin—" Pain splits my brain, so I press both palms to my temples as it brings me to my knees.

"I'm in your head, big brother."

"No!" I roar, exploding up off the floor. Red invades my vision, and I can see nothing but Sheelin's laughing face in front of me. I charge. "Sheelin!"

A body hits me with the force of a train, and my back slams into the wall. Warmth trickles down from my temple as I fight against the hold. Power burns through me, and the body disappears, slamming back away from me.

"Fearghas!"

Her voice stops me in my tracks. "Eira?"

Tears burn in my eyes, momentarily blocking my vision. But when I blink them away, I see her standing less than two yards away, her cheeks pink from the cold outside.

"Stop," she whispers.

"Fucking-a, Fearghas, what the hell is wrong with you?"

Tearing my gaze from Eira, I turn to Rainey as she helps Elijah off the ground. Blood trickles from a wound on his temple, and he glares at me as he gets to his feet. "I don't—where is she?"

"Who?" Eira questions, as she takes a cautious step toward me.

"Sheelin."

"She's not here, asshole," Rainey snaps.

"I don't understand what the fuck is going on." I turn back to Eira and rush forward. She moves back, resulting in my steps pulling us farther apart. "You're okay?"

"Yes."

"Were you here last night?"

Her jaw tightens, violet eyes hardening. "No. I was with Elijah. At my club."

"I saw you, though. You and..." I trail off as I fight to recall the name of the man from last night. The one she'd been so terrified to see—"Conrad."

Eira's gaze darkens, and she takes a step back while her entire body goes rigid. I can feel her fear even from here—her anguish.

"What the fuck did you just say?"

I whirl on Elijah, surprised to see the hunter has

moved closer to me now, his gaze murderous. "Who the hell is Conrad?"

"How do you know that name?" he demands.

"He was here last night. With Sheelin and—" I turn around as Eira begins shaking violently, the tremors rocking through her body like tidal waves.

"Easy," Elijah coos as he shoves past me. His arms come around my siren, and it's all I can do not to rip him off of her, even as I know there's nothing but platonic affection between them. He's the only one I've ever seen her not pull away from.

"Care to fill us in?" Rainey crosses her arms.

"He is the one who captured you, isn't he?" I ask, anger, pain, and guilt all assaulting me at once. I never want to be the one to bring her pain, and here I am, delivering blow after blow these days.

I am undeserving of her love; something that's never been more apparent until now.

"Yes." Elijah is the one who answers. "He's dead," he tells her.

"You weren't here," Rainey adds. "Which means it's likely Sheelin is fucking with Fearghas and trying to get to you through him. We already know she's behind every damned thing that's happened the past few months."

That's news to me. I turn to Rainey. "Excuse me?"

"Sheelin paid Eira and Elijah a little visit at the

club last night. It's why we're here. We tried calling to fill you in, and you didn't answer."

"What do you mean 'everything?'"

"The humans? Sheelin is the one feeding them information. The voicemail at Eira's club? Also, your sister."

I turn toward Eira. She still hasn't spoken, though her fear has subsided. The shock has worn off. Honestly, I feel like an idiot for not putting the pieces together before. Of fucking course, it was all Sheelin. How else will she tear me apart?

"I'm so sorry, Eira." I move closer. She swallows hard and pulls away from Elijah in an attempt to remain strong.

"I was not here," she repeats. "Sheelin is targeting all of us because she blames us for what happened to her mate."

"He was not her mate," I snarl.

"She thinks he was. Whether or not we agree with her is a moot point." She clears her throat and looks away. "It's safe to assume we're all targets at this point."

"Has she come after you?" I ask the question, already knowing the answer.

Violet eyes meet mine. "Yes." There is so much weight in that single word, that single syllable uttered from lips I've been dying to taste for centuries. I hadn't believed her before, not when she'd said she was done with me. Even after that fight, I still had a sliver of hope. But no more. In this moment, this instant, all hope of a future with Eira fades to black—leaving behind a gaping hole.

But as it fades, so does my hero complex. Winning is no longer my goal; surviving no longer my desire.

I will put an end to Sheelin, once and for all, and I can only hope I'll die alongside her, as I should have all those years ago.

CHAPTER THIRTY

EIRA

Darkness clouds Fearghas's expression as the air between us shifts.

"Then it's time to deal with her. Have a good day." He turns away from me, and I don't know why, but for whatever reason, it feels as though he's taking a part of me with him.

"What are you going to do?" Rainey demands.

"Whatever I need to," he replies. "She has the ability to force you to do her bidding. Avoid confrontation at all costs." Then, he slams the door behind him.

Rainey turns to us. "Am I the only one confused?"

Elijah shakes his head. "No."

"Sheelin is trying to break him," I tell her. "We all need to be careful. Any one of us could be next. And after this morning, Fearghas is clearly not seeing things the way they are."

"He attacked me," Rainey whispers. "If Elijah hadn't—"

"Sheelin is the root cause of this," I remind her. "Not Fearghas."

"I know that, but a loose cannon who happens to be a fae? I saw what he did to Elijah. He fucking threw him across the room without even touching him."

"They can manipulate the energy of living things around them," I explain. "But had he been at full power, neither of you would have survived."

"That's comforting."

"It should be," I tell her. "Fearghas is driven by his need to do good—to be good. Sheelin showing me what she did only showcased his reasoning behind that drive. And because of it, hurting those he cares for is something he can't do. Which is why Sheelin is still breathing. Fearghas can't bring himself to kill her."

"I sure as fuck can. We need to find her."

"And what of her ability to control?" Elijah demands, looking more flustered than I've ever seen him. "That can be a pretty deadly trick, don't you think?"

"There has to be a magical way to block it," I say.

Rainey's lips tighten in response.

"Otherwise we're as good as fucked."

"I'll talk to Bronywyn," Rainey offers.

The brown door separating us from Fearghas has

never felt thicker. “He may not survive losing her—not for good.”

“He will because he’s not alone.” She pulls out her phone. “I need to call Del. Can you try to get ahold of Ridley again? We could use him and Rachel.”

Elijah nods in response and pulls out his phone. After tapping on the screen, he puts it to his ear. Less than a second later, though, he is ending the call. “Still voicemail. They’re probably still in Faerie.”

“Shit. Del’s not answering, either.” She turns to me. “We need to head over there. You good?”

I nod, embarrassed that I reacted the way I did. Hearing his name, though—it’s the first time I’ve heard it since the day he took me. I was never allowed to refer to him as Conrad, and doing so humanizes a man my mind has decided is a monster.

Truth is, he’s one and the same. A man who is a monster. Logically, I know the sooner I realize that as fact, the sooner I will be able to move past the debilitating fear.

“Thank you for calling me,” I tell Elijah.

“I shouldn’t have.” He shakes his head. “I should have waited, had I known about what he saw—”

Shaking my head, I hold up my hand and interrupt, “Had you not, he could have killed you. Fearghas unchecked is—he’s deadly. He was out of his mind; I saw that much written all over his face.”

"Like last night," Rainey adds. "He's seeing things that aren't there."

"Yes." Which makes what I'm about to do very, very stupid. "I will see you both later."

"Are you sure that's such a good idea?" Rainey asks as I move toward Fearghas's apartment.

"I guess we'll see."

For the second time since I've known her, fear passes over her dark gaze. "We can hang out for a bit."

I shake my head. "It's better if you go. Warn Delaney. Fearghas is too stubborn to realize he's the most vulnerable, and I might be the only one who can convince him."

"Eira—" Elijah starts, but I shake my head.

"It's still Fearghas." My reminder does nothing to ease their discomfort though, so I opt to keep moving forward, instead. The truth is I've faced so much worse than what Fearghas can deliver, and I might be the only one who can keep him grounded in reality when Sheelin wants so badly to bury him in fantasy.

I don't bother looking behind me to see if they've gone, nor do I knock. As I'm pushing open the door, Fearghas is coming down his hall, shirtless.

My mouth dries—a feat for a woman who controls water.

Taut skin stretched over hard muscle invades my vision, and it takes nearly all my self-control to force my gaze up to the angry expression on his face. Wait, no...not angry. He should be enraged. Pissed. Instead, he looks annoyed.

What the hell?

"What do you want?" he asks as he moves past me and into the kitchen.

"Are you okay?"

The water faucet squeaks on as he fills a glass then turns it off and faces me. "Great. Haven't felt this clear-headed in..." he trails off and takes a deep breath. "Well, I don't even know how long it's been. Feels good, though." He takes a drink of water, throat bobbing after he swallows it down.

My eyes are drawn to his throat as he swallows. "After what happened, it's normal to be upset."

He lowers the glass. "Upset? Why the hell would I be upset? Pissed? Sure. But upset? Come on, Eira, you know me better than that." He chuckles and sets the glass down to cross both arms. "I have things to do, so unless you're here for something that will entertain me, I suggest you leave."

His callous words shock me. Unease churns in my belly as I stare back at a man I've always believed to know better than I know myself. But now? His demeanor is completely different. Disconnected.

"What's going on with you?"

"I really do not have time to talk in circles, love." He winks. "Let me know if you ever want to have a good time though, yeah?" He moves past me and into the hall. "Though I suppose you made your stance on that quite clear."

I reach down and grip his arm.

He stops in his tracks and looks down at me. The expression on his face, the ferocity in his gaze—it terrifies me. "I love it when you put your hands on me," he whispers. "It's so fucking hot."

I release him and step back.

His dark chuckle chills me to the core, and he takes a predatory step toward me. "I know you want me, too," he says. "You try to hide it, but I can feel it every single time we're near each other."

The wall hits my back, and I swallow hard as terror prevents me from moving any further. "Back off, Fearghas."

"Or what?" He slams both palms to the wall on either side of my head and drops his head down so it's mere inches from me. "You going to give me a shower?"

My gaze drifts to the cup of water on the counter. I consider it—I hate myself for it—but I consider filling his lungs with it, if only long enough to get him away. Every nerve in my body is afire, every muscle quivering with fear. I can't be a victim again, *won't* be a victim again.

"Come on, Eira, we keep dancing around each other, and it really is pathetic. Let's just get after it. Knock one out for old times' sake?"

"No." The word has never made me feel more helpless. The water begins to rise out of the glass.

"No?" Warm breath fans against my cheek as he moves in closer. "Then get the fuck out of my apartment, and stop wasting my time." He shoves away from me, and I sprint toward the door, wiping away the tears streaming down my cheeks.

Thankfully, Rainey and Elijah are both gone, giving me a brief moment to try to pull myself together. Breathing ragged, I suck in breath after breath as I try like hell to shut the panic attack down.

I've known Fearghas longer than I've known anyone, and because of that, I believed that I knew him better than I knew myself.

But then Sheelin showed me another version. A man who spent his days high, surrounded by women. A man who should have helped protect her and had been unable to do just that. I'd felt bad for him, angry that she wanted to taint who he was in my eyes.

Now, he's the one showing me another side. The man back there is not one I recognize—not one I ever want to know.

Both of those are making it impossible to believe I ever really knew him, at all. Is he the hero I've painted him as? Or is he the villain as Sheelin believes?

"Barr, Marx." I wave at the two guards standing over the private sector of my club. Without question, they fall into line with me, their heavy footfalls echoing down the long hall as we make our way to my office. The moment we're inside, I shut the door and turn to face them.

The huge dragon shifters are imposing even in their human form, and of all the supernaturals I have on staff, they are the strongest. Even as the last of their kind, the magic they can draw on is ancient, making them the only two who would stand a chance at going up against a pissed-off fae.

"You both know Fearghas?"

Barr snorts. "Bastard cleaned me out in a game of poker last week. Yeah, I know him."

"Same."

"He steps foot in this club, I want to know about it."

All joking aside, both men straighten. "Something happen?" Max demands. "Did he hurt you?"

I close my eyes, remembering the image of Fearghas looming over me; the overwhelming feeling of being trapped momentarily overwhelming me.

"Boss?"

"No. He didn't hurt me, but he's—" I search for an apt word. "—troubled at the moment. Don't confront him. Don't remove him. But I want to know about it."

"You got it." Barr pulls on the lapels of his coat. "You sure you're okay?"

"I'll be fine." My response is curt, but I can't be bothered to fake normalcy right now. Not when my entire world is falling apart. "No one outside of this room is told of this conversation, understand? None of the other staff need to know."

"If he's a threat—" Max starts.

"He's not a threat to anyone in this building." *No one but me.* "As I said, he's going through some things at the moment, and I want to be made aware if he shows up."

"Understood."

"You are both dismissed." I turn toward the massive one-way window and stare down at the club as the door shuts.

The heavy music is mute up here in my tower, but below, I can see the bodies moving together. Hips gyrating beneath strobe lights make each of their movements appear more jarring than normal.

I swallow hard as I allow myself to recall Fearghas's expression in that hall when I'd first shown up. He'd been panicked at first, then angry, and then—I don't even know how to describe what he'd been when I'd gone into his apartment.

I do know one thing though. Our dynamic has changed for good.

Nothing will ever be the same. And that kills me.

CHAPTER THIRTY-ONE

FEARGHAS

"Please, man, I know nothing!"

I tighten my grip on the shifter's throat, and his face turns beet red in response. Or is it beet purple? I never truly understood why they are described as red when they are more akin to a violet.

He sputters, and I release the pressure just enough that he can get air. "Sorry, mate, my thoughts were elsewhere. I believe you were just getting ready to tell me where I can find a dark fae."

"I don't know," he manages, eyes half-shut from lack of oxygen.

"I think you do. I think all you fuckers do." I gesture to the bodies littering the basement around me. Necks snapped, throats open, their deaths were carried out in different manners, and still, no one has talked. "Now, you're the last of your little fucking group alive, so I suggest you tell me what I want to know before I wipe out your entire line."

"I. Don't. Know."

"Wrong answer." His windpipe is crushed in my hand before I toss him to the side. He lands on top of the pack alpha, a man who'd been snorting cocaine when I'd come in. "Fucking pathetic."

Carefully, I step over the bodies and into the hall that will take me back up to the humans who'd been hiding them. The woman, man, and the teenaged girl are all three sitting exactly where I'd left them, tears streaming down their cheeks. "Don't worry. I handled your pest control problem."

"Why? They were protecting us!"

"They were using you. And the alpha was fucking your wife."

The woman's eyes bulge, and she gapes up at me, shaking her head. "No. No, we weren't!"

"I can smell you all over him, and vice versa."

"Sally?"

"No!" She turns back to me. "You bastard!" she pushes to her feet and charges at me, but I stop her by gripping her throat much like I'd held the shifter less than two minutes ago.

"Please, don't hurt her!" the man roars.

"Mom!"

I glance at the teenage girl. She looks to be around eighteen or nineteen, her eyes circled heavily with bags, likely from drugs. Every single one of these humans is haunted by addiction. I can smell it on their breath, see it in their eyes.

Do they deserve to die for it? I turn back to the man. "You'd damn well better clean your act up, or I'll be back, and the only one walking out of here with me will be her." I point to the daughter, who leans into her father.

He wraps his arms around her. "Please don't kill my wife."

I turn to her as she claws at my hands, the contact so damned light I can barely feel it. "I won't. This time." Tossing her to the ground, I wipe my hands on the black t-shirt I'm wearing. "Think twice before hosting any more supernaturals. They'll eat you for dinner if they can." I wink and move out into the bright afternoon sun.

Three packs, one succubus den, and a hive of vamps later, and I'm still no closer to finding what it is I'm looking for. Opting to walk, I move past my car and stroll down the sidewalk, enjoying the warmth of the sunshine on my face.

Even in the cold chaos that is my life, a ray of light is always appreciated.

Nights spent hunting with Rainey then lying awake beside Eira have made way to stressful days for nearly a week now. While I'm exhausted, I also know there's no resting until Sheelin and the humans are stopped.

Then, we can rest.

Then, I can try to convince Eira that I would make an epic permanent sleepover pal.

Someone honks as I cut across the street, but I pay them no mind as I make my way over toward a convenience store directly across the street from the precinct. A little bell dings as I move inside, heading straight for a red bag boasting the logo of Rainey's favorite candy.

After I drop them on the counter, the young human woman working it grins up at me.

"This all?"

"It is, lass, thank you."

"Irish, huh?"

"You bet."

"It's on my bucket list to go there," she tells me as she rings up the candy. "Five dollars and forty cents."

I hand her a twenty. "Maybe I'll see you over there one day." I wink, enjoying the way color floods her pale cheeks. "Keep the change." After retrieving the bag of Skittles, I step out onto the street again and head over toward a parked car a few yards away.

She may have turned in her badge, but I know there is a part of Rainey Astor who will always be a cop. And that part is currently staking out the police department, wearing massive sunglasses and a baseball cap.

I open the passenger door and slide into her car. “Cliché much?”

“What the fuck are you doing here?”

“Can I come in?”

“You’re already in.” She tosses her cell onto the dash. “What the hell do you want, Fearghas?”

“To apologize.” I hand her the bag of Skittles, and she wastes no time opening it and dumping some into the palm of her hand.

“For?”

“Yesterday. You were coming to check on me, and I attacked you and Elijah.”

“Eira believes you were seeing something.”

“I was. Remnants of the nightmare, I’m sure.”

She crosses her arms and arches a dark brow. “Nightmare.”

“That’s what it must have been. Eira claims she wasn’t there.”

“Then how did you know the name of that man?”

An ache blooms in my chest alongside the image of Eira nearly in tears. “Must have heard it in passing.” I set the Skittles onto the dash beside her phone. “I need your help, too.”

“There’s the meat of it. How the hell am I supposed to help you? My police background does not give me the license to counsel you through whatever the hell you’re going through. And, in case you forgot, I don't even have a badge anymore, so any kind of law enforcement help is out of the question."

"Then I suppose it's a good thing I need the help of a hunter."

Her eyes narrow. "What kind of help?"

I lean back against my seat and redirect my gaze to the humans strolling past us on the sidewalk. "Going against Sheelin has put me at quite a disadvantage, given that she can dematerialize and I cannot."

"I don't have a time machine, Fearghas. Not like I can go back and help you un-rescue Cole."

"And I wouldn't, even if it were possible."

"Good to know."

"You think I regret saving him?"

"I think I don't know you anymore. You're so determined to prove you're not the man she says you are that you're becoming just that."

Her words hurt, but I push the sting aside. After clobbering Elijah last night, I'm pretty damn grateful she hasn't killed me. "I want to stop her."

"What advantage is it that you are looking to gain over her? Sounds to me like the bitch has an entire deck of cards to our single one."

"You recall the dark fae we ran into a few months ago?"

She snorts. "You mean the one who nearly made Bronywyn and me kill each other? Yeah, she's a bit difficult to forget. But Rachel killed her."

"I have a theory that she is not the only one in Billings."

"Her mate was killed, too."

"Dark fae thrive on chaos; it's their life force. What place is more chaotic than Billings right now?"

"New York? Chicago? I can think of a few places."

This is only one of the reasons I adore Rainey. She's blunt—beautifully so. "Billings is where supernaturals were outed. Humans are hunting us, and in return, we're slaughtering them. We know Sheelin is behind it, but what if the chaos has drawn more?"

Rainey's gaze narrows on my face. "And if there was one, it could be dead by now. Sheelin stole that power from someone."

"They rarely travel alone."

"What are you getting at, Fearghas?"

"Finding the dark fae here in Billings solves both our problems."

She's silent a moment, her wary expression unwavering until, finally, she tilts her head to the right side. "And how exactly will a dark fae solve your problem?"

"Because, if we find one, I can steal its magic."

Rainey audibly gasps—a rare thing for her. She's almost never surprised. "Excuse me? Haven't we had enough dark magic transfer these days? Or did you forget Bronywyn trying to kill everyone half a year ago? And how about what you told me would happen to Sheelin now that she's taken in that magic?"

"This is different," I assure her. "Fae magic is not as volatile as witch magic. We draw on the energy of the living things around us. It boils down to how we use it. I will use it to defeat Sheelin; to keep her from hurting the rest of you."

"You said yourself that Rafferty is the only fae who's survived a transfer like that."

"But he did survive it. Which means there's a chance I can, too."

"Are you fucking kidding me, Fearghas? What if you can't? What if it does to you what it's doing to Sheelin? Then, not only will I have lost my best friend, but I'll also have *two* fucking crazy fae on my hands. How is that solving anything for me?"

"I'm your best friend?"

"*That's* what you take away from it? Fine. Not anymore. You're fucking fired." She leans her forehead against the steering wheel.

"Will you help me?"

"Fuck no. There is another way."

"Sure." My temper begins to rise, frustration fueling it, but I shove it down as best I can. Getting angry will do me no good—not with Rainey. So, instead, I rely on logic. "We can wait until she's killed Delaney, Cole, their baby, Bronywyn, Tarnley, Mags, Drex, Elijah, you—then when there's no one left in my life, I'll have no reason to play things smart, will I?

Then I can just throw all my chips into the game and take us both out."

A muscle in her jaw ticks. "There has to be another way. There is *always* another way."

"Just because there has been in the past doesn't mean there is now. But, hey, if you want to look for one, be my guest."

"Promise me you'll let me think of something," she pleads. "I know I don't say it often, but I really don't want you to die."

Had I not shoved all feeling aside—buried it deep down with the pain I carry over my past—her words would have resonated with me. But as it stands, I believe my only option is to make myself an even match.

And I'll do anything to gain that power, even if it means lying to one of my closest friends. "I promise."

She visibly relaxes. "You okay now?"

"I am. So, what are we looking for?" I peer out toward the precinct, and Rainey shrugs.

"Anything out of the ordinary. I'm hoping the humans are watching this place, too, since they seem to be evading Jillian easily enough."

"How exactly do you know that?"

"She's been keeping me relatively in the loop."

"How nice of her."

Rainey snorts and eats another handful of Skittles.

"She's trying to keep me from going on a murder spree."

"Smart woman."

"Honestly, I'm just ready to be able to take a bubble bath without being worried your sister is going to drop a toaster in."

I stiffen, pulling in a deep breath that brings me down from the dark joke. "I didn't realize the great and powerful Rainey Astor took bubble baths."

"They are great for aching muscles."

"What kind of bubbles do you use?" She glares at me, and I grin widely at her.

"How is the sleepover going?"

After letting out a long sigh, I shake my head. "I don't know how she doesn't see that we'd be good together."

"She will."

"Perhaps."

"Maybe you should get her a gift. I hear orchids are in full bloom this time of year." Her wicked grin makes me laugh even as I despise the very fact that she knows the story involving me, my mother, a lover to-not-be-named, and an enchanted flower.

Rainey's phone rings, and she presses it to her ear. I can hear the words plain as day, my supernatural hearing making it loud enough it's as though the receiver is right in front of me. "There's been an accident," Cole growls. "Get to our house." Adrenaline surges through my body at the sound of his voice, the broken tone.

My first thoughts are of Del, of the baby. What if—

Rainey throws her phone to the dashboard and turns the car on. Within seconds, we're peeling away from the curb and heading toward the highway.

"If she hurt her, I fucking swear—"

"We don't know what happened," I remind her, trying to keep my own panic at bay.

Ten minutes in complete silence. Ten minutes of mute panic, and we're finally screeching to a stop in front of Delaney and Cole's two-story house.

Rainey and I throw open our doors and race toward the front where Cole is standing with Elijah, Tarnley, and Bronywyn beside him.

"What the fuck happened?" Rainey demands.

"Where's Delaney?" I ask Cole. His expression is tight. His face is pale. Even without his pain, I can't sense the witch anywhere in the vicinity.

"I don't know."

Rainey lunges toward him. Elijah wraps an arm around her waist, banding her against his body. "What the hell do you mean you don't know?" she roars.

Bronywyn closes her eyes, and power surges around us. "Sheelin was here."

I whirl on her. "How long ago?"

“A few minutes.” Eyes the color of jade land on my own. “No longer than that.”

Cole hands Rainey a sheet of paper, and she opens it, her face reddening further with every passing moment. “That fucking bitch.”

“What is it?” I ask, and she offers it to me.

The witch and I are having a little play date. See you soon, big brother.

I crumple the paper in my hand as rage burns through me hotter than I’ve ever felt. Sheelin has poisoned my soul more times than I can count over the years, but there’s no way I’m allowing her to steal anyone else.

These are my people. My family.

“‘See you soon, big brother.’ That note was meant for you,” Cole says, as he takes a step toward me. The tattooed shifter and I have never really seen eye-to-eye, but there is one thing we can agree on: Anyone who touches Delaney has just signed their own death warrant.

It doesn’t matter that Sheelin signed hers months ago; she just added another notch to the unsavable column. “I bet she’s back at my apartment,” I tell them.

“Then let’s fucking go.”

I shake my head. “We all go busting in there, and she could hurt Delaney.”

“You can’t expect us to stay put.”

"I'm not, but you'll stay the fuck in the hall until I can get her safe."

"No." Cole's jaw tightens, his gaze full of fear.

"I get that Del is your mate, your wife, and that she's carrying your child. But you're doing no one any favors by running in their half-cocked. Sheelin is after me. She may be using you all to get to me, but you aren't her end game. The moment you step into that room, she can gain control over you."

"Actually." Bronywyn reaches into her pocket and withdraws a plastic bag containing what looks to be costume jewelry. "I just finished these this morning."

"What is that?"

"In theory? They are warded to prevent Sheelin from manipulating any of us."

"Seriously? You did it?" Rainey asks as she accepts the gift from Bronywyn.

"Again...in theory. Obviously, I had no dark fae to test it on, so just remain cautious."

"Thank you," I tell the witch.

She smiles softly. "The only problem is that they contain iron. I don't know if you can even use one."

"You protected those I care for, and that's all I wanted." I turn to Rainey. "If she manages to control me, you damn well better have a bullet with my name on it."

"Fearghas—"

"I'm counting on you, Rainey Astor. Don't let me down."

"Can you keep your head in there?" Elijah questions.

It's a fair inquiry, but it pisses me off. "We can't all be level-headed, can we?" I ask as I turn toward him.

"We'll be right in the hall," Rainey tells me. "And I will be putting a bullet in her head—not yours—the moment I get the shot."

"You get the shot? Take it."

CHAPTER THIRTY-TWO

FEARGHAS

Head and heart as clear as they can be, I step into my apartment. Delaney is seated on the armchair across from me with tears slipping down her cheeks. "Del, how nice of you to stop by." The iron bindings on her wrists anger me, but I don't let it show.

"It's a trap," she chokes out.

"I know, honey. Come on out, Sheelin. Rude to keep family waiting."

She pops into view right behind Del, holding a knife in her hand. "Took you long enough, brother. I was just getting ready to start cutting pieces off of your honorary sister just to keep myself entertained." She presses the blade next to Del's ear, and she winces, closing both eyes so tightly more tears spill out.

"You're going to want to refrain from injuring her, Sheelin. She has quite the fan club."

Sheelin disappears and reappears right in front of me. "What's different about you?"

"I don't know what you're talking about."

She stares at me for a few moments until a wide smile spreads across her face. "You've finally broken, haven't you?"

"Hardly." I move toward Delaney, and Sheelin blocks my path once more. "You're going to get out of my way so I can let her go. It's not her you want."

"Maybe not at first. But that baby of hers, can you feel its power?" She inhales. "Delicious. And none of my magic works on her. Watch this." Before I can stop her, she flings a vase across the room at Del. She screams, but nothing happens. The vase hits an invisible wall in front of her and crashes to the ground.

Unfortunately, that's all the others need to come barging in. Rainey, gun drawn, is first with Cole in his wolf form right beside her.

Rainey takes aim and fires, putting two holes in my wall since Sheelin dematerializes even faster than the bullets can fly.

She reappears right behind Delaney, blade at her throat. "My magic will not work, but my blade does just fine." In demonstration, she presses it into Del's throat, and a bead of crimson wells against the silver.

Cole growls. Tarnley blurs across the room, but

Sheelin slams her palm into his chest and sends him flying into the wall.

Bronywyn's magic pulsates around us, the violet snapping up and down her arms like lightning.

Sheelin giggles. "My, oh my, how I do love an audience." She pulls the blade back, perching it on the other side of Del's throat. "Did you ever tell her lover how you tried to get her to run away with you?"

I wince, forcing myself to keep my gaze trained firmly on her, even though I feel the eyes of everyone else on me.

"I had so much fun reading her mind." Delaney's eyes clamp shut, and another tear slips free. Her swollen belly protrudes out in front of her, and Sheelin takes her free hand and rests it on the top.

Cole snarls.

"Move your fucking hand, bitch, or I swear I will cut it off."

At Rainey's threat, Sheelin throws her head back and laughs. "You think you'd be used to seeing your sister bleed out by now. Let's have some fun. Shoot your sister, Rainey Astor."

Rainey's arm doesn't even budge.

Sheelin's eyes widen, and she turns to Elijah. "You. Kill her."

"Fuck you."

My sister straightens, her head cocking to the side. "Interesting."

"Sheelin—" I start.

She shifts her golden gaze to me. "You really are pathetic. So desperate to be loved you're willing to run off with whoever will have you. Say bye-bye to your sweet friend, Fearghas."

"No!" Rainey rushes forward.

A man appears behind Sheelin and rips her backward, sending her flying into the wall just as a woman appears beside Delaney. She grabs her, and the two of them disappear.

Sheelin snarls and disappears, and Ridley turns to me. "Have I told you how much I fucking hate your sister?"

Rachel appears right beside him, accompanied by Delaney, now free of the iron chains. She rushes forward as Cole's bones pop; his shift complete by the time his mate reaches him. She wraps her arms around him and sobs, shoulders shaking.

The sight of her so broken, so agonized, tears me the fuck apart. But it also sets me free as one solid truth cements in my brain.

If I'm going to beat Sheelin, I have to take emotion out of it. My attachments are the reason she's coming after everyone. They're the real reason she's so much more dangerous than I am.

It's why Rainey nearly died in that succubus den.

Why Del nearly died today.

Sheelin has no emotion.

No feeling.

No attachment.

So instead of running forward, I ignore every single instinct I have and turn away, making my way toward the door. Every step makes my heart ache, but I keep going, one foot in front of the other.

I'm just reaching the end of the hall when I hear a door slam. I turn, half-expecting to see Delaney. Instead, it's Rainey, arms crossed, jaw hard.

"If you're out here about what Sheelin said, I tried to take you with us."

"This can't happen again."

"I'm going to make sure it doesn't."

"I will help you with the dark fae," she says, eyes shut tightly. "But it stays between us. No one else can know what we're looking for, you got it?"

"Not even Elijah?" It's a low blow. I know it. She knows it. But I need to know for sure where we stand.

"He'd never let us go through with it."

"Then why are you?"

"Because I will do anything to save my sister, you asshole. Nothing is worth Delaney's life."

"Great. We'll meet up tomorrow."

"What the fuck is going on with you?" she asks as I turn away. "Why aren't you in there right now, making sure she's okay?"

"If today taught me anything, it's that I don't have

the luxury to feel right now, Rainey. You know better than anyone what emotions get you."

"So, what, you've just decided not to care that Del nearly died?"

I whirl on her. "I care way too fucking much—which is exactly the reason Delaney was put in the position she was in. Ever since the day my sister was raped, I've done everything I can not to care. I put nearly everyone at arm's length, turned my back on any friendships, and kept my feelings buried way the fuck down. The only person I bothered to show anything for wants nothing to do with me, and those I've let in since..." I trail off and gesture toward the door. "You see what the hell has happened there. So you'll excuse the fuck out of me if I don't want to hold hands and sing kumbaya, or whatever the hell it is you people do at summer camps. This is real life, Rainey—real, deadly, life—and I won't be broken by my attachment."

Her gaze doesn't waver, not even when she takes a step forward. "When this is over, I'm going to kick your fucking ass, Fearghas."

Two hours later, and I'm just walking back into my apartment when Ridley appears in front of me. "Where have you been?"

The dark-haired fae looks more relaxed than I've ever seen him, which is saying a whole hell of a lot. "Faerie. Hunting your sister."

"Took you long enough to get back," I snap.

"I hear you're feeling quite volatile these days."

"Where's Rachel?"

"With Delaney, making sure she and the baby are okay. I decided to come by alone just in case you need your teeth kicked in."

"Come the fuck on and get it over with, then."

"You know, I went to Eira's club, looking for you."

My stomach churns, but I shove it back down. "Good for you."

"Heard you made quite the ass of yourself."

"She tattled on me, then? Good to know we're going by schoolyard rules."

He snorts. "She didn't have to say a damn word. Her reaction to just hearing your name was enough."

I'm damn grateful my back is turned to him because, had it not been, I imagine he would have seen the agony his words caused written all over my face. "I figured it was well past time she knew where I stood. She didn't care for it. Here we are." I turn toward him.

Ridley's gaze stays trained on me. "Sure. We'll go with that." He props a hip on the countertop. "Tell me about this plan of yours."

"What plan?"

"How are you going to beat Sheelin?"

"By hunting her down." The half-lie comes out far smoother than it should have.

"And?"

"I have you now, right? You can pop in and grab her."

His expression darkens. "We both know that's not possible. Not with what she's capable of."

"Still unwilling to risk your neck?" I retort, referring to the man he was when we first met.

Ridley straightens and takes a step toward me. "I've risked my ass more than once for you assholes, and I'll happily do it again—if there's a chance of success. Sheelin is far from a sure thing these days."

He's not wrong, and I know that much. It's the reason why I'm willing to go to the lengths I am in order to stop her—but telling him my plans to capture and drain a dark fae seem a little risky.

"Then what do you suppose we do?"

"*Running* out of the question?"

"You know as well as I do running will do no good. Sheelin will find me."

"Then you run. Take Eira, and you go wherever the hell you want."

"Sheelin will kill everyone here if I leave. The only reason she hasn't yet—your rescue of Delaney aside—is because she's toying with us. We need to take a stand. I just don't know how."

"Bronywyn said she found a way to block Sheelin's dark fae capabilities from them."

"She did, but it won't work for us because it's embedded iron."

"No, I get that, but what if she can find a way to neutralize Sheelin?"

"We know how to neutralize her. An iron crossbow bolt straight to the heart."

"Who has gotten close enough to do that?"

"No one," I admit. "She always manages to show up when I'm not prepared."

"But if we can lure her—like we did Bronywyn—into a warded circle, we might be able to take the shot."

"In case you've forgotten, that plan massively backfired on us and nearly ended up getting the both of us roasted."

He begins to pace. "Fair enough."

After retrieving my whiskey from the cabinet, I pour some into two glasses and slide one across the island.

Ridley stops pacing long enough to take a drink.

"Did you, uh, see my mother, then?"

He turns to me. "I did."

"How is she?"

"Good. Misses you; was pissy I didn't bring you with me."

"I bet she had your ass for that."

"She did, at first. Then I explained to her how you couldn't leave your lovely siren, and she understood. Got a bit misty-eyed, even. Then there was a feast, I nearly clobbered Taranus, and now we're here."

I blow right past the mention of his younger brother. "You did *not* tell her of Eira."

"I did. Though I regretted it as soon as I realized you fucked that right up." He takes a seat on one of the stools and crosses both arms on the white marble countertop. "Tell me again how you did that?"

"Not in the talking mood."

"You're never in the talking mood when it comes to Eira."

"Then I suppose you should be used to it by now." Now, it's me who begins pacing. "We need to get close enough to Sheelin that she cannot make a counter-attack plan. Especially given that she's behind everything that's happened lately. The humans, the phone calls to Eira—all of it."

"Rainey filled me in on all of that."

"She tell you of the succubus who came here?"

"She did. The magical implosion that sent her husband to his ass, too."

I cringe. Not one of my best moments. "Sheelin had a grand time screwing with my mind. And when Eira and I got closer—"

"Closer?"

“I was staying with her, helping watch over her while she slept.”

“Always the good lap dog,” he replies, coolly.

A muscle in my jaw ticks as I glare at him. “It’s all done now. I told her how I felt; she shut me down.”

“Seems like it’s all over,” he replies. Why the hell he’s pushing my buttons, I don’t know, but he’s getting dangerously close to getting his ass kicked.

“Regardless, it’s done.” I down the rest of my whiskey. “Now, if you’ll excuse me, I have some sleep to get before I try to find and murder my sister tomorrow.”

“Fair enough.” Ridley grips my arm as I go to move past him. “You need to keep your head, Fearghas. We already have one unhinged fae on our hands. Let’s not up that count by one.” He releases me and disappears, leaving me staring at an empty apartment with my plan weighing heavily on my mind.

I reach into my pocket and withdraw my cell. After tapping Rainey’s contact info, I press it to my ear.

“What?”

“Meet me in an hour. Alley beside Eira’s club.”

CHAPTER THIRTY-THREE
FEARGHAS

Headlights shine over my car, illuminating the inside as Rainey comes to a stop right behind me. As soon as she shuts off her engine, I climb out and meet her on the sidewalk.

"Why are we here? Aren't you currently unwelcome?"

"Probably. Which is why you're the one going in."

"Why?"

"We need a dark fae. I've seen some in here a handful of times over the years. You're going to go see if there's one inside."

"Why not just call Eira? You can grovel, can't you?"

"She can't be involved. No one can know what we're doing, Rainey."

"Yeah, yeah." She turns away from me, and her

breath forms a small cloud in the cold air. "What do you want me to do to get one out here?"

"Shouldn't be too hard. They love having their egos stroked."

"As long as that's all you're expecting me to stroke."

"It absolutely is," I reply, quickly. "Tell her—or him—how pretty they are, and they'll follow you damn near anywhere."

"And how do you plan to trap them?"

Reaching into the backseat of my car, I withdraw a crossbow. "With this."

She studies it appreciatively. "Fine, but when this is over, you are so letting me play with that."

I grin. "Anytime."

Her expression changes, and she crosses both arms. "When we find Sheelin, what's the plan? She doesn't make logical moves. She's all over the damn place, which means tracking her is going to be difficult."

"She won't get a chance to get away again," I assure her.

"You already stabbed her once, and she managed to survive."

"I'm not going to drive a blade into her gut the next time I see her. It'll be going straight into her heart."

"Shit, Fearghas." Rainey shakes her head and turns

away from me a moment before her chocolate gaze returns to mine. "Why don't you let one of us take care of her? She may be bat-shit crazy, but she's still your sister."

"My sister died over a millennia ago," I tell her. For whatever reason, the memory of that little bird pops into my head. "I should have killed her the first time I realized how far she'd fallen."

"She's your sister—" Rainey starts.

"She was. And I failed her. Do you know how many innocents she's killed? Do you know how many fae bodies I've cleaned up to keep her name clear? How many times I've tried to reason with her; to get her to see the man she was loyal to was a murderer and those she was killing at his orders were innocents? My sister has been dead for a long time. The monster wearing her face is no family of mine."

"With Ridley and Rachel back, things are different though, right? Maybe we don't need—"

"No. We still need the dark fae."

"Why? Your reasoning for needing one was because you couldn't dematerialize. We now have two fae who can."

"A lot of good that will do if she shows up here and they aren't around."

"But if it's risky—"

"It is risky," I cut her off. "But it's the only way to ensure we don't lose."

"I just want to make sure you're doing this for the right reasons."

"Sheelin needs to be stopped by any means necessary."

"Even if it costs you your life?"

"It might," I tell her. "But my end has been a long time coming, Rainey. Should this be the hill I die on, then so be it."

After the first hour, I gave up standing outside and opted to hide out in my car. So far, no one has come in or out of Eira's since Rainey walked in, but all that could change at any moment.

Something moves out of the corner of my eye, so I shove open my door and face off with Eira. Her expression is angry, but even with the red cheeks, it's still so fucking good to see her. "Eira."

"What in the hell are you up to, Fearghas?"

"I don't know what you're talking about." Crossing both arms, I lean back against the car. It's then I notice the two security guards lurking a few yards away. "Can't be around me without protection?"

Her eyes flash with color. "Not after last time."

"Don't trust me? Well, probably for the best. I am my sister's brother."

"You are nothing like her."

"Sure. What do you want?"

"You sent Rainey into my club, alone—why."

"I'm not welcome."

"You're being an ass right now, but that doesn't mean you're not welcome."

Pushing off the car, I take a step toward her, and her gaze flickers to the guards. She offers them a tight nod then refocuses on me.

"I'm an ass because I no longer want to pad around behind you like a pathetic lap dog?"

"You were never a lap dog. We were friends—we are friends."

I snort. "No, Eira. We're not friends. I was your comfort blanket, and you kept me close by, knowing how I felt about you. You led me on, did you not?"

She swallows hard. "I did. I'm sorry."

"Did you ever bother to ask yourself why I had that effect on you?" When she doesn't reply, I move in closer. This time, even as I move, her gaze never leaves mine.

"I suppose you know why."

"I do. I've known about it since the moment we first met on those cliffs. The instant I saw you, I knew."

Her eyes widen, and her mouth falls slack.

"My magic chose you as its mate. My soul claimed you as its other half. And as long as I live, I'll never be able to love another. Trust me, I've tried." I'm leaning back against my car when my phone dings.

Pulling it out, I check the text from Rainey. *I found one.*

My heart hammers against the inside of my ribs as adrenaline surges through my veins. I shove the phone back into my pocket and meet Eira's gaze for what is quite possibly the last time. "I would have done anything for you, Eira. Would have given you everything—been whatever you needed. All I needed you to do was give me a chance."

The front door opens, and Rainey stumbles out alongside a woman wearing a skin-tight black dress.

I reach into the back of my car and pull out the crossbow.

Eira's eyes widen. She glances back to Rainey, then to me. "No. You can't be serious."

"I am." Raising the crossbow, I put the dark fae in my crosshairs.

"Fearghas, no." Eira starts toward me.

I pull the trigger.

A woman screams.

"What the hell did you do?" Eira screams loudly, as she follows my sprint across the parking lot. I reach Rainey first as she glares down.

The dark fae writhes on the concrete, her black eyes wide, teeth bared. She hisses over and over again, and I reach down to grab her by the arm.

Eira steps in my path. "What the hell are you doing? Everyone here is safe!"

"She's not." I drag her across the parking lot, and Eira's bouncers step in my way. "I like you guys, but if you don't move, things are going to get complicated."

They don't speak.

"Rainey, you can't seriously be helping him!"

"There is no other choice. Sheelin nearly killed my sister tonight. If this is how we win, then this is what I'm willing to do."

"Delaney! What happened?"

"Sheelin happened," Rainey replies. "I'm sorry about the violence. But we needed a dark fae."

Her eyes widen, and a tear slips free. "You're going to drain her."

"I am."

"No. Rainey, please...you can't let him do it."

"There's no other option."

"You're turning him into a monster!" she screams.

I wince. "I'm already a monster, aren't I?" The words come out far cooler than I meant, but they do the trick.

Eira takes a step back. "You're not a monster."

"No? That's not why you ran out of my apartment in tears?"

"You were upset—"

I laugh. "I don't get upset, Eira. Not anymore." The dark fae groans, and I keep moving. "Get them out of my way, or I'm going to show you exactly how wrong you are about me."

After a few moments, they step aside.

“You can’t come back from this, Fearghas,” she chokes out. “This is it. This is the end for you. Please don’t do it.”

“Goodbye, Eira.”

CHAPTER THIRTY-FOUR
EIRA

My hands shake as my heart rate skyrockets past the point of normal. Nothing I've felt in recent years comes close to this panic as I shove into Tarnley's pub.

Just as I was hoping, Elijah is sitting at the bar. He, Tarnley, and, to my relief, Ridley, all turn to face me.

The second they take in the likely terrified sight of me, all three are rushing toward me.

"What is it?" Elijah demands.

"Fearghas. He—" I close my eyes. "He and Rainey just abducted a dark fae from my club."

Elijah's gaze darkens, a momentary reminder of the powerful vampire he'd been before being force-fed a supernatural cure and becoming a hunter.

"She did what?"

"What the hell does he want with a dark fae?"

Tarnley questions.

"Stupid son of a bitch!" Ridley bellows and turns to send his glass flying across the room. It shatters. "He's going to drain her."

"He's going to do what Sheelin did," Tarnley says.

"Yes. We have to stop him!" My voice is frantic now—panicked. "If he does this, he'll never be the same." Tears stream openly down my cheeks now, and for the first time, I don't care who sees it.

"We will." He takes my hand and waits as Elijah and Tarnley both touch him, too. Then we disappear... only when we reappear, we're still in Tarnley's pub.

"I don't understand."

Ridley's cheeks flush with anger, and he releases me. "He must be somewhere with a shit-ton of iron. I can't find him."

"Thankfully, we have some powerful witches on our side," Tarnley says as he withdraws his cell. He presses it to his ear and begins to speak as my mind replays every good moment Fearghas and I have ever had.

Starting with that first one.

He's always been there when I needed him, always been by my side.

And I treated him like shit in the one moment he'd begged me to at least try. I'd been a coward, and now I was going to pay for it by losing the one thing that ever really mattered to me.

CHAPTER THIRTY-FIVE
FEARGHAS

"You're sure this is a good idea?"

I strap the dark fae into a chair and glare down at her, trying to see past the human exterior to the caged monster beneath. The power slithers just beneath her skin—the answer to everything.

It's right here for the taking, right in front of me.

So why the fuck does it feel so wrong?

"No," I admit, honestly. "The iron in the rock around us will keep us safe."

"How ironic that you're about to ruin your life in a cave and most of our shittiest moments the last year have taken place in one. It's fitting."

I don't bite. I can't. "If you don't want to be here, you can go. I have what I need."

"Not a chance, asshole. You've got me in deep, and

I'm not leaving until I know whether or not you're going to be problem number two." She reaches behind and withdraws her firearm. "Iron bullets. Come near me and I will put you down."

The ghost of a smile passes over my lips. "Thank you for being here."

She narrows her gaze. "I'm not doing a long goodbye, Fearghas."

Chuckling, I nod. "Understood."

"So how do you do this? Stick a straw in her like a juice box and suck it out?"

I cringe. "That's a horrible mental image."

"Yep. Saw it as soon as I said it. The scene from *Starship Troopers* popped into my head."

Since I've seen that movie one too many times, I, unfortunately, know exactly what moment she's talking about. "Thanks for that."

"You know, it's not too late to back out. We can just kill her and leave. Find another way."

Turning toward the fae, I shake my head. "This is the only way. I need to be an even match. After what she's done to you, to Del, to everyone...I can't risk it."

"You're losing everything. You know that, right? Eira. Yourself. All of it."

"Rafferty didn't completely lose himself."

"One positive outcome does not a good plan make."

"I don't know what else to do," I tell her, honestly.

"Listen to him. He's not wrong."

We both spin as Sheelin strolls in, wearing all leather.

Rainey levels her gun and fires.

Sheelin raises a hand, and the bullets stop mid-air.

"How the hell can she use magic in here?" Rainey demands.

"It's an iron prison. I may not be able to leave, but I assure you I am quite capable." In demonstration, she waves a hand. Rainey slams into the wall with a grin from Sheelin, and I rush toward her.

"What the fuck, Sheelin! Your fight is with me!" I pull Rainey into my lap and check her pulse.

"Go on, then," she says. "Have your fun. I'll wait."

"Rainey? Talk to me."

"For shit's sake." Sheelin waves her hand again, and Rainey is ripped from my grasp. She's thrown clear across the room, and I make a move to rush for her.

Rainey gasps and clutches at her throat, her face turning bright red.

"Let her go!"

"Make me." She gestures toward the dark fae. "Go on, big brother. Join me. The water is quite warm on this side."

I turn to Rainey. Somehow, the idea of what I'd been about to do is even less appealing, and I fucking despised myself for thinking of it in the first place.

"Do it. Or she dies." Sheelin clenches her fist. Rainey's eyes roll back in her head, and my decision is made for me.

Reaching behind me, I grip the handle of the weapon at my back. With one quick move, I draw it out and drive it into the heart of the dark fae. She screams, a horrible sound that is more beast than person.

She fights against me, and I allow my magic to freely mingle with hers.

It's wrong.

Disgusting.

My stomach churns as my soul blackens. The power buried within the soul-matter of the dark fae embeds into my body. It's painless, surprisingly so, but the rush—the toe-curling, stomach-dropping rush—is fucking potent.

And soon, the whirring in my ears stops, and I straighten.

The dark fae's body is slumped, her head rolling lifelessly to the side. I turn to face Sheelin, who's released Rainey from her previous hold.

Now, my closest friend's gaze narrows on my face from the headlock she's currently being held in.

"Let her go," I order.

Sheelin stands firm. "Fun little bit of knowledge: A dark fae cannot be governed by dark fae."

That's unfortunate. "At least, you can't control me."

I dematerialize and rematerialize where she'd been, but she's already across the room, Rainey in hand.

"Tell me, big brother, if you had to choose between this one and your siren, who would you save?"

I take a step toward her as Rainey's eyes widen.

Sheelin reaches up and grips the leather strap of the amulet Bronywwyn outfitted Rainey with. A simple tug sends the thing clattering to the ground, leaving Rainey open for whatever sinister game Sheelin is wanting to play.

"Dematerialize, and she'll be dead before you're solid again," my sister warns. Then, she leans down and presses her lips to Rainey's ear.

A single tear slips down her cheek as she raises her gun and presses it to her chest.

"No! Sheelin, no!"

"Count to two. Then pull the trigger." She grins and disappears.

"One."

I appear behind Rainey in enough time to shove the gun away as she pulls the trigger. She collapses into my arms, body shaking, and I hold her to me as I take us back to my apartment.

"You dumb son of a bitch!" Ridley snarls the moment we take shape near my couch.

"Didn't think we'd be coming home to an audience," I growl back as I release Rainey into the arms of her husband.

"What the fuck happened?" he asks as he looks her over.

"She's shaken, but she'll be okay."

Elijah glares at me. "Then how about you tell me what the fuck is so wrong with you that you had to get my mate tangled in your dumbass suicide plot!"

"It's not a suicide plot. As you can see, I'm still standing." I open both arms.

Ridley steps closer, and the air between us charges with power. Moments later, he recoils in disgust. "You fucking did it."

"I had no choice," I snap.

"There is always a choice!" Ridley roars in my face, his hot breath fanning over me.

"Not this time. Sheelin must be stopped."

Rachel appears behind him, Bronywyn with her.

"At the cost of you?" Ridley demands.

My gaze flickers back to Rachel. "I'm sure Max would have appreciated if I'd done this sooner. Might have saved him some torture."

She whimpers.

"You son of a bitch!" Ridley's fist connects with my jaw with enough power to send me stumbling backward. Dropping my shoulder, I race toward him and slam into his abdomen. Power roars in my veins, so potent, unleashed—like nothing I've ever experienced.

And suddenly, I no longer care that we were friends.

How dare he challenge me? Act like he knows exactly what I'm dealing with! Sheetrock dust rains down on me as his body impacts with what was once my kitchen wall.

But Ridley wastes no time; he dematerializes out of my grasp, and before I can turn around, his fist slams into my side.

"Knock it off, you two!" Delaney's roar is the only thing that breaks through the rage.

I turn, surprised as shit she's here at all.

More pissed off than I've ever seen her, she stands in my doorway, Cole at her side. Magnolia and Drexel are right behind her, the first time they've left Bronywyn's since Bella's death.

"What the hell is wrong with you, Fearghas?" she whimpers as she moves into my place.

I move back. "I did what I had to do."

My gaze travels over all those I am willing to die for. Delaney. Cole. Bronywyn. Tarnley. Elijah. Ridley. Rachel. Shit, even Mags and Drexel. And then, finally, to Rainey. Her eyes are bloodshot, her throat bruised, but when she looks at me—it's as if she's seeing a total stranger.

They're expecting me to lose it.

To lose myself to this darkness. And who knows? Maybe I will. Swallowing hard, I do the hardest thing I've ever done: walk away.

CHAPTER THIRTY-SIX

EIRA

The moon is high, casting an ethereal glow on the parking lot of my club as I make my way toward my car. The white sedan is parked near the back, as always, directly beneath a street light. With nerves consistently frayed these days, I'm seriously regretting my decision to send my guards home.

Even as I know I won't need them tonight. Rainey's text letting me know I needed to get to Fearghas's place lets me know that they're both, at least, alive, even if Fearghas—

"Hello, Ariel."

A deep voice slides over me, filling my ears and icing my spine. I swallow hard and turn to face a group of no fewer than twelve human men. Forcing a smile, I try to appear relaxed even though every alarm bell in my head is going off full blast. "I'm sorry. I'm afraid you have the wrong person. My name is not Ariel."

"Oh, we know it's not." A man steps forward, sporting a massive neck tattoo boasting a trident—the symbol for the human gang Rainey warned me about. "You're Eira. A siren, mermaid, supernatural scum."

My breath catches. She did it. Sheelin outed me. Why the hell am I surprised?

"I am not hurting anyone."

He looks over his shoulder at all the other men, and they laugh. "You are a supernatural. That makes you scum. And honestly, you're lower than that because you're also hiding your kind."

"You're murdering innocents," I growl back. I could drown them now, but doing so would make me no better than them. If there's a way to walk away, I know that's what I need to do. Even if every part of me wants them dead.

"No supernatural is innocent. You're all abominations of nature, garbage, beings that shouldn't exist."

"We're people."

"You're monsters, and we're not willing to allow you to take over."

"No one wants that," I shout back. "We just want to live."

"You're not allowed that right," he says, calmly.

"What's so great about living, anyway?"

I whirl on Sheelin, and she grins at me,

meeting my gaze with eyes so dark I can barely see a few flecks of gold. "What the hell are you doing here?"

"Making my brother choose." She looks past me. "Take her out." Sheelin disappears, and I whirl, not wanting my back to the humans.

They move toward me and I allow my power to surface; water begins to pool in front of me. "This is your last chance," I warn them. "I'm not like the others."

Something pinches in my back, right between my shoulder blades. My power goes dormant in the next heartbeat, allowing the water I'd collected to fall to the ground in a splash.

"You're still unable to tolerate silver, just like the others. Such a perfect weakness."

The voice from behind turns the blade, and I scream as I fall to my knees, overcome by pain exploding through my body—like a series of small landmines all going off simultaneously.

Somewhere in the distance, a man grunts moments before another appears in front of me. Wearing black slacks and a white dress shirt with sleeves folded to his elbows, he tilts his head to the side. "You fucked with the wrong person," Fearghas says. His tone is low, his voice dark, and it takes me a moment longer than it should have to realize he dematerialized in front of me.

Tears burn in my eyes. He did it. He actually stole the power.

The man who'd spoken to me steps forward, twirling his silver blade. "You shouldn't have just done that."

Fearghas chuckles; the sound is so dark, so terrifying, I never would have recognized him.

I suck in a deep breath as the silver poison spreads through my veins faster and faster with each heartbeat. It attacks the magic in my blood, and my vision swims. "Fearghas," I choke out.

He turns toward me, and his eyes—once a beautiful green—are now golden and swirling with dark shadows. It steals the breath from my chest. "You're going to be okay."

"Please. Let's just go."

"Listen to your whore," the man tells him. "Or we'll kill you, too."

Fearghas closes his eyes and takes a deep breath. I can see his fight for control, and it breaks me.

"Please. Let's go," I plead, again. "Just go. They don't understand."

He shakes his head and opens his eyes. "They hurt you, and for that, they will pay."

When he turns away from me, I try to stumble to my feet but fall, scraping my palms against the asphalt.

He holds out both arms. "Come and get me."

The men charge, and Fearghas disappears. He reappears behind the leader and snaps his neck as though it's little more than a toothpick. Then, he disappears and reappears again, this time grabbing the blade from the human's hand and driving it into his gut. He coughs and falls to his knees before landing right in front of me, cheek to the pavement. A single tear rolls down his cheek.

My gaze drops to the wedding band on his finger, and I lose it, my stomach churning with bile. How did the world get so screwed up? War on every corner. People attacking because they don't understand.

We all bleed red.

Fearghas appears in front of me, kneeling down. "Come on."

"You shouldn't have killed them."

His brows draw together. "They would have killed you," he says, simply. "No one can hurt you."

"No one but you, right?" I choke out.

Never in the time that I've known him has Fearghas looked like a true fae. But right now, he's every bit the mythical creature others have painted his kind as.

Inhuman. Unfeeling.

He reaches out and cups my cheek. I try to turn away, but before I can, my hands land on plush carpet. Fearghas stands and moves around behind me. I'm still unable to move as agony takes over every breath.

"This will hurt," he says, a moment before ripping something from my spine.

I scream, the pain fresh fire.

He tosses the blade to the ground beside me and reaches down to lift me. My stomach churns, and I fight to get him to release me.

"I will not hurt you. Be still."

My body obeys him. "You magicked me," I choke out.

"You're going to hurt yourself."

"You promised."

"I promised never to hurt you. Tearing yourself apart to get away from me is hurting you."

Holding my breath, I attempt to calm my racing heart. This man—this isn't Fearghas, and somehow, that's more terrifying than his arms around me.

Moments pass as we move through my house until, finally, he sets me gently on my bed. "Turn over."

Once again, I obey, helpless to deny the hold his magic has on me. While my cheek presses against the mattress, violent tremors wrack my body as terror threatens to overtake me.

"I'm going to heal your wound," he tells me.

"Fearghas, please—"

"Stop talking."

I choke on my next words as tears stream down my cheeks. Fabric tears, and I shut my eyes tightly just before warm hands press against my shoulder blades. Magic swirls around me as warmth spreads through my body, and golden rays fill the room while Fearghas's massive black wings unfurl around him, the tip of one so large it rests beside my face on the bed.

Within the quiet moments of fear, my pain subsides, leaving behind an entirely new ache for the loss of someone I'd loved more than should be possible.

"You may speak and move freely now," he whispers.

Wings receding, he stands and moves across the room as I jump up. I keep my hands on my body, holding up my now-destroyed dress. "Why did you do it?" I choke out through the tears. The agonizing ache in my chest is more than I can bear, even as I realize how much of a hand I had in creating the creature before me.

He turns toward me. "I became what I should have always been. Goodbye, Eira."

The moment he's gone, I fall to the floor, throat burning as I sob. My tears fall to the carpet, and I struggle against the urge to vomit.

I did this to him.

I turned him away when he'd needed me. Discounted what we both felt. And now—no. Even with no one here to see it, I shake my head. He can't be gone—not really. Changed, yes...but we all change.

Even in his darkest moments, when I was at my weakest, Fearghas still saved me. He fought for me all this time, and now it's my turn to do the same.

With shaking hands, I reach into my pocket and pull out my cell phone. Rainey answers on the first ring. "We have to save him," I manage. "And I think I know how."

Can they save Fearghas? Or will his own fear be his undoing? Find out in Healed by the Fae! The FINAL book in the Siren's Blood Chronicles! Available now!

My fear cost me the man I love.

Haunted by perceived failures in his past, Fearghas's attempt to shield us from the wrath of his enemy has backfired–horribly. Now, the stoic warrior who once wanted me as a mate is steadily unraveling, turning into the very monster he set out to defeat.

Unable to let go of what could have been, I refuse to accept his surrender to darkness and set out to find Fearghas's only hope, a renegade fae hunted by his own kind. Unfortunately, he has never stepped foot in our world and crossing the Veil into Faerie is proving problematic.

Saturated with magic, it's thinning at an alarming rate. And if not stopped, it will lead to the end of the world as we know it. The countdown has begun, and every moment counts.

Save Fearghas. Fix the Veil. Or lose everything.

Healed by the Fae is available now!

ALSO BY JESSICA WAYNE

Fae War Chronicles

Ember is dying.

But as she will soon discover, some fates are worse than death.

Accidental Fae

Cursed Fae

Fire Fae

Vampire Huntress Chronicles

She's spent her entire life eradicating the immortals. Now, she finds herself protecting one.

Witch Hunter: FREE READ

Blood Hunt

Blood Captive

Blood Cure

Rejected Witch Chronicles

She's back from the dead. The trouble now, is staying that way.

Curse of the Witch

Blood of the Witch

Rise of the Witch

Dark Witch Chronicles

She sacrificed her soul for her friends...Now they have to save her...or put her down.

Blood Magic

Blood Bond

Blood Union

Sirens Blood Chronicles

He's loved her a millennia, but that love might just be what gets them both killed.

Rescued by the Fae

Healed by the Fae

Mated by Midnight

Barbarian. Beast. Murderer? One thing's for sure, nothing is as it seems in this crazy town.

Midnight Cursed

Midnight Hunted

Midnight Bound

Accidental Alchemy

My job is to keep the things inside these supernatural books from coming out...unfortunately, I suck at it.

Dragon Unleashed

Shadow Cursed

He can have her body. But never her heart.

Savage Wolf

Fractured Magic

Stolen mate

Blade of Ice

Rise of a Warrior

Fall of an Empire

Birth of a Queen

Cambrexian Realm

The realm's deadliest assassin has met her match.

The Last Ward: FREE READ

Warrior Of Magick

Guardian Of Magick

Shades Of Magick

Rise of the Phoenix

Ana has spent her entire life at the clutches of her enemy.

Now, it's time for war.

Birth of the Phoenix

Death of the Phoenix

Vengeance of the Phoenix

Tears of the Phoenix

Rise of the Phoenix

Tethered

Sometimes, our dreams do come true. The trouble is, our nightmares can as well.

Tethered Souls

Collateral Damage

For more information, visit www.jessicawayne.com

ABOUT JESSICA WAYNE

USA Today bestselling author Jessica Wayne was only seventeen when she wrote her first full-length novel. Titled *One Lovers Ill Will (A book that never saw the light of day.)*, it was at that moment she realized she wanted to be a full-time author.

Life had other plans, though. After spending seven years in the Army, Jessica finally had the time to push forward with that dream.

Now, a wife and mother of three, Jessica spends her days crafting worlds in which anything is possible.

She runs on coffee, and if you ever catch her wearing matching socks, it's probably because she grabbed them in the dark.

She is a believer of dragons, unicorns, and the power of love, so each of her stories contain one of those elements (and in some cases all three).

You can usually find her in her Facebook group, Jessica's Whiskey Thieves, or keep in touch by subscribing to her newsletter via her website: www.jessicawayne.com.

amazon.com/Jessica-Wayne/e/B01MQ1OH4O
tiktok.com/authorjessicawayne
patreon.com/authorjessicawayne
facebook.com/AuthorJessicaWayne
twitter.com/jessmccauthor
instagram.com/authorjessicawayne
bookbub.com/authors/jessica-wayne

Made in the USA
Columbia, SC
06 August 2024

39548784R00250